Continue your adventure in history with three FREE historical novels from James Rada, Jr.

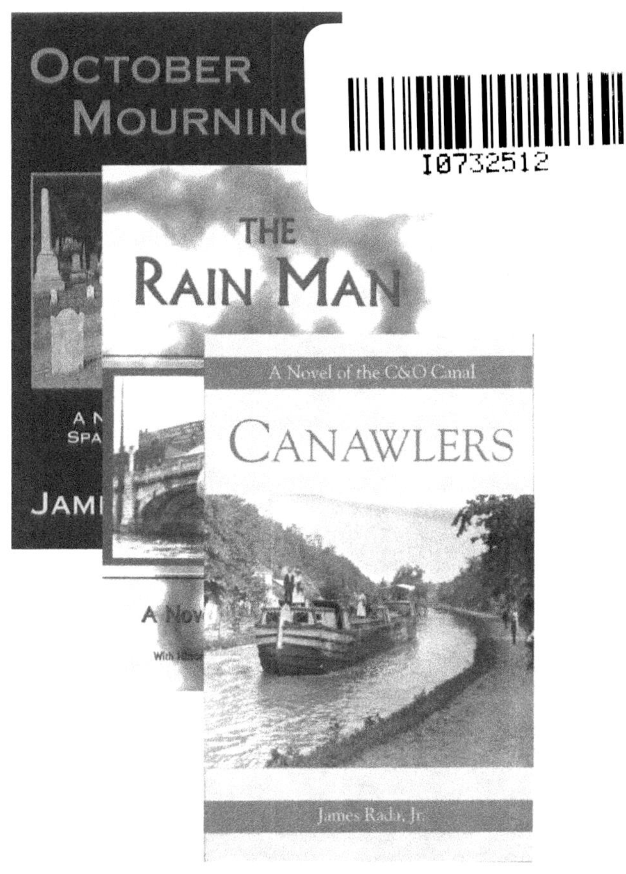

Visit *jamesrada.com / newsletter-email*
and enter your email
to receive your FREE novels.

BLACK FIRE, BOOK 3

FROSTBURG BURNING

Other books by James Rada, Jr.

Non-Fiction
- Battlefield Angels: The Daughters of Charity Work as Civil War Nurses
- Beyond the Battlefield: Stories from Gettysburg's Rich History
- Clay Soldiers: One Marine's Story of War, Art, & Atomic Energy
- Echoes of War Drums: The Civil War in Mountain Maryland
- The Last to Fall: The 1922 March, Battles & Deaths of U.S. Marines at Gettysburg
- Looking Back: True Stories of Mountain Maryland
- Looking Back II: More True Stories of Mountain Maryland
- No North, No South: The Grand Reunion at the 50th Anniversary of the Battle of Gettysburg
- Saving Shallmar: Christmas Spirit in a Coal Town

Black Fire Trilogy
- Smoldering Betrayal
- Strike the Fuse

Secrets Series
- Secrets of Catoctin Mountain: Little-Known Stories & Hidden History Along Catoctin Mountain
- Secrets of Garrett County: Little-Known Stories & Hidden History of Maryland's Westernmost County
- Secrets of the C&O Canal: Little-Known Stories & Hidden History Along the Potomac River
- Secrets of the Gettysburg Battlefield: Little-Known Stories & Hidden History from the Gettysburg Battlefield
- Secrets of Washington County: Little-Known Stories & Hidden History Where Western Maryland Starts

Canawlers Series
- Between Rail and River
- Canawlers
- Lock Ready

Fiction
- October Mourning
- The Rain Man

BLACK FIRE, BOOK 3

FROSTBURG BURNING

by

James Rada, Jr.

LEGACY
PUBLISHING

A division of AIM Publishing Group

FROSTBURG BURNING

Published by Legacy Publishing, a division of AIM Publishing Group.
Gettysburg, Pennsylvania.

Printed in the United States of America.
First printing: February 2022.

ISBN 978-1-7352890-3-8

Cover design by Grace Eyler.

315 Oak Lane • Gettysburg, Pennsylvania 17325

Chapter 1

June 29, 1922

Matt Ansaro stopped paying attention by the third time someone told him President Warren Harding would be driving through Eckhart Mines.

The first time was when he walked to the lobby of the St. Cloud Hotel in Frostburg to check if he had any mail. The front desk clerk with naturally curly black hair asked, "Did you hear the news, Mr. Ansaro? The President is coming here."

Matt didn't believe him. Why would the President of the United States come to a coal town of a few hundred people? Eckhart Mines was a small western Maryland town that had a sense of familiarity and quaintness Matt appreciated, but in the grand scheme of things, it meant nothing to President Harding. Of course, with the national coal strike for better wages and safer working conditions nearing the end of its third month, maybe he was coming to make an announcement about the strike. Although it wouldn't make sense for him to make the announcement here. The Maryland mines weren't unionized. The United Mine Workers was using the national strike as way to unionize the Maryland mines. UMW organizers were keeping Maryland miners on strike until the mines recognized the union.

Then Matt's Uncle Samuel mentioned the story as the family ate dinner. Matt didn't believe him, either, but Samuel showed him the article in the *Cumberland Evening Times.* It said the President was going to be driving home to Marion, Ohio, from Gettysburg, Pennsylvania, this weekend. He would stop in Cumberland for lunch with Mayor Koon before continuing west. It didn't take a genius to know his route along the National Road would carry the President through Eckhart Mines and Frostburg. So, it wasn't a visit or an announcement. Harding was just passing through, like so many cross-country travelers did.

The third time Matt heard the story was when a coal miner Matt didn't know walked up to him in front of the hotel and asked Matt if he had heard about the President coming. Matt just nodded and crossed the street. He didn't need to hear the story told for a third time in an hour.

He wondered if people were actually excited about the visit, or if it was just something different to talk about other than the three-month-long coal strike.

Frostburg was noisy as he walked through the town on his way to see his girlfriend Samantha Havencroft. Lots of people were on the streets as the retail stores closed down for the day, and the restaurants, theaters, and dance halls were starting their evening business. Having recently lived in Baltimore, Matt was used to this type of noise and more. To him, it was the heartbeat of a city. The louder it was, the stronger the heart was and the healthier the city was.

Frostburg was not Baltimore. With 6,000 residents, it was barely large enough to be considered a neighborhood in Baltimore, but its heartbeat was strong. It was a coal town on a mountain ridge in Western Maryland, which gave it its own unique energy.

He browsed some windows as he walked. He saw a red and beige ratine dress in the window of the Hitchin Brothers Store. Samantha wouldn't like it, but Matt thought it might be something she could wear when she became a teacher. It was more conservative than the shimmering flapper dresses she favored.

He also saw a toy drum he considered buying for Jacob Spiker.

Jacob and his mother, Laura, were living with Joey McCord. The thought of how crazy Jacob pounding on a toy drum would drive Joey brought a smile to Matt's lips.

He walked along College Avenue until he came to a three-story Georgian home with six bedrooms. It was as large as the family boarding house in Eckhart, except the boarding house had been home to eight people. That house had burned down ten days ago, leaving Matt's family homeless. They were living in the St. Cloud Hotel until a new house was built in Eckhart Mines.

This home was for three people. It was far larger than the Havencrofts needed since only Samantha, her father, and their cook lived there. Mrs. Fratelli lived on the third floor, and her room there wasn't counted among the bedrooms. Samantha and John Havencroft each had a bedroom, which left four bedrooms that were furnished and rarely used. Mr. Havencroft could have used all his extra space for a college dormitory.

That wouldn't happen. John Havencroft had come from money, and he liked to live in a way that fit his expectations of life and his job. He was the president of Frostburg College. It wasn't a large school, but the job had a lot of prestige in the area because residents were proud that a country town could support a college. Miners, merchants, and housewives had donated the money that was used to purchase the land for the college in the 1890s. Many of those donors still lived in the area and could point to the school and claim it as a personal achievement that would outlive them.

Matt went around the side of the house and knock on the kitchen door of the Havencrofts' home. This was the safest way for him to visit Samantha, since John Havencroft had made it clear he thought his daughter was too good for Matt, who he believed was just a poor coal miner, and one without even a home right now. Matt doubted the man's opinion of him would change, even if he knew Matt was a Pinkerton undercover detective. He might even think worse of Matt for keeping secrets.

Not that Mr. Havencroft could talk. He had his own secrets that Matt knew and also kept.

Mrs. Fratelli answered the door. She was in her fifties, but she still had flaming red hair untouched by any gray. She held a wooden spoon dripping with yellow batter.

"Good evening, Mrs. Fratelli. Is Samantha ready?" Matt asked.

The cook waved Matt inside with the spoon, flinging some of the batter on him. "Come inside, I'll fetch her for you." She put the spoon in the mixing bowl and disappeared up the back stairs to the second floor.

Matt stepped into the kitchen, but he didn't sit down. He wanted to step out onto the porch if he heard John Havencroft coming toward the kitchen. It would be easier on Samantha if her father didn't see Matt.

Samantha came down dressed in a sleeveless white dress trimmed in red. She spun around so the knee-length skirt flared at the bottom.

"Do you like it? I bought it in Cumberland," she asked.

"You look beautiful, but don't you think it's a little much for a movie? It will be dark inside the theater. No one will see your dress."

They were going to see *Her Night of Nights* at the Palace Theater. It was a comedy starring Marie Prevost, but from what Matt had heard about it, he thought Samantha might identify a bit too much with Prevost's character. The actress played a New York model torn between her boss's successful son and a lowly clerk from the country. If Samantha was the model, then Matt was the lowly clerk and Professor Williamson from the college was the successful son. Mr. Havencroft certainly preferred him over Matt as a suitor for his daughter.

Samantha ran her hand along Matt's neck scar, a wound from his time in the Great War. "I'm hoping you'll take me dancing afterward," she whispered in his ear seductively.

Matt closed his eyes and sighed. She certainly knew how to get to him.

"We'll see," he said.

She wiggled her eyebrows up and down. "Oh, yes, we will."

Matt was half-regretting his leg wasn't still in a cast from the cave-in three months ago. At least then he had an excuse not to dance. It would also mean that Pete Spike and two other miners wouldn't have been killed when the mine tunnel collapsed on them. Matt had been lucky to survive.

He held the door open for Samantha and followed her outside.

As they walked into Frostburg, he noticed some businesses along Main Street, which was part of the National Road, were decorating their store fronts with red, white, and blue bunting. Matt wondered if it was for the president or the Fourth of July.

"Did you read that President Harding will be in town on Sunday?" Samantha asked when she noticed the decorations.

Matt rolled his eyes and sighed. "He won't be in town. He'll be driving through it from one end to the other in a minute. Two minutes, tops."

"Maybe so, but I've never seen a President in person before."

"I have."

Samantha stopped walking and turned to face him. Her blue eyes were wide open. "You have? Really?"

Matt nodded. "Remember, I told you I was engaged before I came back to Eckhart?"

"Her name was Priscilla, right?" Then her tone turned a bit frosty. "You said I reminded you of her."

When he had first seen Samantha trying to create support for women's rights by giving a speech on Main Street, he had thought of Priscilla. The impression hadn't lasted long, but it had been long enough to draw Matt to Samantha.

Matt held up his hands. "That was a first impression. Now that I know you, I don't look at you and think of her."

Samantha's eyes narrowed a bit. "Uh, huh."

Matt quickly changed the topic. "Her family was what I would call rich, and while I was dating Priscilla, we went to a party her parents threw at their home one evening. The President was the guest of honor."

"President Harding?"

Matt nodded. He had been as uncomfortable at that party as he was on the dance floor. The party attendees had been made up of local politicians, successful businessmen, society woman, and

Matt, a hard-working Pinkerton detective.

"Did you talk to him?" Samantha asked.

Matt shrugged. "Not really. I shook his hand, introduced myself, and said it was nice to meet him. I didn't run in his social circle, and he probably knew that. Oh, he was polite, but he didn't try to have a conversation with me or anything."

They started walking again, and Samantha said, "If my father knew that, he might think differently of you."

"I doubt it."

"Don't. My father was in his office all day, making phone calls to see if he can arrange to meet President Harding. You already have." She laughed.

"What?"

"I'm imagining my father's face when he finds out you've met the President, and he can't arrange a meeting."

"I can't provide an introduction for your father, though. Not that he would ask me."

Samantha laughed. "If he had a chance to meet the President, he would even let you marry me."

She realized what she said and suddenly went quiet, her cheeks turning red. Although things were back to normal between them, they still had a tender spot in their relationship where Jenny Washington was concerned. She had torn Matt and Samantha apart for a time, although she hadn't meant to. Whenever Matt and Samantha got truly intimate again, Samantha pulled away. She never mentioned Jenny, but Matt knew that was who Samantha was thinking about at those times.

Matt pretended he hadn't noticed Samantha's silence. "Your father will probably have to go to Cumberland if he wants to meet him. That's where the luncheon will be. The newspaper said nothing about the President stopping in Frostburg."

"That wouldn't be so bad. It's not like he doesn't go to Cumberland for meetings once in a while."

Matt shrugged. "Maybe not, but the people holding that luncheon are going to want to show off Cumberland, not Frostburg."

"You don't seem so excited about the President's visit."

Matt didn't see that there was anything to get excited about. President Harding would drive through town. He would be here and gone. Nothing would change because of the visit.

"I guess not," Matt said.

"Why?"

"I can't help but think that this is the man who sent the U.S. Army against the striking miners in Matewan last year, and he okayed the army to bomb them. That doesn't sit right with me. The military isn't for use against our own people. It's supposed to protect Americans like we did in the war."

"I'm sure he had his reasons."

"Maybe so, but I don't think he'll get a warm welcome at this end of the county. Miners remember what happened at Matewan. It's probably a good thing he is driving through and not stopping here."

Their conversation stopped as they arrived at the movie. Matt was glad it was a comedy. He had enough drama and tragedy in his life. He didn't need to pay to see more.

After the movie, Matt gave in and they went dancing at the Gunter Hotel. Matt hoped it was still too early for Jenny, or rather, Calista, to be working the room. The last thing he needed was for Samantha to see Jenny dressed to the nines and attracting the attention of men. However, Matt realized he wasn't sure if Calista was still working as a prostitute. He had seen her during the day more often. If she had been working during the night, then she would have spent the day sleeping. He had even seen her some evenings, not dressed up to go to the dance halls and speakeasies. He would have to ask her about that.

After dinner, Matt and Samantha made a date to watch the President drive through Frostburg. Samantha would come by the St. Cloud Hotel, which sat on Main Street at the Depot Street intersection. They could watch the procession from the hotel's front porch, which was a couple steps above street level, so they could see the President if a large crowd formed on the sidewalks.

Matt walked Samantha to the front door of her house and kissed her goodnight on the front step.

"Thank you for the dancing," she whispered as she hugged him and laid her head on his shoulder.

He wrapped his arms around her and enjoyed the feel of her body against his. "My pleasure."

"Liar."

"No, as long as I'm with you, it's a pleasure."

That earned him another kiss.

Matt walked to the St. Cloud Hotel and went upstairs to his family's rooms on the second floor. He had convinced his Aunt Toni to allow him to pay for their rooms while their new house was being built. He shared a room with his Uncle Enos. Uncle Samuel and Aunt Myrna shared a room. Aunt Toni had her own room, and Matt also paid for a room for Jenny since he had agreed to help her.

When Matt came into his room, Enos snoring in his bed surprised him. His uncle was usually out drinking or running moonshine at night. In a switch, everyone else seemed to be out this evening.

Matt heard a train whistle blow, marking the arrival of the evening train on the Cumberland and Pennsylvania line. Curious whether more strikebreakers would be arriving, he hurried down the steep hill to the train depot and took a seat on a bench on the platform as porters opened the doors on the passenger cars.

Matt scanned the crowd and saw three men wearing holstered pistols. He watched some people on the platform look nervously at the men as if they expected them to pull their guns and start shooting. They had the look of Pinkerton agents, and Matt should know, since he was also one. Unlike these men, however, he was working undercover.

He hated the image these men were creating for the Pinkertons. They came across as thugs. Matt just hoped no one discovered he was one of them.

He watched as a half dozen shabbily dressed men—strikebreakers, he thought—came off the third-class car and looked around. The Pinkertons walked over to them. Matt didn't hear what they said, but the group left the platform together with the strikebreakers following the detectives.

Matt waited, expecting one of the Pinkertons to accompany them. With all the violence that had been happening during the coal strike, it wasn't unheard of for miners to attack strikebreakers and try to run them out of the town. The Pinkertons were supposed to be protecting them.

Matt followed the men to make sure they would be all right. Most people ignored them. A few cursed them, but things remained relatively calm.

He stopped walking and shook his head, sorry for that last thought. Given the problems the strike was causing, thinking that things were relatively calm also made him think it might simply be the calm before the storm.

Chapter 2

June 30, 1922

Laura Spiker opened her eyes and lay still in the feather bed. She stared at the bare white ceiling. It helped her clear her mind and focus as she started her day. It reminded her that every day was a clean slate and a fresh start—right before she got up and started making the same poor choices again.

She tried to sense whether Joey was still in bed beside her. She didn't feel a sag in the mattress from his weight or the warmth of another body near hers. She turned her head to the side and slowly rolled over.

He was already up and gone.

When she had been married, she had been the first one up in the mornings. Sensing Pete next to her, the warmth of his body and the familiarity of his scent were comforting no matter how poor they had been. She would slide out of their bed and go get breakfast ready for him before he went off to the mines. When she came back into the bedroom to let him know breakfast was ready, she would wake him with a kiss or nibble on his ear.

Laura exhaled, not realizing she had been holding her breath. She raised her fingers to her temples and rubbed. Her head throbbed and the light coming through the windows didn't help any.

What time was it? She looked at the clock on the wall. After nine in the morning. Jacob would be up and hungry. She needed to get him breakfast.

She sat up, and her head spun so quickly she thought she might fall back. She took a deep breath and stood up. She picked up her robe draped over the back of the chair and put it on over her nude body. She had nice nightgowns now, but even if she wore them to bed, they rarely stayed on once Joey joined her in bed.

She walked down the hall to Jacob's room and opened the door. The room had an oversized bed in it, but it didn't look like a child's room, let alone a bedroom. The bookshelves held books Jacob couldn't read. The bed was far too large for a child. The furniture looked too nice for Jacob to touch. It wasn't an inviting room. Jacob might sleep there, but it wasn't his room.

Her son bounced on the bed, playing with his toy soldiers.

"Mama!" he said when he saw her.

Squinting at the bright light in his room, Laura came into the room and sat on the bed next to the three-year-old boy. She hugged him and kissed the top of his head. He was a miniature version of his father with the same brown hair and eyes. Sometimes, he would smile, and Laura thought it was exactly the way Pete used to smile. She could look at her son and remember Pete.

"Good morning, my boy," she said. "You must be hungry."

Jacob shook his head. "I ate breakfast."

"Really? What did you eat?"

"Maizy cooked me pancakes with syrup. I ate two big ones."

Maizy Middleton was Joey's housekeeper and cook. While she allowed Joey and Jacob to call her Maizy, she insisted Laura call her Mrs. Middleton. Laura wasn't even sure whether the woman was married. Laura had heard no one mention the housekeeper's husband.

"Did you thank her?" Laura asked.

"Yes."

"Good boy."

Laura hugged him and headed downstairs.

Mrs. Middleton was in the kitchen kneading dough when

Laura walked in. Locks of her gray hair had pulled loose from the bun tied at the back of her head and dangled in front of her face. The older woman glanced at her, but said nothing. She rarely did, at least to Laura.

"Thank you for feeding Jacob," Laura said. "He loved the pancakes."

Mrs. Middleton said nothing, although she lifted the dough she was kneading and slapped it down hard against the table. The noise rattled through Laura's head. Perhaps it was better that Mrs. Middleton said nothing.

Jacob and Laura had been living with Joey for a couple of weeks now, and Mrs. Middleton hadn't warmed up to Laura. Laura tried to be pleasant with her, but the woman treated Laura much like the women in Eckhart treated her. Mrs. Middleton seemed to enjoy Jacob's company, though. She even let him help with her cooking sometimes.

As Laura turned and left the kitchen, she thought she heard the cook mutter, "Tramp."

Laura walked back to her room and drew the shades to darken the room. Then she went into her armoire and lifted the lid on a shoe box at the bottom of the closet. She pulled out a bottle of gin she had found hidden in the basement, along with a lot of other bottles of pre-Prohibition liquor.

She looked at the bottle and joggled it. It was still half full. She uncapped it and took a drink. It hit her with a kick. She felt nauseous since she hadn't eaten breakfast yet, but her headache faded.

She crawled back into the bed and took the bottle with her. She had never been much of a drinker when she was married to Pete. Not that they could afford liquor. Pete had been known to take a drink from time to time, but she had never liked the taste. Truth was, she still didn't like the taste, but she did like how it made her feel, or rather, not feel.

After a couple drinks, she didn't have to worry. All her problems and worries went away. It was just her and her happy thoughts or no thoughts. She didn't have to deal with the loneliness of not having Pete around. She didn't have to deal with the scorn from people in town who thought she was betraying the miners by being with Joey. She didn't have feel shame for being here with Joey. Everything was fine.

Joseph McCord came into the house, bouncing on his feet. He was so excited he had forgotten to drive his Renault GS up the hill from the mine office. The short walk had left him huffing, with a slight sheen of sweat on his forehead.

"Laura! Laura, where are you?" he called.

Not seeing her in the parlor, he rushed upstairs to the bedroom. He opened the door and saw her lying on top of the blankets asleep. Her light brown hair fanned out around her head and her robe draped open, showing just enough her body to make him smile.

Then Joseph noticed the glass and bottle of gin on the nightstand. Maybe not asleep; she was probably passed out.

When had she become such a drinker? She hadn't seemed that way in school or when she was married. She was probably too young to drink much in school, but had Pete Spiker kept her in check while they were married?

"Laura!" he shouted.

She moaned and rolled back and forth on the bed.

"You don't need to shout," she mumbled.

She opened her eyes and pushed herself up on her elbows. She glanced at Joseph and out the window.

"What time is it?" she asked.

"It's one o'clock."

"Isn't it early for you to be home?"

"Yes, but that's not important. I have news. The President is coming," Joseph blurted.

Laura's brow furrowed. "The president of Consolidation Coal?"

Joseph sat down on the bed next to her, grabbed her by the shoulders, and gave her a shake. "Focus! Not the president of the mining company. The President of the United States."

"The President of the United States is coming to Eckhart?"

"Well, he's coming to Cumberland and then driving west,

which means he'll be driving through Eckhart. I'm going to arrange to meet him. I will show him the mines and get his support to end this damnable strike!"

And if Joseph could get his picture taken with President Harding, he could certainly leverage that to his benefit in some way.

"Can you do that?" Laura asked. "I mean, arrange a meeting with him?"

Joseph drew his shoulders back. "Of course I can. I will invite him to the house for coffee. We can't have drinks because of Prohibition. That means you can't be drinking when he is here." He shook a finger in her face. "You have to be sober, and you have to dress in your best dress."

Laura nodded. "Of course, Joey."

"And you'll have to keep the boy in his room."

She frowned. "Why? I'm sure Jacob would love to meet the President."

"This won't be a social meeting. President Harding and I have business to discuss, and we may not have much time."

Joseph stood up and started pacing the bedroom. This would work. He could meet with the President and show him the impact the strike was having on small towns across America. He could show the President that the problems from last year hadn't been solved yet and he needed to stay strong against the United Mine Workers. If Joseph could bring about an end to strike, he could get a job with any coal company in America.

He would have to reassign the strikebreakers from the mines to help the mine guards and make sure the union miners wouldn't protest the President's arrival. He wouldn't have enough guns for them all. Weapons were in short supply since the strike had started. Joseph would have to get the strikebreakers' clubs to use if they needed them.

He looked at Laura, who had slumped back onto the bed. The harder part might be making sure that Laura was presentable enough to meet with the President of the United States. How was he supposed to show himself as a man of influence when he couldn't even control his mistress?

Chapter 3

June 30, 1922

Enos Ansaro shuffled the playing cards and began dealing them to himself and the three ladies sitting with him around the table in the lobby of the St. Cloud Hotel in Frostburg. He had his back to the front desk so he could watch people passing by on Main Street. When he had dealt out the deck, he looked at his dwindling pile of bobby pins, which they were using for chips.

"This is unfair," he said. "I'm a man. We don't know anything about bobby pins."

"I think it's more obvious you don't know anything about playing hearts," Jenny Washington joked. She sat on his right, and she wasn't wrong. He had told them he would rather play poker, but his sister-in-law Myrna Ansaro wouldn't hear of it.

"Your pile isn't much bigger than mine," Enos told Jenny.

His gaze drifted from her small pile of pins to her bustline. Jenny caught him staring. She picked a pin up from her pile and poked him in the hand.

"Ow! That hurt." He stuck his hand in mouth.

"It's not a straight pin, Enos," Jenny told him. "It's a bobby pin. It's not pointy, so stop whining and play cards."

"Has anyone ever told you that you are overly competitive?"

Enos asked.

She waved at the pile of pins in the center of the table. "I need to win back my bobby pins, or I won't be able to put up my hair."

"I think it looks fine."

His compliment earned him a smile. "Thank you. Now let's play cards."

Enos picked up his cards and arranged them by suit. She caught him casting glances at her, although he was careful so she wouldn't poke him again. She was used to men staring at her, but she usually wore outfits to attract their attention at those times. Jenny was barely wearing any makeup, and her auburn hair needed to be brushed out.

Across the table from Enos, his sister Antonietta Starner fidgeted in her seat. It was quite unlike her to act so uncomfortable. His brother's wife, Myrna Ansaro, sat across the table from Jenny. Myrna laid a four of clubs in the center of the table. Everyone followed suit, and Jenny took the trick with a ten of clubs.

As Toni considered her cards, Enos said, "Toni, what's eating at you? You look like a rabbit about to bolt."

"I just can't get used to sitting around with nothing to do. No cooking. No cleaning. Very little sewing but no laundry," she admitted. "It doesn't feel natural."

"I can get used to it," Myrna said.

Jenny tossed her card on the table. "I can get used to it, too. Usually, I'm too busy to relax and do something fun like playing cards."

"Why aren't you working?" Myrna asked. "I thought you were a maid for someone in town."

Jenny froze. She and Matt had concocted that story to cover up her work as Calista, the persona she adopted as a prostitute, and have a respectable reason to have money. Actually, Matt had been paying her room and board as a way to help her get out of Frostburg and allow him to funnel money to his family without them knowing it. Then the boarding house in Eckhart Mines had burned down, or rather, David Lakehurst had burned it down. Matt had felt obligated to continue their deal, but now Jenny was back in

Frostburg, and Matt's money wasn't helping his family as much as it was the owners of the hotel.

As for Jenny, she couldn't tell this group what she did for a living. Matt knew, but he hadn't told his family. She liked these people, and if they found out she was a prostitute, they might start treating her differently. That's what happened when John Havencroft had found out his maid had been a prostitute. It hadn't mattered that she had stopped when Samantha Havencroft had hired her. Mr. Havencroft had fired her on the spot.

"They had to let me go," Jenny lied. "They have lost a lot of business because of the coal strike and couldn't afford hired help any longer."

"I'm so sorry," Myrna said as she patted Jenny's arm. "This coal strike is hurting everyone, not just the miners."

The strike had been going on for three months and showed no signs of ending. Jenny wondered how many businesses would close and how many families would leave the area before it ended. She had been a coal miner's wife once. She felt for the miners' plight.

"I'm sure I'll find something else to do," Jenny said.

Not that she had looked. Even if she had found another house-keeping job, someone would eventually recognize her from her other work. She had gotten used to working a job where she didn't have to hide what she did from most people. Since the fire, though, she had been going back to her night work occasionally. She wasn't sure how long Matt could afford to support the family in a hotel. She wasn't family, and if he had to cut back, asking her to give up her room would be his first cut.

Enos sniggered. Jenny looked at him. Why did he laugh? Did he know she was lying about her work? That was what worried her about being back in Frostburg with the Ansaros. How long would it be before someone saw her and recognized her? She rarely worked in this hotel, but she find men here from time to time.

"Do you find this poor girl losing her job funny, Enos?" Myrna asked.

"No, Myrna, not funny at all. I just happened to be thinking about something humorous at the wrong time." He turned to Jenny and said, "No offense, Jenny."

Was she mistaken, or did his brown eyes twinkle with mirth? It was hard to tell with Enos. He was a cheerful man whom she enjoyed being around.

"Well, I'll be glad when the new house is finished, and we can move back home," Toni said.

"Will it be home, though? It will be all new. It won't have all the old memories," Myrna said. "The rocking chair my grandfather built burned. The quilt you and I made is ash." She stopped talking when she felt her eyes tearing up.

"It will be new, but it will be our home. We'll make it our home and fill it with new memories."

Jenny was just happy they would soon be out of this hotel. Joseph McCord and the Consolidation Coal Company had offered to build a new house for the Ansaros because David Lakehurst had been employed by the coal company. The coal company didn't admit responsibility for the fire, though. They said Lakehurst had been acting on his own, which Jenny could believe. The man was a monster.

Myna nodded. She tossed in a card and reached out and took the trick with a single heart in it. Her bobby pin pile grew even larger. Jenny wondered if Myrna was a card shark disguised as a kindly, middle-aged wife.

Jenny thought of another reason she felt content and happy: David Lakehurst was gone. That brute of a man had beaten her, broken Matt's leg, and burned the Starner Boarding House down. Matt had finally thrashed him, though, and Lakehurst had fled town, probably to avoid the trial for assaulting Jenny and who knows how many other women. She was surprised at how she had felt a burden lift off her shoulders when she heard he had left. It meant she didn't have to testify in court about her work and what Lakehurst had done to her. Then everyone would have known what she did to earn a living.

Jenny had been living in a happy limbo for the past couple of weeks. She didn't have to work as Calista unless she wanted to.

Even living in the hotel as she did was so much better than the ramshackle house she had been renting. And she had friends. This was something she hadn't felt in a long time. How long had it been since she really trusted anyone, especially a man? The last time probably would have been before her husband, Gregory, had been killed in the war. After that, she had worked odd jobs until loneliness drove her to seek other men. Then she had decided to make money from it.

Now, Matt paid for her meals and room and asked nothing for it. He had even rebuffed her when she had tried to climb into bed with him; the second time, not the first time. The first time it had happened was when they had met.

She knew it would have to end at some point. She needed to earn a living, even if it meant more prostitution. The Elks' and the Maryland State firemen's conventions were both coming to town this summer. That would certainly offer her all the business she wanted while those men were around.

For now, though, she was happy just playing hearts.

Chapter 4

June 30, 1922

It was a short walk from the St. Cloud Hotel to the Junior Mechanics Hall in Frostburg. The United Mine Workers local had called a special meeting for its members, and word spread from miner to miner as they saw each other throughout the day.

Only Matt and Samuel went from their family. Enos said he wanted to sleep because he had deliveries to make that night. Matt thought that odd. Enos had joined the union, but Matt and Samuel were still undecided, and yet, they were the ones going to the meeting. Enos had joined the union out of convenience and for the free booze that was offered as a "sign-up bonus."

When Matt and Samuel reached the hall, it was standing room only inside. That only drove up the temperature in the room on an already warm evening. With 150 unwashed men gathered in a hot, small space, the smell was acrid.

Since the miners were on strike, most of them had nothing better to do than attend the meeting. Plus, most of them wanted to know when they would be going back to work. The strike had been going on for three months, and the miners needed money to pay bills, feed their families, and pay their rent. They had used up their savings—the few who had any—and were living primarily on vegetables and meat their wives had managed to can. Those stores of food were running low, too. They were waiting for the next shoe to drop. Would the coal company evict them from their homes? Would their food run out? It had already happened to some of them.

The older miners remembered the local strikes of 1900 and 1894 that had failed to unionize Western Maryland's miners despite the promises of the union organizers. Although they joined in this strike in a show of solidarity, they were the most skeptical about the strike's chance of success. The unions hadn't fully supported the local miners, but the mine owners had remembered which miners had fully supported the union. Those miners had lost their jobs when the strikes had failed.

The UMW had set up a food commissary to help the struggling families, but it wasn't supplying miners with an abundance, since miners across the country were out of work and needed help. Also, it was in Frostburg, which meant those miners further down the Creek had to find a way to get to Frostburg other than spending money to ride the trolley if they wanted food from the commissary.

The coal companies and the UMW were negotiating, but the news didn't sound promising. John L. Lewis was determined to win this battle and cement his authority in the union. He had started his association with the UMW back in 1906, when he was elected a delegate to the UMW national convention. Five years later, Samuel Gompers hired him as a full-time union organizer. He became the acting president on November 1, 1919, and soon thereafter called his first major coal union strike. During that strike, 400,000 miners walked off their jobs. Since becoming president of the UMW in 1920, Lewis had been aggressive in asserting the power of unionized coal miners.

Matt and Samuel talked to a few miners they recognized as they made their way to the back wall near an open window. The breeze coming through the window was barely cooler than the temperature inside the room, but the smell wasn't as bad.

Samuel wiped his forehead with a kerchief. "Makes you appreciate the coolness of the mines."

Matt never thought he would get used to the fifty-degree temperature below ground. "There has to be a middle ground," he replied.

"Maybe the mines are the coal companies, cold and dark. This is the union, hot and getting hotter."

Matt cocked an eyebrow at his uncle. "When did you get so philosophical?"

Samuel blushed, or maybe it was the heat. "I'm not. I read it somewhere, probably in the newspaper."

Matt doubted that. His uncle was intelligent and thoughtful, but no one expected wisdom from a coal miner.

Matt listened and caught snippets of conversations around him. The men were angry at the union and the coal companies. The union had told the miners the strike would be short, and they would prevail. The union always said that. It was rarely true. The miners weren't happy the strike was still ongoing. That was no surprise. What surprised Matt was that some men were losing faith that the union would prevail, which meant the recruiters' jobs were on the line. Not only would Lewis not be thrilled to lose a strike, the union's image in Western Maryland would be weakened again. Maybe beyond recovery.

At the front of the room, Brian Kilpatrick, the head of the Frostburg Local, stood up and waved for the crowd to quiet down. Although he wore a clean, white shirt and pleated pants, he couldn't escape the air of a coal miner, which he was. He had a thick, black beard that reached his chest and the slight hunch that many miners developed from working in mine shafts with low clearances. His position with the local wasn't a full-time job. He still worked in the mines when they were open, although he probably wanted to advance to a position that took him above ground.

"Thanks for coming out tonight, everyone." Kilpatrick said. "I know it's a Friday night, and you would rather be out having some fun, but we have some important things to talk about. I'll let Paul explain it to you."

Paul Tomlinson stood up. He had replaced Harvey Thomas as the union organizer in the area when the strike started. Matt thought that must mean something, but he wasn't sure what. Unlike Kilpatrick, Tomlinson didn't look like a miner. He reminded Matt of a banker or a huckster.

Paul adjusted his sports coat and said, "Some of you know me. I'm Paul Tomlinson, the UMW representative for Maryland and West Virginia. I suppose you all read the newspaper this morning."

"Can't afford it. We're not working," someone called out, and a few people laughed.

Paul grinned and nodded. "Well, President Harding is traveling from an event in Gettysburg to his home in Ohio. He will stop for lunch and a meeting with the mayor of Cumberland on Sunday afternoon. From there, he'll be driving west and that means he'll be coming through Frostburg."

Some of the crowd had booed at the sound of Harding's name. What had started with private detectives evicting union miners from their homes in Matewan, West Virginia, last fall had turned into a full-blown civil uprising at Blair Mountain. The fighting between miners and company men pulled in the police and U.S. Army. At its peak, about 40,000 people were fighting. About 130 people had died. It had been the first time since the Civil War that armed troops had been sent against civilians. Harding had even allowed soldiers to drop bombs on civilians from airplanes. It had helped end the strike, but it had also caused a lot of animosity toward the administration among union miners and many Americans who thought the government had overstepped its authority using federal troops against civilians. Although the Stone Mountain Coal Company had won the battle, it won no friends. Things in West Virginia were still tense; more so with the national coal strike ongoing.

Tomlinson held up his hands for quiet. "I'm not saying you need to line the streets to greet the man." He shook his head. "Feel free to boo him. Lord knows he's no friend of the miner. No, I have something different in mind. I want him to feel the fear our brothers in West Virginia felt when they were bombed." He bowed his head as if holding a moment of silence. It felt wrong to Matt, like fake grief. "I want him to know we are serious about our demands."

"What can we do?" someone called out.

"I'm glad you asked," Tomlinson said, perking up. "I want to find the best shot among you and have him shoot at the President."

That caused just as big an uproar as mentioning President's Harding's name. Matt straightened up, unsure he had just heard what he heard. Was Tomlinson calling for assassination? That was one sure way to turn all the country against the coal miners and any union members against any union!

"Hear me out! Hear me out!" Tomlinson slammed his hands down on the podium. "I don't want to kill the President or even have a bullet hit him. I just want him scared, scared like the miners in Southern West Virginia were when soldiers marched on them and bombs fell from sky. I want the President to think about his actions. Maybe then this strike will be settled sooner rather than later, and with some consideration for us working men."

Matt thought it interesting that Tomlinson included himself as a working man when it was obvious he had had never worked in a coal mine. Matt wondered if the man had ever even been below in a mine shaft.

"I know you all hunt, so I need the names of anyone who is a great shot. Leave them with Brian, and I will contact you privately. We don't want to hurt or kill anyone, but other people will be around. That's why I need a crack shot. We just need you to put a hole in a car or blow out a tire," Paul said.

That brought more raised voices. Some men even walked out. Beside Matt, Samuel hung his head and shook it. It wasn't a popular decision, but Matt also saw some men going up to Brian Kilpatrick. He was writing on a small pad.

This was not good news. It was dangerous news, and he had to let the Pinkertons know.

Chapter 5

July 1, 1922

Antonietta Starner walked down the National Road from Frostburg to Eckhart. She made the trip at least once a day. It was more than just needing to have something to do, although that was a large part of it. She couldn't get used to sitting around the hotel lobby or her room with nothing to do. Eckhart was her home. Her friends lived there, and she hoped she would, too, one day soon.

Her first stop, as always, was to walk by the boarding house. She felt a need to see the progress with her own eyes. It had reassured to see the frame go up, then the sides and roof. It already looked different from their home that had burned down. She wondered if this would feel like home when it was complete. Although she had managed to save many of the family photos and the family Bible, they had lost nearly everything else. Her mother's wedding dress that she had worn when she married Michael Starner. The quilt her grandmother had sewn. The rocking chair her father had made her mother when she was pregnant with Samuel.

Enos and Samuel had also saved some things, too, but Myrna had been overcome with smoke. She and Samuel had been lucky to get out of the burning house alive. Luckily, Matt had helped them. That brave, foolish boy... It was hard to stay mad at him. She wanted to. He was standing on both sides of the coal strike and trying not to get dirty. It just wasn't possible when coal was involved.

Toni watched the workers climb on the roof, and she also heard hammering from inside of the house. Joseph McCord was using some strikebreakers to rebuild the boarding house for the Ansaros. Hopefully, they were better at building than they were at mining.

Toni wasn't sure how she felt about strikebreakers building the house. It somehow felt disloyal to the miners, but if the strikebreakers were building a house, could she even call them strikebreakers? Too bad they couldn't find full-time work like this to do for a living.

One man walked out of the house to a bucket of water that sat on the porch. He wiped his face off with his handkerchief. Then he used a dipper to get himself a drink. As he turned to go back to work, he saw Toni and stopped.

"Good day to you, Mrs. Starner." His hand reached up to tip a hat that wasn't there.

Toni smiled despite herself. She had met Patrick a few weeks ago when the strikebreakers had started coming to town. She had lumped him in with the rest of that group and taken an instant dislike to him, but he had shown himself to be polite and persistent where Toni was concerned."

"Good morning, Mr. Kennedy."

He smiled and hopped off the porch. He was a light-skinned man with blond hair that was almost white. He had an erect posture, which marked him as military in her mind, because she had seen other former soldiers with the same bearing. Matt had that posture, come to think of it.

"What do you think?" he said, waving a hand at the house.

"I think you men are probably better carpenters than miners."

He nodded his agreement. "I know I am. I much prefer this over mining. I miss the sun when I am underground, but a person has to make a living." He spoke hesitantly, as if English wasn't his native language. More likely, he was trying to speak clearly and minimize his accent. "This is your house, isn't it?"

"It will be my family's house when it's done."

"Then perhaps you might want to walk through it next week. We should be well into the interior work, and you may want to suggest things that will make it feel like home. Mr. McCord wasn't too specific about what we should build." He winked at Toni. "I doubt Mr. McCord will even notice."

Toni's eyes widened. "Don't you need to work from plans?"

Patrick grinned. "That we do, and I got a set from the man who sold us the lumber. He said he would just add it on his bill."

"And you all are carpenters?"

Patrick shrugged. "Some of us are. Others are just laborers. We all know how to use the tools if you're worried about that."

She pressed her lips together in a tight line. Then she said, "I've been wondering if it will ever feel like home again and if I will ever truly feel comfortable in the house."

"Because of the fire?"

Toni nodded. "I never thought about the possibility of the house burning down before. We were lucky no one was killed."

Patrick said, "Quite right, but then, there's nothing to stop this house from burning, or the house next to it, or the one next to it."

"Why say that? Do you want to give me nightmares?"

"Not at all. I want to take them away."

"How is making me think about fire going to do that?"

"Because I'm reminding you that everywhere you have lived up to the point where this happened could have burned down as well. It only happened once, and that, from what I've been told, was an unusual set of circumstances. So there's no reason to think it will happen again in your life. It can, but it's unlikely, and it's something you can't control other than by taking normal everyday precautions."

"You have an odd way of looking at things, Mr. Kennedy."

"I learned a long time ago that so much of my life is beyond my control. I'm not going to waste my time on this earth trying to control it. What I can change, I do, hopefully for the best. What I can't, I do my best not to let it get to me."

They talked for a little while longer until another worker called Patrick back to the house. He said goodbye and went back to work.

As Toni walked down the hill to Louis Chabot's store, she found herself thinking about Patrick. He had expressed an interest in her, and she had turned him down. Was that because she wasn't interested or because he was a strikebreaker? She told herself it was the former, but she wasn't so sure now. She had been a widow for more than a year, and in that time, Patrick was the first man to pay her any attention, or at least the first one who had made his feelings known. He was attractive enough and a friendly, kind man, but she couldn't get past the fact he was a strikebreaker.

Still, she had to wonder how much longer men would pay her any attention. She was a miner's widow in her mid-forties. She would make a man a good wife, but she certainly had no money or influence to bring to a marriage. She was also past her child-bearing years or nearly so.

She walked into Chabot's for a cup of homemade ice cream to ease some of the heat from the day. She wasn't the only one with the idea. Five other people were in the store, including Laura Spiker and her son, Jacob.

Jacob waved when he saw Toni and ran over to her.

"Miss Toni!"

Toni reached down and scooped the boy up in her arms. "Hello, Jacob. I have missed you." He gave her a hug with one arm, since the other held an ice cream cone.

Laura started toward her, but staggered and had to steady herself.

"Hello, Toni."

"Are you all right?"

Laura nodded. "I'm just a bit tired. This little guy keeps me busy." She rubbed Jacob's hair. He just licked at his ice cream cone.

"Well, when we move back into the house, you can bring him by. Myrna and I had fun watching him."

"You don't have to do that. I have a cook now. She also keeps the house clean and plays with Jacob."

Toni thought it was interesting Laura, who had been a starving widow a few weeks ago, now claimed Joseph's cook as her own. Toni wished Laura all the happiness and security she could get, but Toni doubted the young mother had either one.

Laura looked over at Cora Jacobs and Mary Corsini, who were whispering at one side of the store. Laura lifted her son from Toni and set him on the floor.

"We have to go," Laura said. "It was nice to see you, Toni."

They walked out of the store. Toni watched them go, smiling.

Cora walked over to Toni. "How can you talk to that woman, Toni?"

Toni's smile turned into a frown. "Quite easy, actually."

"She betrayed this community and her husband."

"How did she do that?"

"She became Joseph McCord's mistress."

Some people had nothing better to do than criticize other people's choices without knowing why they made them. The thought gave her pause. Wasn't she doing just that with Patrick and his decision to work as a strikebreaker?

"Maybe she loves him." Toni knew it was doubtful. Joseph McCord wasn't a very likeable person, but she had to admit she had only seen him be kind to Laura.

"It's Joseph McCord," Cora said. "What she likes is his money. She is nothing but a whore, and that poor boy will suffer because of it."

Toni doubted that. One thing she knew for sure was that Laura loved her son and would do nothing to hurt him.

Chapter 6

July 1, 1922

Matt ate pancakes with maple syrup in the St. Cloud Hotel dining room before rushing out to catch the Cumberland and Westernport trolley on its loop back to Cumberland. The trolleys made hourly trips during the day between Cumberland, Frostburg, and Westernport. The trip to Cumberland from Frostburg was twenty-six miles and took an hour.

He could have made a phone call to take care of this business, but he didn't want to risk an operator overhearing his conversation. Besides, the discussion might take some time as he and William Singletary decided on how to proceed. Matt read the *Cumberland Evening Times* on the ride, searching for more information about President Harding's visit on Sunday. He saw nothing. It wasn't a huge event with planned speeches. It was a quick luncheon with the Cumberland mayor and city council on President's trip home. Better for everyone that it stay low key.

Matt had read articles on the problems the coal strike was causing across the county. People at all levels of society were suffering, and much of the blame was being placed on the United Mine Workers. That was enough to keep Paul Tomlinson committed to sharing the pain with the President. Tomlinson and John

Lewis both acted as if this was a religious crusade to make miners' lives better. Matt never saw how they could justify themselves to those whose lives seemed to get worse. It was all about control and power. Should those who mine the coal or those who own the coal mines have the power?

Matt hopped off the trolley at the Centre Street stop in downtown Cumberland and walked around the corner to Baltimore Street. He checked the numbers on the buildings and found the door he wanted. It opened to stairs that led to offices on the floors above the ground-floor store. He walked down the hall to a wooden door near the back. The small sign on it read "PND Agency."

This differed from the regular office of the Pinkerton National Detective Agency, which also had offices on Baltimore Street. However, Singletary was coordinating the undercover agents in coal towns along Georges Creek. He needed a separate office in which to meet privately with the local agents like Matt, who were undercover in the area coal mines.

Matt walked into a small office. A young woman, perhaps in her late twenties, sat at a desk filing papers. If she was young, what did that make Matt, who was twenty-three? Her brown hair was carefully pinned on top of her head.

She stopped her work and looked up. "May I help you?"

Her right hand drifted slowly below the level of the desk. He wondered if she was reaching for a pistol. She might need it in her line of work.

"I'm here to see William Singletary."

"Is he expecting you?"

Matt shook his head. "No, tell him Matt Ansaro from Eckhart Mines is here."

The woman stood up, knocked on the door to the adjoining office, and then went inside. She came back out a few moments later.

"You can go in, Mr. Ansaro."

"Would you have shot me?" Matt asked.

She smiled. "I wouldn't have tried to kill you."

So it had been a pistol.

"Your mistake. If you shoot, shoot to kill," Matt told her.

She raised an eyebrow. "Even if it's you?"

"Better not to draw on me. I'm harmless."

She looked him up and down. "Somehow I doubt that."

Matt walked into an office that was no larger than the secretary's. It had a single window that looked out on an alley. William Singletary stood behind his desk. He was a small man with thinning hair. The secretary shut the door.

"I'm glad to see your leg has healed, Matt. Have a seat." He waved to one of two chairs in front of his desk. Matt sat in the one that didn't have files on it.

He'd been out of the cast for a few weeks now. His right leg had been broken in a cave-in in March. It still ached if Matt walked for long distances, but he considered himself lucky. Pete Spiker, Laura's husband, had been killed in the same cave-in.

"Thank you." Matt sat in a wooden chair in front of the desk.

"So what is so important that you show up at my office instead of calling or sending a letter?"

Matt explained what had happened at the union meeting as simply as he could. Singletary's frown deepened with each new detail.

"So they're going to kill the President?" Singletary asked when Matt finished.

Matt shook his head. "No, they want to scare him. As angry as they are with the President, I don't think they would try to kill him... at least not any of the miners."

"Are you sure? They've been killing each other during this strike."

"Some of them. Most of them are willing to fight for what they want, but they don't want to kill people."

"It is risky. If someone was shooting at me, it would scare me, and it might also kill me."

Matt nodded. "That's what I'm worried about. Whomever Tomlinson picks to shoot at the President will be firing near a crowd of people. After his first shot, all hell will break loose. People will be running around. If he plans more than a single shot, the second bullet will have to be very carefully placed to avoid hitting anyone."

Singletary drummed his fingers on the desk. "What do you think we should do?"

"Can we divert the President's party? Have him take a different route once he leaves Cumberland?"

Singletary snorted. "What route? There aren't a lot of ways through the mountains. Plus, if word gets out that he changed his route because of a threat from the miners, he will look weak, or he'll look like he's trying to blame them for something they can say they weren't going to do. It would probably accomplish the same things the union is hoping to achieve by having someone shoot at him."

"But no one will be in danger of getting shot." Matt rubbed his forehead. He was getting a headache. "It was easier in the Marines. If someone shot at you, you got out of the way."

Singletary frowned. "This is not the Marines. It's politics and a lot worse. Your enemies like to come at you from behind."

"Do you have any suggestions?"

Singletary removed his wire-frame glasses and rubbed his eyes. "The President will have a police escort, but I can certainly bring in more agents and call in the ones already in the area. With more protection, the shooter will probably be scared off."

Matt shook his head. "That would make things worse. There are enough guns walking around the county already. If people see more agents, they might start thinking the coal companies are cracking down even harder. People are tense and armed. If the shooter fires near a crowd, people might pull their guns and start firing back or at each other." He paused. "Let me handle it."

"What can you do?"

"I'll find out who is going to be doing the shooting and stop him."

"How? You said there were more than a hundred miners in that meeting, not counting the ones Tomlinson might have approached before and after the meeting. A lot of them would probably be willing to take a shot at the President, too."

"Not as many as you think, and whoever does it will be alone. He won't want anyone else to see him. The more people who know what he is doing, the greater the chance someone will tell the police about it. I was trained to watch for suspicious activity, tactical positions, and ambushes. Let me put those skills to use to find a coal miner rather than a German."

Singletary was quiet. Finally, he nodded. "Fine. You have today and tomorrow to come up with something. Let me know the situation by noon, or I will flood the area with agents. We can't take any chances. This is the President of the United States we're talking about."

Matt was aware of the stakes on both sides. "I'll get right on it."

Matt stood up, but Singletary held up a hand. "One more thing." Matt sunk back into the seat. "David Lakehurst."

"What about him?"

"I heard about the fight you and he had."

Matt had wondered if he would hear more about Lakehurst. He wondered if Lakehurst had said something to the Pinkertons about Matt having family in Eckhart.

"Did you hear he burned down the home where I was staying?" Matt chose not to say it was his family's home. If Matt had told the Pinkertons he had family in Eckhart Mines, they wouldn't have allowed him to work undercover there.

Singletary nodded. "I did. Did you know he was a Pinkerton?"

"Yes, he wasn't undercover. He lorded the fact that he had a badge and pistol over everyone. I was having trouble with Lakehurst for a couple of months. He hurt a friend of mine. A woman."

Singletary frowned. "Sadly, she is probably not the only woman he has hurt."

"Pinkertons aren't angels. I know that. They need to be tough, but they shouldn't be brutal or sadistic. If you want to know one reason having more Pinkertons in the area would cause problems now, it's because you sent someone like Lakehurst in the first place. He bullied and beat people when he didn't have to. Now, everyone looks at the uniformed agents with suspicion and fear."

"Some would say Lakehurst got the job done."

Matt raised an eyebrow. "Did he? What did he accomplish? He

might have kept the strikebreakers safe, but because of the tension he brought to the area, they are still in danger. Maybe even more so. He also endangered other Pinkertons."

"How so?"

"People who had run-ins with Lakehurst spread the word about him. It made them more cautious in public, and it made them more likely to attack any other Pinkertons with an overwhelming force in case the Pinkerton is another Lakehurst."

"Then I guess you won't be surprised to hear that has happened at least twice. In Pekin and again in Mount Savage."

Matt shrugged. "Are the agents all right?"

"They were injured enough that they had to be replaced." Matt kept silent. "Lakehurst was fired. Not that it matters. No one has seen him since he jumped bail and left the county. The reason I'm letting you run with your idea is we need to cool things down in the county, not heat them up more."

"I agree."

Singletary nodded. "Good luck, then."

They shook hands, and Matt left the office. He headed back to the express office for the Cumberland and Westernport Electric Railway to a catch the next trolley, but he detoured to the Liberty Trust Bank at the intersection of Centre and Baltimore streets. At six stories, it was taller than the Queen City Station for the Western Maryland Railroad, but not as impressive. It was a simple brick design with slightly rounded corners.

Inside, he found a clerk to take him to the safe deposit boxes. He unlocked number 407 and looked through the contents. He had started using the box when he arrived in Allegany County to store things he didn't want the residents of Eckhart to see, like his Pinkerton National Detective Agency badge. The box also held his old engagement ring from his unfinished wedding to Priscilla Bankert. He wasn't sure why he kept it or Priscilla's picture. Maybe he wanted to remind himself of good memories. Maybe he wanted to caution himself about giving his heart to the wrong person. He didn't know which, but until he did, he couldn't get rid of them.

What he wanted from the box was the largest item in it. He

pulled out his revolver and a box of ammunition. He had kept his Colt M1917 from the war. Matt loaded the six cylinders with .45-caliber cartridges and slipped the pistol into his waistband behind his back. Given that there might be shooting this weekend, he needed to be prepared, and a hunting rifle wouldn't do the job.

Matt started returning everything else to his box. He paused and eyed his roll of emergency cash. He picked it up and shoved it into his pocket. It was getting expensive to feed and house his family while Joey McCord's men built their new home.

He closed up the safe deposit box and headed over to the trolley office to catch the next trolley. He got off the trolley car below Eckhart. He walked along the National Road, following the path the President's motorcade would take and scanned the hills and buildings. He quickly ruled out a sniper in any of the houses in town. Any of the buildings that were close enough for the shooter to be accurate with his shots were also close enough that police could capture the shooter before he got too far away.

Matt decided the sniper would take up a position somewhere in the hills above Eckhart. The high ground would allow the shooter a better angle for a clean shot at the President's car. It also offered many more places to hide and potential cover when the sniper tried to escape after he took his shots. The sound of the shots would also echo off the hills, making it harder to detect where the shooter was hidden.

Matt marked half a dozen places in his mind that were high enough so the angle of the shot wouldn't cause the bullet to deflect off the car. The locations also had to provide a good field of view so the car could be tracked as it started up the hill through Eckhart and be within accurate rifle distance. All the potential locations Matt identified were south and west of the National Road.

It would be a long shot, and he tried to think of someone who would be good enough to make the shot. Not that he knew all the miners in the county. A lot of them would be veterans and hunters. They would have the skill to make the shot.

Matt left the road and hiked up the side of the mountain to visit each of the potential shooter sites. He wanted to look at the road from the perspective of the sniper to see which one offered the best angle. He also wanted to scout out the sniper's cleanest exit paths. Too much brush would slow him down, and rustling brush would mark his path. Matt eliminated a few spots from his list.

He thought he had a good idea of the area where he would find the shooter, and he could also guess a rough time the shooter would arrive. Now, he just had to hope Paul Tomlinson used only one shooter and not a group of shooters.

Matt walked back to the National Road and followed it up the mountain toward Frostburg. He did not relish Sunday afternoon and hoped his vigilance wouldn't be necessary.

As he walked past Joey McCord's two-story brick house between Eckhart and Frostburg, he saw Laura standing on the front porch. She saw him and waved. She started down the steps and staggered but caught herself before she fell.

Matt hurried over to check on her.

"Good morning, Laura. Are you all right? It looked like you were about to take a fall."

"I'm fine, Matt." She waved him off. "What are you doing here?"

Had she seen him come off the hillside on the other side of the National Road? That would be hard to explain. Instead, he tried a different excuse. "I'm just checking on the progress of the new house and enjoying the scenery in the hills."

"Do you want to sit for a spell?" She waved to the wicker chairs on the front porch.

"I'd like that, but I had better not. Joey wouldn't like it if he saw me here," Matt said.

Laura dismissed his concern with a flick of her hand. "He's taking a nap inside. He said he was tired when he got back from the mine this morning."

Tired? With the mine barely operating, he couldn't have much to do while the strike was ongoing.

"That must be nice to have that much leisure time, but that's all the more reason for me not to stay around," Matt said. "He might wake up and see me. I wouldn't want to cause an argument and complicate things between the two of you."

Laura snorted and laughed. Matt caught a whiff of her breath. He was sure she was drunk. What he wasn't sure of was why she had been drinking. He couldn't remember ever seeing Laura impaired from too much liquor.

"How are you doing, Laura?"

"Oh, I'm good. Can't you see that I'm good? I live in a nice house with plenty of room for Jacob to play, and I have clothes that don't have holes in them." She turned in a circle to show off her dress and point at the house. "And I don't have to worry about having food to eat. Everything is wonderful."

Matt noticed that one thing she left out of her list of great things was Joey. He wondered if he was reading more into that than he should since she was drunk.

He just couldn't imagine Laura with him. Matt knew Joey was attracted to Laura. Who wouldn't be? She was pretty, but she had been happily married. However, since Pete had been killed in the mine cave-in, Laura had had a tough time. Joey had taken the opportunity and ingratiated himself with her. Matt wondered if she loved Joey or simply felt obligated to him.

"I have to say, I miss seeing you and Jacob at the boarding house, and I know my aunts do, too. They enjoyed looking after him when you needed them."

"Now Mrs. Middleton can watch him. She hates me, but she loves Jacob."

"Why does she hate you?"

"She doesn't approve of me living with Joey."

"Maybe Joey should find a new housekeeper."

Laura shook her head. "He won't"

"When we move back to the new house, you'll have to stop by with Jacob."

Laura nodded. "I will." She paused, then asked, "Do you miss being here in town?"

Matt shrugged. "I suppose I do, but we're not that far away. I am walking back to the hotel now. I do know Toni and Myrna are chomping at the bit to have something more to do. They can't wait to be back home. They are used to doing all the cooking and cleaning for the family. Samuel keeps himself busy looking for work, and Enos is just enjoying the easy life. He loves hotel living."

"Do you miss me?"

"I just said we did."

"You said your aunts missed seeing Jacob and me, but do *you* miss me?"

He looked into her eyes. Did he see yearning there? Not for him. That was behind them. They were just friends. But she seemed to want him to say something in particular. He just wasn't sure what.

"Of course, I do."

Laura smiled. "You might be the only one."

She turned and trudged back to the front door, weaving only a little. She paused to lean against the door frame.

"Are you sure you're all right, Laura?" Matt asked. "Do you need me to stay a while?"

She shook her head, but she didn't turn around. "No, this was my decision. I guess I just didn't realize the cost."

She walked inside the house and shut the door behind her. Matt stared after her, hoping she would come back outside. He was reluctant to knock on the door to check on her because he didn't want to risk waking Joey. Any conversation they had wouldn't go well.

Finally, he walked back up the road and headed to Frostburg. It didn't take him long to reach the St. Cloud Hotel. It was on the southern side of the town, which meant it was closer to Eckhart than the Gunter Hotel further north on the road at the other end of Frostburg. It was where he and Samantha went dancing. With only twenty-two rooms, the St. Cloud was smaller than the Gunter Hotel, but it served good food in the dining room. It also wasn't as expensive at the Gunter, which was something Matt thought about more often of late.

When Matt walked into the lobby, he saw Samuel sitting in a chair near a window. He was the tallest and oldest of the Ansaro children. He also carried himself with an almost regal bearing that hid the fact that he had been a coal miner for decades. He hadn't let the low ceilings of the mine tunnels give him the hunched appearance many miners had.

He was reading a copy of the *Cumberland Evening Times*. He was probably searching for any job openings he might be qualified for.

"What are you doing down here, Samuel?" Matt asked his uncle.

Samuel folded the newspaper closed. "Believe it or not, it's quieter down here. Between Myrna worrying over whether a war will erupt along Georges Creek and Toni fretting over having nothing to do, it drives me a little crazy."

"So, I guess I shouldn't let them know that I'm back."

"That would be my advice, but you should know, Enos is sleeping, which means he'll probably go out running moonshine tonight."

Matt shook his head. Enos was too willing to take chances delivering orders for Vincent Gambrill, one of the largest moonshiners in the area. Matt wasn't sure whether his uncle did it for the money, the moonshine, or the fast cars.

Matt clapped his uncle on the shoulder and headed toward the stairs.

"Matt." Matt stopped and turned back to his uncle. "Not that I'm not grateful, but how are you paying for all this? It can't be cheap."

Matt knew he couldn't tell Samuel the truth. It was bad enough Toni had figured out Matt was an undercover Pinkerton. The more people who knew the truth, the more dangerous the situation was for Matt. He needed to lie.

"I have savings," Matt said. "I didn't have much to spend my Marine pay on during the war, and I didn't need a lot when I was living in Baltimore. So I saved my money, particularly when I thought I was getting married to an upper-class girl. I wanted to be worthy of her."

"Married? You are a man of secrets, Matt."

Matt sighed and shook his head. He was a man who had fallen in love with a woman too far outside of his social class. "No secrets, Samuel. It just hasn't ever come up. Samantha knows about her."

"So who was this woman who broke your heart?"

"Her name is Priscilla Bankert. She is a lovely girl, and we got along well. We had a lot of fun together. We met at a function for her father's company, and I thought my life would be very different today. I expected to be married. We would have a child on the way. We'd be living in a small house in Baltimore."

"So what happened?"

Matt hesitated, but he had started the story. He needed to finish it. "She realized she was too good for me, or maybe her parents convinced her. The result was the same. She called off the wedding. She sent me a letter with her ring, and I haven't seen her since. I tried to see her and work through things, but her parents sent her off somewhere and wouldn't tell me where. That's when I realized I couldn't stay in Baltimore anymore, so I came out here."

"I'm sorry, Matt."

Matt shrugged. He had put Priscilla behind him, or at least he thought he had. "It is probably for the best. We lived in different worlds. Her parents didn't like me or at least what I represented to them."

"You must have loved her, though, if you wanted to marry her."

Matt nodded. "I did at the time. Given all that happened, I have to wonder whether I really knew her or not. And if I didn't know her, how could I have loved her?"

Samuel's eyes widened a bit. "That's pretty deep for a coal miner."

"You should know, Samuel, coal miners go deep, and we have a lot of time to think while we're down there." He patted Samuel on the shoulder. "I'll see you in the morning."

Matt turned and walked to the staircase that led to the second floor. He unlocked the door to his room. It was dark inside, and he could hear Enos softly snoring. He would wake in another few hours to get ready to make moonshine deliveries tonight. No one was thrilled he was working for a moonshiner, but he was making money and he liked the work. He especially loved being able to drive. It was better to let him get a good sleep, so he would be alert and not get caught again.

Matt changed clothes as quietly as he could. He picked up the items he wanted and then slipped back out of the room. He was going to enjoy some time with Samantha because he had an idea he might be busy this weekend.

Chapter 7

July 1, 1922

Enos stretched his arms over his head while he lay in his bed. He opened his eyes and immediately shut them. The sun shone brightly through the window.

"Matt, close the curtains!"

No answer. Enos turned his head and squinted. He was alone in the hotel room. It seemed like Enos and his nephew missed each other more often than not. Matt slept at night and was out during the day. For Enos, it was the opposite. He delivered moonshine most nights and slept during the day. Given how little daylight he saw, he might as well have been back in the coal mines, except now he earned a lot more money and got to drive Vincent Gambrill's Duesenberg.

Enos rolled out of bed and staggered to the window that looked out the back side of the St. Cloud Hotel toward Cumberland. With a jerk, he pulled the curtains closed. Then he hurried back to fall onto the bed.

When his eyes finally adjusted to the dim light, he looked at the alarm clock on the nightstand next to his bed. It was eleven-thirty in the morning. It was early for him, but he hadn't had many deliveries last night, so he had gotten back to the hotel around four in the morning.

He washed and dressed and headed out behind the hotel. He needed to look at his car. Vincent allowed Enos to drive the black Duesenberg Model A, but only as long as Enos worked for Gambrill. The car had a straight-eight engine that could push the car to eighty-five miles an hour. Enos would love to drive it that fast, but none of the roads around here were long and straight enough for him to get the car up to its top speed. He kept watching for one, though.

That's not to say, Enos didn't put the car through its paces. He knew well what the car could do, which is one reason he wanted to look at it now. The engine had been running rough last night. Since his freedom and business success depended on the car running at optimum, Enos needed to figure out what was wrong. He had been learning how to maintain and repair the car since he had learned to drive a couple of months ago. He needed to know. If the car ever broke down, it would most likely be in the middle of the night on a back road far from a mechanic. He couldn't trust the police to help him since he would also most likely have a load of illegal liquor hidden under his seats.

Enos opened the trunk and took out his toolbox. Then he lifted the hood panels to look at the engine. At least he had plenty of light to work by.

The engine was cast iron, although the lower crankcase and oil pan were made from aluminum. He checked for an oil leak, which could account for the rough sounds even though the engine hadn't been running hot. The level was fine, so he began inspecting the parts themselves. Since he was still new with all this, he might have to take it to a garage and watch what the mechanic did to fix things.

"That's a beautiful car."

Enos jumped back from the engine and straightened up. He saw Jenny Washington standing on the other side of the car. She wore a red dress that was pulled in a bit at the waist. It wasn't as loose as most gowns nowadays and it showed off her figure. She looked like she was going out for a night on the town.

"I didn't mean to startle you," Jenny said.

"It's fine. I didn't see you standing there."

"Is this your car?" Jenny asked.

Enos hesitated, tempted to impress this woman. "I drive it for my boss. He lets me keep it."

She let her fingers trace the contours of the car. "Is it fast? It looks fast."

Enos grinned. "It can go eighty-five miles per hour, but I've only had it up to sixty."

Jenny's eyes widened. "I can't imagine going that fast. You could go from here to Eckhart in a minute or two."

Enos waved her over. "Here, look at the engine. It's a beautiful piece of machinery."

Jenny walked over and bent over the engine. Enos started pointing out the engine block, cylinder heads, crankshaft, and pistons to her. He wasn't sure whether she understood what he was showing her, but she seemed interested, which was enough to keep him talking. He enjoyed having her near him. Her perfume smelled delightful, and he admired the curve of her neck and back side when she bent over to get a closer look at the engine. She caught him staring once, and she grinned.

"Would you like to go for a ride?" he asked suddenly.

Jenny straightened up. "Really? I've never ridden in a car before. The closest has been the trolley."

Enos knew that was false. She had ridden to the hospital in a car earlier in the year when he, Matt, and Samuel found her beaten in an alley. Of course, she probably didn't remember that ride. She had been barely conscious and suffering from exposure. He wondered if she even remembered him being there.

"That's like saying the closest thing you've done to dancing is walking," he said.

"Well, I want to dance."

Enos walked around to the passenger side of the car and opened the door for her. Jenny smiled and slid into the car. Her skirt pulled up a bit as she did, and Enos got a good look at her shapely calf.

He closed her door, put the hood down, and climbed in behind the steering wheel. He started the engine. It rumbled loudly and then settled. Apparently, he still hadn't fixed the problem with the engine.

"Ready?" he asked.

"Let's go!" Jenny said with a smile.

Enos pulled into the alley and then onto the National Road. He headed south. He knew of a long, straight stretch of road below Eckhart. It was where he had had the car flying along sixty miles per hour.

"Where are we going?" Jenny asked.

"Let me surprise you. By the way, you look very nice."

She beamed. "Thank you."

"Why are you so dressed up?"

Jenny hesitated. "I was coming home from some work I was doing last night."

"I'm a night owl, too."

She hesitated again. "May I ask you something personal?"

Enos nodded. "You can. It doesn't necessarily mean I'll answer."

"I understand. Your family says you are a moonshiner."

Enos chuckled. "They would say that. I'm not a moonshiner. I deliver moonshine in this car, actually."

"Does it bother you that you're breaking the law?"

"No, but I don't consider it breaking the law. It was not even two years ago drinking was legal. Despite what my family believes, I don't do this for the liquor. I do it for the money, which is great, and I love driving. If I could drive a car in the coal mines, I might not mind the work so much."

Jenny bounced in the seat and giggled. "I don't blame you. This is wonderful."

"Well, hang on. You're about to see why I like this job."

The road straightened out to the east, and it looked clear of any other vehicles or horses for the moment. Enos pressed the accelerator and shifted gears. The needle on the speedometer climbed, and he watched for a police car. It was second nature to him from his work.

"This is great! How fast are we going?" Jenny asked.

Enos glanced at the speedometer as it crept past fifty-five miles per hour.

"Fifty-five miles per hour."

She stared out the window. "Can we go faster?"

"A woman after my own heart." Enos pressed the gas pedal further down and the car surged forward.

Jenny laughed. She leaned her head out the window, letting the wind blow her brown hair back like a comet's tail. Enos smiled. Jenny was showing the same joy he felt when he drove.

They sped along the road at a little over sixty miles per hour. He saw an occasional horse and rider or car. The horsemen got off on the side of the road to avoid having their horses scared or pebbles thrown at them from beneath the car's tires. Enos zipped around the other cars as if they were parked. Jenny waved at each one they passed.

Enos watched for ruts in the road. He didn't want to hit one going this fast and bounce Jenny out of the car.

He finally slowed the car as they came into Lavale and traffic started increasing. Jenny slid back into her seat. Her wind-blown hair settled all around her head in every direction. She smoothed it down, but didn't seem bothered.

"Can you teach me to drive?" she asked.

"What?"

"This was amazing. I want to learn how to drive. I want to be able to go fast like that on my own. I feel like we were going so fast I was outrunning my troubles."

"You have troubles?"

"Doesn't everybody?"

Instead of following the National Road to Cumberland, Enos headed north to drive through Mount Savage and back to Frostburg. He kept his speed up as much as possible, but the road wasn't straight enough or smooth enough to go truly fast—at least not fast enough for Jenny to lean out the window again. He loved her free spirit.

As they approached Frostburg, Enos said, "Would you like to

go to lunch with me, Jenny?"

She said nothing, and Enos thought she might not have heard him over the wind blowing through the car.

"Yes, I'd like that, but I have to change first," she said. "I probably need to brush my hair, too. The wind must have blown it every which way."

"It did, but I think it looks fine because I know how it got that way," Enos said with a smile.

"It was worth it."

Enos parked the car behind the St. Cloud Hotel. Then he and Jenny went upstairs to get ready for their lunch date. Enos washed his face with water, but he used soap and water on his hands, trying to get the grease off his fingertips.

When he was ready, he walked down the hall to Jenny's room. She opened the door and stepped out into the hall. She was wearing a simple everyday calico dress, a far cry from the beaded dress she had worn earlier. She had brushed her hair and pinned it up in the back. She looked beautiful, if not as glamorous as she had looked earlier.

"Where are we going?" she asked.

"I haven't had pizza in a while. I thought we could go to the Italian diner next door and then get some ice cream afterward."

"Oooh, ice cream. I could almost skip the pizza for that, but I love cheese pizza with lots of vegetables on it."

They walked to the small diner next door to the hotel. It didn't have a name, just a sign outside that read "Pizza." They sat at a table in front of the restaurant and ordered a pizza with green peppers and mushrooms. They talked about cars and driving while they waited for their food. They also made plans for when Enos could start teaching Jenny how to drive.

When the waitress brought the pizza out, it smelled of oregano and melted cheese. Enos's stomach rumbled with anticipation. They started eating and Enos found himself enjoying the afternoon. He couldn't remember the last time he had courted a woman. Usually, he was too busy working to worry about a relationship. Plus, he enjoyed spending time with his friends and not having to worry about someone else. He loved Myrna, but she took up most of Samuel's free time, not that Samuel seemed to mind.

They finished their first slices and were pausing before starting on their next slices.

"That is delicious pizza," Enos said. "It's better than anyone in Eckhart makes, but then this pizza probably doesn't have coal dust in it." Coal dust or dirt seemed to cover everything in Eckhart.

"This had better be good. It's the only thing this restaurant sells," Jenny said.

"Calista?"

Jenny's hand froze with the slice of pizza halfway to her mouth. Enos turned to see who had spoken. A man walking down Main Street veered over to stand in front of the table. He was dressed like a merchant in a shirt and tie. He wobbled a little. It was a move Enos recognized. He had done it enough when he had had too much to drink.

"I'm surprised to see you here. Will you be at the Gunter tonight? I got paid today," the man said.

Jenny flushed. "I'm sorry…"

The man glanced at Enos and the pizza. "If you aren't too busy now, we can have a go in the alley."

Enos jumped up and grabbed the man by his tie. He didn't care if the man was drunk or not, Enos wouldn't allow him to be vulgar with a lady.

"Mister, you had better keep walking down the street, or I will throw you down it."

Jenny stood up and put a hand on Enos's arm. "Enos, don't. You'll just get in trouble."

"I won't get in trouble. Anyone would hit him after what he just said."

"But… but he's not lying, Enos."

She turned and ran off. Enos let the man go and pushed him away. The man started to say something, but then he saw the expression on Enos's face and thought better of it. Enos took a dollar from his wallet, laid it on the table, and hurried after Jenny.

He thought she was running back to the hotel, but she ran past it and turned into the alley.

"Jenny, wait!"

He turned the corner and saw her leaning against the side of the building, sobbing. Enos walked over and stood next to her.

"I'm sorry, Enos. I didn't mean to embarrass you," Jenny said.

"You didn't," he told her. "If you think that was embarrassing, you haven't been around me long enough. I got so drunk once, I went running through Eckhart in my long johns."

Jenny stopped crying long enough to laugh briefly.

"So, I know that guy wasn't your husband, and I don't think he's an ex-boyfriend, is he?" Enos asked.

Jenny shook her head, but she didn't look up. "He's paid me before to have sex with him."

Enos took that in and leaned against the building beside Jenny. "Oh... I didn't ask you to dinner because I wanted to—"

"I know. Are you going to tell your family?"

"Why would I?"

"So they don't let me stay in the new boarding house. I'm sure you want to protect the reputation of your family."

Enos sighed and pressed his head back against the wall. "As long as you don't treat the boarding house like your place of business, I don't see the need to say something."

Jenny buried her face in her hands. "You must hate me."

Enos took a deep breath. Then he reached over and took one of her hands in his. "People call me a drunk or a moonshiner. I don't think I'm either, but I can see why they think it. So who am I to judge what's in your heart or why you do what you do?" He paused and let the silence settle between them. Then he added, "Even when I was giving people a reason to think I was a drunk and a moonshiner, it never was all I was, even at those times, and it's not who I wanted to be. One day I won't be driving for a moonshiner, although I doubt I'll ever give up drinking. I can when I need to drive, though."

"You sound like you believe what you're saying."

"Oh, I do. I've had Samuel and Toni lecture me enough about my behavior, but I only saw it from my side. Now, with you, I see it from their side, and I'm trying to act like I wish they would act with me. I'm not going to tell you what you're doing is the best decision you can make, but I know you must have your reasons. Just keep your dreams alive. There's something out there that's going to be important enough that you make better decisions, like me not drinking when I'm driving. When you figure that out, I think things will fall into place. Not get easier, mind you, but you'll know what you want to be, and you'll have something you'll be working toward."

She wiped the tears from her cheeks. "Do you know what you want to do?"

Enos grinned. "I want to run a taxi, and lately, I've been thinking about racing cars."

Jenny patted his hand. She pushed herself off the wall and started walking toward the street.

"Jenny?"

She stopped and turned.

"When you want your first driving lesson?"

She smiled. "As soon as possible."

Chapter 8

July 2, 1922

Having identified the general shooting area, Matt felt he could find and stop the shooter before he took any shots at President Harding. William Singletary wasn't so sure. He wanted someone under arrest before the President even reached the county. That would not happen. Only Paul Tomlinson and the shooter knew who the shooter was. Matt knew where the shooter was going to be, so his only option was to watch the area until the man showed up and stop him.

Singletary still worried that one person watching wouldn't be enough, but Matt told him that the more agents he put on the hill, the easier it would be for the shooter to see them. If that happened, the shooter would just take up a secondary position.

"The shooter might abandon the idea altogether," Singletary had suggested.

"Or he might try something that would endanger more people," Matt had replied.

Matt understood the pressure Singletary felt. Matt felt it even more. If the worst happened, and the sniper shot at the President, Singletary could always blame Matt for his failure to stop the man. Matt had no such person to blame.

The United Mine Workers was feeling empowered right now. Besides coal miners, railroad shipmen across the country had gone on strike to support the coal miners and because of their own labor issues.

Nearly 400 men, from foremen down the ranks, had laid down their tools at the B&O Railroad and walked off the job at ten o'clock in the morning yesterday. In addition to supporting the coal miners, the railmen were protesting the wage cut that the United States Railway Labor Board in Chicago had ordered. The strike affected 1,246 men in Cumberland and nearly 2,000 in the Cumberland Division. However, only the B&O workers walked out in Allegany County. The Western Maryland Railroad men were still on the job for now.

Unlike the coal strike, the railroad strike was peaceful so far. Singletary worried that with even more striking men on the street wanting to have their grievances heard, and the President of the United States coming to town, violence would soon follow. The Pinkerton manager wanted to flood the area with agents or detour the President. Matt had gone round and round about both options with Singletary. The former would increase the tensions in the area and the latter would make the President look weak in his negotiations.

Singletary had finally agreed to Matt's plan, but with the stipulation that he would be on the scene to order the Pinkerton agents already in the town into action if need be.

Matt hoped there would be no need.

He ate a hearty breakfast Sunday morning and had the hotel kitchen prepare him two ham sandwiches he could take with him. He also filled a canteen with water. He picked up a bag of supplies he thought he might need and set out for Eckhart.

He actually walked past where the National Road turned east through Eckhart. He kept walking for another quarter mile or so until he found a game trail off to the side of the road. He hiked up over the ridge and made his way through trees and brush toward Eckhart. Approaching this way, no one would see him walk off the National Road near Eckhart and onto the mountain. And if no one saw him, no one would mention it to the wrong person.

He climbed a sycamore that got him above the brush. It also allowed him a clear view to watch the road and the side of the mountain from cover. He pulled out a pair of binoculars and scanned the countryside. Satisfied with his field of vision, he settled down to wait. Although President Harding wasn't even expected to arrive in Cumberland until three o'clock, Matt figured the sniper would want to be in place by then, so Matt made sure to arrive two hours earlier. He wanted to get a sense of the land so any movement would catch his attention. He also wanted nature to get used to him, so it would stop being silent. That way, when the sniper approached and the birds quieted or flew off, it would be a signal for Matt.

All this was happening around the same time Cumberland Mayor Thomas Koon and members of the Cumberland City Council were meeting the President's motorcade east of the city. The President, his wife, and about thirty others were on their way to the President's hometown of Marion, Ohio, to relax for a few days and celebrate the town's centennial. They had attended a special re-enactment of the Battle of Gettysburg presented by U.S. Marines and were now on their way west along the National Road.

The *Cumberland Evening Times* had reported the group was expected for a late lunch at the Fort Cumberland Hotel at three o'clock before heading west to the Summit Hotel in Uniontown, Pennsylvania. The route between Cumberland and Uniontown followed the National Road through Eckhart and Frostburg and into Grantsville before veering north into Pennsylvania. The article had also said a motorcycle police escort would accompany the President's party to help control any crowds and to keep the streets clear.

That police escort was why Matt knew the sniper would be somewhere on the mountain. He had to be somewhere far enough away from the crowd that he could escape the police, who would quickly hunt for him as soon as they made sure the President was safe.

Sitting in the tree reminded Matt of a case he had worked in Baltimore. He hadn't been in a tree then. He had been hidden in a building watching the Baltimore docks from a dark window. His assignment was to catch a group of thieves who had been stealing shipments from the dock. It hadn't been a case of national security, but it had involved a lot of sitting and watching. He had caught those men with no one being shot, and he would catch this man the same way.

Matt watched the National Road and even stared through his binoculars at the activity on the streets of Eckhart. He scanned the faces to see if anyone was paying too much attention to the hills. He could see the new boarding house just off of Store Hill on Porter Road. All the framing was up. It might be ahead of schedule. Joey McCord probably wanted to get it built as quickly as possible since the longer it remained unfinished, the longer people would be reminded that it was someone who had been working for Consolidation Coal who burned it down.

Truth be told, it made Matt uncomfortable, too. It was a reminder that the Pinkertons might not be on the right side of this fight. It didn't matter so much to men like Singletary as long as they were paid their fees, and the agents like Matt were expected to do what they were told. Matt had already stepped over the line for this assignment. If his bosses knew he was an Eckhart boy, they would pull him out of the county quickly and probably fire him for withholding information. Matt had come to Eckhart to help his family, but the longer this strike continued, the more danger he would be in.

He took out one of his sandwiches and unwrapped it from the butcher paper. It was a ham and cheese on sourdough bread. He lifted the bread and saw mustard. He ate it quietly and sipped from his canteen.

The number of people in the street noticeably increased around three o'clock. A few of them brought chairs out to the edge of the National Road and sat down to wait for the President and his motorcade.

Matt also noticed uniformed Pinkertons on the street. He worried Singletary had ordered more agents to patrol the town, but the Pinkertons disappeared into the mine office and stayed out of sight. Singletary was probably holding them back in case of trouble.

Now, as long as he didn't jump the gun and cause the shooter to take a shot from somewhere else.

Matt was watching the mine office when he heard rustling. He lowered his binoculars and looked around slowly. Movement on the ground caught his eye. He saw a man carrying a rifle walking through the woods.

Matt froze and watched as the man make his way down the hill closer to Eckhart. Judging by his direction, Matt could guess which of the spots the sniper had picked out. He wasn't sure whether to feel joy or relief that his assessment of the situation had been correct.

He put on his hat and tied a kerchief around his face. He couldn't risk being recognized. He was still undercover among the coal miners. If they discovered who he was, not only would Matt be at risk, but so would his family.

Matt climbed down the tree and crept down the hill, watching where he put his feet. He didn't want to snap a twig and warn the sniper he was coming.

Matt stopped when he saw the man ahead of him. He lay on the ground, sighting along the barrel of his rifle, which rested in the V of two crossed sticks stuck in the ground. Matt looked past the man at the road. It was empty of vehicles, so the man was only planning his shot and figuring out the best angles.

Matt pulled a lead-filled leather sap from his pocket, one of his tools of the trade for his Pinkerton work. He pulled his pistol out and held it in his left hand. Hopefully, he wouldn't need to use it because he wasn't left handed.

The sniper rose to his knees to adjust the sticks in the ground, and Matt hit him across the back of the head with his sap. The man dropped to ground unconscious. Matt pulled his satchel off and reached inside to pull out a small coil of rope. He tied the man's hands behind his back and ejected the bullets from his rifle. He tossed the bullets off to one side and the rifle off in the opposite direction. Finally, he checked his knots again, and satisfied, he headed back over the mountain the same way he had walked in.

Instead of heading back to Frostburg, though, Matt headed down the National Road to Eckhart.

He saw Singletary standing back from the crowd gathering at the edge of the road near the mining office. Matt walked over and stood near the man, but not too close. They looked like a pair of spectators.

When it appeared no one was paying them any attention, Singletary asked, "Is everything okay?"

Without turning to face the man, Matt said, "Yes, I found him. He won't cause a problem."

"Are you sure?"

"I wouldn't be down here if I wasn't."

"Good work then."

Matt nodded and moved off to mix with the crowd. He heard a murmur start and grow in volume. He looked down the road where he saw some people pointing. He could see the motorcycle police leading the presidential convoy toward Eckhart. Then he saw Paul Tomlinson, the union organizer. He stood out from the crowd because he wasn't getting excited, and he wasn't looking at the procession. He stared up toward where the sniper hid.

The vehicles approached and people began waving and cheering. Matt also heard a group of miners booing the President.

The vehicles made their way up the mountainside. Matt glimpsed President Harding as he passed. Then the cars were past him and moving further west toward Frostburg.

Matt saw Singletary standing on the porch of the company store. He smiled at Matt, then turned and went inside.

Matt looked around and found Tomlinson in the crowd. He was still staring up the mountain with a look that was somewhere between confusion and anger.

Matt grinned and started walking back toward Frostburg.

As Matt walked by Joey's house, he saw Joey and Laura standing near the road. Joey was wearing an expensive suit and Laura had on a fancy yellow dress. Her hair was styled in an elegant bun on top of her head. It looked like they were ready to go to a grand ball.

Laura waved when she saw Matt. Joey put his arm around her waist and pulled her closer. Matt waved to Laura, but he kept on walking. Joey didn't look happy, and Matt didn't want to spoil his good feeling at stopping the shooting.

Joey stood at the edge of the National Road, hearing the crowd cheer. The President was on his way. He smoothed out his suit coat and sucked in his stomach.

Joey hadn't been able to get in touch with the President's people to arrange a meeting. His only hope was to catch the President's attention as the motorcade passed and hopefully have him pause long enough for Joey to make the coal company's case.

He had placed a sign reading "Consolidation Coal Company Eckhart Superintendent."

Laura was in her best dress and sober. He also had Maizy Middleton take the brat into the backyard and play with him, so the child wouldn't disturb Joey's meeting with the President.

"Hurry up and get over here, Laura," Joseph called.

Laura hurried down from the porch. She walked over to stand next to Joseph. She didn't stagger. She had kept her promise and hadn't been drinking.

"Just smile. Let me do the talking."

The motorcycle police approached first and passed. Joey coughed as their motorcycles raised dust off the road.

He saw the President's car and began waving.

"Mr. President, why don't you stop for a drink?" Joey called.

He saw Harding in the back seat of the car. The man saw him and waved.

"Mr. President, please stop for a moment."

The car didn't even slow. It stirred up even more dust than the motorcycles as it passed. Joey watched the cars go by and swore. He stood there as people from the dispersing crowd walked up the hill. He saw Laura wave to Matt and pulled her closer.

"I'm sorry, Joey," Laura said.

Joey looked at her. He took her by the arm and led her back into the house, straight to the bedroom. He pushed her back onto the bed. He quickly undid his pants and nearly jumped on her to vent his frustration on her body. There was no romance in what he did, no seduction, like he had used their first time.

Laura didn't resist, say anything, or even try to kiss him. She just laid back, closed her eyes, and let him have her. When he finished, he stood up and redressed.

He looked at Laura. Her eyes were still closed, and a tear rolled down the side of her head. He realized he didn't care. He didn't care if he had hurt her or upset her. He just didn't care for her. He might have at one time, or it might have been a case of wanting something he couldn't have.

He had been romantic with her and worked hard to seduce her, but since he had succeeded, he realized his goal had been in the chase and to have someone he had once loved.

He finished dressing and left without so much as a goodbye.

Laura waited until Joey left before she let a sob escape her lips. She had wanted to scream the whole time, but she didn't dare with Jacob playing outside. She rolled onto her side and drew her knees up and cried. She stood up and looked at the dress Joey had ripped off her body. He had had her buy it special for today, and now it was ruined.

She put on an everyday dress she had and went to the basement where Joey had been hiding his liquor. She tried the door and found it locked. It had never been locked before. Joey must have tired of her drinking his liquor. She leaned against the door and sobbed. She needed the liquor. She needed to forget.

She went back to the bedroom and picked up her purse. She looked inside and saw she had some money, but she didn't know how much it would buy her.

She left the house saying nothing to Mrs. Middleton and walked into town. She knew of a speakeasy in the basement of a house on Neff Street. She walked around to the back of the house and knocked on the door.

A middle-aged woman with unkempt hair answered. "What do you want?"

"A drink."

"Well, you're not getting one here, missy."

"I've got money." Laura rooted around in her purse for the bills. She found them and waved them at the woman. "I can pay."

"Might as well put that away. We're not serving you. This is a miner's place."

"I was married to a miner."

"And now you're the superintendent's whore, and we don't want you in here."

The woman slammed the door, and Laura looked around to see if anyone had been listening. She appeared to be alone.

What should she do now? She should have been sipping her first drink and calming down by now, but things had just gotten worse.

She needed to be where fewer people knew her. She walked over to the road and waited for the trolley. She rode it to the Hotel Gunter, where she had heard about a speakeasy Matt had mentioned.

She would be able to drink there.

As Matt approached Frostburg, he saw more people than usual, but then, a crowd had also gathered here to watch the President's motorcade. He was supposed to have met Samantha here. He needed to explain why he hadn't showed up.

He scanned the faces in the crowd, but he was fairly sure Samantha would have already headed home. He walked to Samantha's house and knocked on the kitchen door.

It surprised him when John Havencroft opened the door. He frowned when he saw Matt.

"Mr. Havencroft," Matt said.

"Proper guests call at the front door," Havencroft said.

"Knowing how you feel about me, I figured it would be better to come in this way."

"And yet, knowing how I feel about you, you came anyway."

Matt sighed. He couldn't figure out why Havencroft was so against him. The man acted like Samantha was too good for Matt, but both men were former military, even if Havencroft had family money.

"I just came to see Samantha, sir."

Samantha came rushing down the back stairs and halted when she saw her father.

"Oh, Father, I didn't know you had answered the door," she said.

John turned and frowned at his daughter.

"So I guessed."

Samantha walked over to Matt and stood next to him. "Did you know Matt has met the President?"

John Havencroft's gray eyebrows rose. "Really?"

Matt wasn't sure what Samantha's goal was in saying that, but he doubted that it would work the way she wanted. She knew Matt's meeting with the President had barely qualified as a meeting.

"Yes, sir, he was at a function I attended in Baltimore," Matt said.

"What sort of function would both you and President Harding attend?"

Matt couldn't say he was providing security at the event because it would give away his cover.

"It was a fundraiser George Bankert threw for the President."

"But surely you didn't have the amount of money to contribute in the way that would be expected at such an event."

Matt hesitated. "No, sir, I was accompanying Priscilla Bankert."

John's chin lifted a bit. "Ahhh, I see. You seem to have a type."

"Father!" Samantha said.

He shook his head and picked up the glass of water he had come into the kitchen to get.

Matt wondered what Havencroft would say if Matt told him he had just stopped a sniper from shooting at the President. He could even do it without revealing he was a Pinkerton. The problem was he was a Pinkerton. No one other than Matt, Tomlinson, the shooter, and William Singletary knew about the failed intimidation attempt, and Singletary wanted to keep it under wraps so he didn't embarrass the President. Matt wanted to keep it quiet because he didn't want it reflecting badly on the area. Still, it would be nice to tell.

"I just wanted to apologize for not being able to meet you today, Samantha. Something came up at the last minute."

"I understand, Matt. I'm sorry for my father's rudeness."

"Don't apologize for me, Samantha," John said.

Matt glanced at John. The man's tight-lipped expression and narrowed eyes warned him that he should leave before John slammed the door in his face.

"Your father's right, Samantha. He shouldn't have to apologize for speaking his mind in his own house. I will talk to you later," Matt said.

Matt turned and left. Samantha hurried out after him.

"Wait, Matt." She ran up next to him. "Do you want to take a walk?"

Matt looked over his shoulder, half expecting John Havencroft to follow them.

"Sure, would you like to stop for some ice cream?" Matt asked.

"Yes."

Undercover work was hard at times because of all the lies Matt had to tell, so he appreciated the times when he could tell the truth and relax. He didn't like undercover work because of that, but he was single and capable, so he was often asked to take on those tough assignments. He was beginning to think that pretending to his family and friends would be his toughest assignment ever.

Chapter 9

July 2, 1922

Paul Tomlinson saw the President's procession coming up the National Road, and he glanced up the side of the mountains to where Brian Purcell hid. Paul didn't know exactly where the miner was among the trees, only that it was somewhere on the mountain. Purcell had volunteered to shoot at the President. He harbored a grudge against Harding because Purcell had family in southern West Virginia who had been involved in the Battle of Blair Mountain. He was also an avid hunter who bragged about his skills with a rifle. He was just the sort of person Tomlinson needed for this job.

Tomlinson held his own grudge against the President, although it wasn't as personal as Purcell's. Tomlinson would have much preferred seeing Eugene Debs in the Oval Office. Debs was a union man. He was a founding member of the Industrial Workers of the World and had helped found the American Railway Union. He had worked with the unions and led strikes. He supported the unions so strongly that he had defied a court injunction to lead men in the 1894 Pullman Strike. Debs had been in jail for protesting the country's participation in the Great War during his 1920 campaign for President, but he had still managed to get over three percent of the vote.

Harding, on the other hand, backed business and considered the unions a conspiracy against the country. Why people, even some union members, liked the man was beyond Tomlinson's understanding. The President's speeches were filled with vagaries and platitudes, nothing that could be held against him later. When he brought the unions and businesses together last year to find a way to lower unemployment, he had promised no federal money to back up any of the group's decisions, and so, nothing came of the meeting.

Tomlinson saw hope in the union strike when the railroad workers joined with their own picket lines yesterday. Harding had already offered them more concessions than he had ever offered the coal miners. The railmen had rejected the offers, so Harding was going to play hardball. There was talk that Attorney General Daugherty was trying to convince a federal judge to issue an injunction to break the strike. He could try, but it would only strengthen the resolve of union men and cause more walkouts.

Tomlinson watched the President's motorcade approach. He tensed, waiting to hear a shot. He wouldn't even mind if Purcell accidentally shot Harding. He did worry that in the confusion the shots would cause, one car might swerve into the crowd and injure an innocent person. If that happened, Tomlinson would have to find a way to keep the blame from falling on the United Mine Workers.

"Do it," Tomlinson muttered to himself.

But the cars passed without a shot being fired. They moved slowly, so as not to stir up any dust on the road. The President and First Lady waved at the cheering crowd.

Tomlinson shook his head. These people liked Harding, even though he worked against their best interests.

In a few moments, the cars and the President were out of range of Purcell's rifle.

What had happened? If Purcell was where he was supposed to be, he should have had an unobstructed shot at any of the vehicles on the road.

The crowd started separating as people went back to their homes or their jobs. Tomlinson swore. Then he crossed the road and walked up the side of the mountain. He wasn't sure where Purcell had chosen to shoot from or if he was even here. Maybe he had gotten cold feet. If so, Tomlinson would have him beaten for throwing away a prime opportunity to put the fear of God and the union into the President.

"Purcell!" he called out.

"Over here!"

The union organizer walked in the direction of the voice, but he didn't see the man.

"Where are you?"

"Here! I need help."

Tomlinson rushed forward and found Purcell laying on the ground with his hands tied behind his back. He was rolling around, trying to pull his hands free. Tomlinson kneeled down beside the man.

"Be still."

He untied the rope. Purcell sat up and rubbed his wrists.

"What happened?" Tomlinson asked. He looked around, expecting police to converge on him.

"Someone snuck up behind me and hit me with something." He rubbed the back of his head and winced. "Then he must have tied me up."

"Did you see who it was?"

"If I had, I would have shot him. Has the President come by yet? I was unconscious. I don't know how long."

Tomlinson looked around. Someone had stopped Purcell but done nothing else. Why?

"The President's gone. That's why I knew to come looking for you," Tomlinson told the miner.

"What do you want to do?"

"Nothing we can do… at least with shooting at Harding. It's a missed opportunity. I would like to know who did this to you and how he knew to find you here."

"It was probably a Pinkerton," Purcell guessed.

Tomlinson nodded. It made sense, at least partially. "How would the Pinkertons know what we were going to do? Only the miners knew, and they didn't even know about you or where you would be. And why didn't they haul you off to jail?"

"Maybe because I hadn't done anything wrong when they stopped me."

It still didn't sit right with Tomlinson. Parading a potential Presidential assassin through town would have improved the Pinkertons' image and harmed the UMW's.

They walked off the mountain. Tomlinson found his parked car. He watched Purcell walk off to his house in Eckhart.

Someone had figured out what the plan against the President was. True, the miners knew what the plan was in general, but only Purcell and Tomlinson knew Purcell would be the shooter and on the hill above Eckhart. Even then, only Purcell knew precisely where he would be.

Tomlinson drove back to his hotel room in the Hotel Gunter. He had had the management bring in a desk where he could work from, and it was piled his with letters, telegrams, newspapers, and reports.

He rooted through the papers until he found the one he was looking for and pulled it from the stack. It was a letter written on Pinkerton National Detective Agency letterhead.

> *Mr. Tomlinson,*
>
> *We have never met, but my name is David Lakehurst. I work for the Pinkertons. You probably recognize my name because I have been beating up your miners for the past couple months, and if truth be told, enjoying myself doing it.*
>
> *I doubt you're a dumb man, or you wouldn't be in the position you are in. You must know the uniformed Pinkertons aren't the only agents in the area. We have undercover agents who are coal miners watching what you do and reporting on it.*
>
> *You're probably wondering if you can believe*

me. You can, because I am no longer a Pinkerton, and I have no loyalty to them. It was one of them who betrayed me and got me in trouble. I would like nothing more than to return the favor.

That's why I'm going to tell you this. I don't know who the undercover agents are in the county. They never reported to me. I did figure out who one of them is, though. He's the one who caused me the trouble. His name is Matt Ansaro. He lives in Eckhart, or he did, until I burned his family's house down. I'm sure you know about that.

Matt Ansaro is no friend of mine and no friend of yours. Check him out if you don't believe me. He used to live in Baltimore. You probably know someone there who can confirm what I'm saying.

You can do with this information what you want, although I wouldn't mind if you kill him. Don't matter to me. He's the reason I need to leave town.

David Lakehurst

Tomlinson had thought the letter a trick from a disgruntled Pinkerton who was upset that Matt Ansaro had publicly beaten him. After all, the Ansaros were a mining family. They were from this area, and if Matt Ansaro was a Pinkerton, why would one Pinkerton have burned down the home of another Pinkerton?

Could Tomlinson really trust anything Lakehurst had to say? The man had made it his mission to torment miners and make them afraid of joining the UMW. Tomlinson and so many other miners had dreamed of what they would do to Lakehurst if they had the chance. Among those who had the chance, many had wound up beaten to a pulp with broken bones.

Except for Matt Ansaro. Lakehurst had beaten him once, but Matt had won the second fight and driven Lakehurst out of the county. Ansaro was a hero among the miners.

This could easily be Lakehurst's revenge against both the miners and Ansaro by pitting them against each other.

But what if Lakehurst was right? Would the miners actually need to thank Lakehurst for helping them?

Tomlinson shook his head.

It made little sense.

But someone had revealed the plan to scare President Harding. Tomlinson remembered seeing Ansaro at the back of the room during the union meeting where they had discussed the plan, but there had been a hundred people in the room. Any one of them could have done something or told someone something that revealed the plan. It might have even happened accidentally; someone overheard two miners talking.

However, if it had been a cop or Pinkerton who had discovered Purcell, they would have arrested the shooter. An unknown person had attacked Purcell. That could mean the person didn't want to be seen either by Purcell or police. An undercover operative like the ones Lakehurst had mentioned.

Tomlinson rubbed his chin and re-read the note.

Even if Ansaro was a Pinkerton, it didn't mean he had stopped the shooting. Even Lakehurst said there were other undercover agents in the county. If Ansaro was a spy, though… Something needed to be done. Tomlinson decided he needed to get control of or get rid of Ansaro.

Chapter 10

July 18, 1922

Enos turned the Duesenberg off the National Road and drove up the narrow road past Parkersburg. He slowed his speed as the road became rougher, but his engine still roared because of the steepness of the grade. He didn't mind washing dirt off the car, but he didn't want to throw up pebbles that might damage the car's elegant body.

He took another turn onto a dirt road and followed that uphill. A short distance along the road, two men holding rifles casually draped across their arms appeared out of the shadows. Enos stopped and waited for one of the men to walk close enough to identify him. He kept his hands in sight.

"How's it going, Ross?" Enos asked when he recognized the guard.

Ross spat a wad of tobacco off to the side. "It's busy."

"How so?"

"You'll see when you get up there."

Ross turned and waved to the other guard. The man grabbed a gate hidden by brush and swung it open. Enos drove through and continued up the mountain. He crept along, driving with his headlights off, in case a revenuer might be watching the hills for lights where there shouldn't be any.

Vincent Gambrill had set up a new still operation above Parkersburg since the police had raided the one on the hill above Eckhart. This new site wasn't far from the old one as the crow flies, but it required descending one mountain slope and climbing another. Vincent wanted to stay close to Frostburg because most of his biggest buyers were in the town. That Vincent could operate so close to the old site just reinforced the general feeling among Vincent's men that their boss was paying off the police to look the other way.

Too bad the federal agent in the county wasn't willing to look the other way, but at least the police must have tipped Vincent about the raid in May. When Enos had arrived to warn his boss, men had already been packing up operation.

The 500-gallon still from Eckhart was reassembled in the clearing, one of at least a half dozen large moonshining operations around the county. There were also hundreds of small stills people hid in their basements and barns, but these produced a fraction of what Vincent's operation did.

Enos parked and got out of the car. He unlatched the panels in the back of the car that revealed the compartments under the back seat where Enos hid his moonshine deliveries. The hiding space seemed secure, and it certainly wasn't obvious, but Enos had never had police try to search his car. Nor did he intend to.

He watched Vincent speak with a group of men filling bottles with moonshine and stuffing the tops with rags.

The wiry man walked over to Enos and handed him a list of the deliveries he needed to make tonight. It seemed shorter than usual.

"Why so short? Are those men also delivering?" Enos asked.

Vincent glanced over his shoulder. "Those guys? They're making bombs."

"Bombs."

"Molotov cocktails. They light the rags and throw the bottles. Either the burning rag ignites the moonshine, and it explodes, or the bottle breaks, spilling the moonshine over something and the fire ignites it."

Enos knew better than to ask who the men were. He could guess they were union miners who wanted to cause trouble. Not that the company men were so saintly that they wouldn't try something. They just wouldn't use a local moonshiner. Also, they would probably use gasoline.

"Seems like a waste of good moonshine, if you ask me," Enos said.

Vincent shrugged. "As long as they pay for it, they can bathe in it for all that I care. We'll just make more."

"That would be the most enjoyable bath I've ever had," Enos said with a smile. "So why is the list so short tonight?"

"This is a business, Enos, and when business is good, you get competition."

"So? You've always had competition, but your brews taste the closest to the real thing than anybody else's around here."

He had tasted most of the moonshine from the larger local still. Not that he claimed to have a discerning palate, but Enos thought he knew enough to proclaim Vincent's moonshine superior.

"True, and it still is, but we're dealing with more than who's got the best booze. There're some guys over the line in Pennsylvania looking to expand into Maryland. They've been bringing in cheap stuff to steal customers and ratting out any moonshine operations they find to cut out the competition."

"Not very neighborly."

Vincent nodded. "Not at all. I'd return the favor if I knew when they were making their runs. It would give the police something to do other than look the other way."

Enos walked over and picked up a pair of jugs and stowed them in his car. Then he repeated the process until he had a dozen gallons hidden. He had only four stops tonight. He wouldn't even need to stop back here to refill his car.

He thought about Matt's friend, Jenny Washington. She was a beautiful woman with short auburn hair and dark eyes. She had a great sense of humor, and on the occasions when he had seen her dressed to go out in the evenings, she was stunning.

Matt said she was a widow, but why no one had married her again was beyond Enos. Then he realized that a lot of men wouldn't be able to get past what she did to earn a living. They didn't mind paying for sex, but they wouldn't have a serious relationship with the woman they had to pay for sex. If Jenny even wanted a relationship. If she had had many encounters like the one she had had with David Lakehurst, she might consider men a danger she had to endure, like miners dealing with rock falls, dead spots, and methane explosions to earn their living.

Enos thought he could get past her other life, but not if she continued doing it if they got serious. And that was the catch. If they started dating, she would still need to earn a living. How could she do that? Did he have the right to ask her to stop and gamble her livelihood on the chance that they might some day get married?

Married? Had he really just thought that in relation to himself?

Enos shook his head. He had figured he wasn't going to get married if he hadn't already. He hadn't wanted to tie a woman he loved to the uncertainty of his life as a miner. Now that he might have a different future and brighter prospects, marriage might be an option, although most women his age, unless they were widows, were married.

He drove into Frostburg, where he made two stops; one at the Gunter and the other in the speakeasy in the basement of Mason and Franklin Furniture. Then he headed out to Grantsville along the National Road to make the other two stops on his list. Now, there were closer stills where the speakeasy owners in Grantsville could buy their liquor, but like Enos had said, no one could come as close to real whiskey as Vincent. His reputation had grown with each satisfied customer and so had his profits.

Between Frostburg and Grantsville, National Highway was an eighteen-mile lonely stretch of road. Enos enjoyed racing along deserted roads. The problem was the National Road gently wove back and forth as it crossed Big Savage Mountain and Meadow Mountain. Also, while Enos managed to pick up speed on the downhill slopes, the uphill climbs taxed his engine and slowed him down.

As he started up Big Savage Mountain, the night was darker than usual because clouds blocked the stars. He saw headlights far behind him and not headlights ahead of him. People traveled little between towns late at night.

He rolled down his window and enjoyed the wind blowing through the car. He kept his eyes open in case a hidden police car pulled onto the road. His moonshine was well hidden, but a suspicious cop might know how to check the car thoroughly.

He noticed the car behind him drawing closer. It wasn't the smartest thing to drive so fast when the night was this dark.

Enos maintained his speed even as the road rose ahead of him. The engine roared as it strove to maintain speed.

The lights behind him grew larger as the car continued to close the gap. Enos knew it wasn't a police car. They couldn't go that fast.

The car came up behind him and started to pass Enos on the left. As it came abreast of Enos's car, Enos looked over, wondering what model car was so powerful. When he did, he saw the man sitting in the passenger seat stick his arm out the window.

Enos caught a quick glimpse of a pistol and instinctively slammed on the brakes. The other car shot past him just as the man fired. The other car slowed as Enos sped up again. He approached car on the driver's side, hoping the driver wasn't armed. He hit the rear corner of the car on the driver's side, and the car spun to the right and slid off the road.

Enos kept going and pressed the accelerator to the floor. The road might be dangerous, but staying here would be worse. As if to reinforce the point, he heard another shot from behind him. He ducked, knowing it really wouldn't do any good, but it was an instinctive reaction.

He considered not making his stops in Grantsville. What if the men in the car knew where he was going? Who were they?

He decided to make his deliveries since he was in the town, but he kept his eyes open, carefully watching the few cars that passed along National Road. None of them slowed or turned in his direction.

Once his deliveries were done, Enos debated how he should get home. He doubted those men were waiting for him. They couldn't know if he was going to return the same route or not. He took the Frostburg Road that headed south through Avilton before turning north to go to Frostburg. It would take him a lot longer to get back to town, but he wouldn't have to worry so much about a bullet hitting him.

He had been hoping to be back in his room by two o'clock, but it was past three o'clock when he got safely back to Frostburg. He was too wired to sleep, though. Who were those men who shot at him?

As he came off the stairs and onto the second-floor hallway, he saw Jenny getting ready to go into her room.

"Jenny," Enos said, waving.

She looked up and smiled at him. She was in that shimmering tight dress she wore at night. He guessed she must have been working. He wondered if the fact she was alone meant she had had an awful night.

"Going or coming?" he asked.

"I'm coming home."

Enos held up a bottle of moonshine he had picked up for himself when he loaded up his car. "Need a drink?"

Jenny smiled. "Really?"

"Matt will be sleeping, so we can pour some of this into a pitcher and go out onto the porch and relax." He held up the jug to show her he had the moonshine.

"What if the police see us?"

"Not likely this time of night. Besides, as long as we don't tell them it's liquor, how will they know?"

"Let me get a couple glasses and change. I'll meet you on the porch."

Enos nodded. He crept into his room, careful not to wake Matt. He filled the water pitcher on the dresser with moonshine and then set the jug on the floor. He would return it to Vincent tomorrow. Empty, of course.

He left the room with the pitcher and headed downstairs. Outside on the porch, he sat down in one of the wicker chairs and set the bottle on the floor.

The night was quiet and the streets empty, but it was three in the morning. The buildings were dark, and the only light came from the streetlamps along Main Street.

Jenny came out a short time later, carrying two glasses. She had changed into a calico dress and brushed out her hair. She sat in the chair next to Enos. Enos filled the two glasses with moonshine.

"So were you making deliveries tonight?" Jenny asked.

"Yes. In Frostburg and Grantsville."

"Were you speeding like we did the other day?"

He tipped his chair back on its back legs. "I don't do that unless I have to."

"Like when you're trying to get away from the police," she said with a laugh.

Enos nodded. "Yes, tonight I did it because someone shot at me."

"Shot at?"

Enos grinned. He could find humor in the situation now that someone wasn't shooting at him. "You sound just as surprised as I was."

"Why?"

"My best guess is they knew I was making deliveries and either wanted my money or my moonshine."

"Were you hurt?

"No, I ran their car off the road and then hightailed it over the mountain."

"You are really a great driver."

"Did you doubt me?"

"I don't know many drivers."

"Well, now you know a great one."

Chapter 11

July 30, 1922

Matt balanced the pieces of the bed frame in his arms and sidled through the door into the new Starner Boarding House in Eckhart Mines. Toni stood in the empty living room, looking around.

She felt like a queen surveying her kingdom. In a way, she was. Opening the boarding house had been her idea. It gave her a way to earn a living and stay in Eckhart after her husband Michael died in a mine accident and she lost her company housing. She managed the house while her brothers and Myrna helped when needed.

"Where do you want this, Aunt Toni?" Matt asked.

Toni eyed the frame. "That one goes into Jenny's room."

Matt nodded and headed for the stairs. Since Jenny Washington was their only paying boarder, Toni wanted to make sure she got the best of what little they had to refurnish the house. She wanted Jenny to stay on. It meant at least they weren't starting quite from scratch to fill their empty bedrooms on the second floor. They probably wouldn't get any additional boarders until the strike ended. In a way, that was a good thing. It meant they had some time to furnish the rooms.

The new house was designed with the same number of rooms and the same layout as the house that David Lakehurst had burned down. She hadn't had any say in that, but she had visited and taked with Patrick Kennedy about baseboard and crown molding, type of wood used in the floor, the wallpaper patterns, and placement of the fixtures in the house. The house was so new that it still smelled of paint and fresh-cut wood. Since the fire had destroyed most of the furniture, they were getting by with donations from other families in town and furniture left behind when other families had moved away to find work. Toni still wouldn't accept direct donations from Matt, and she even refused Enos's moonshining money.

The first thing she had done when she was told the new house was complete was to buy new picture frames and rehang the family pictures she had saved from the fire. The glass in many of the frames had broken in her rush to escape the burning house.

"The pictures will make the house seem more like their home than anything else I can do," she had told the family.

Even with the pieces of donated and saved furniture, the house would still look bare. Who knows how long it would take to refurnish the house like it had been? With only one boarder and Matt, Samuel, and Enos out of work because of the coal strike, it could be some time before they saved enough money to buy the things they needed.

Kitchenware was the next priority. They needed to prepare meals so they wouldn't have to keep eating out. Then would be dishes and silverware and rugs and curtains. Clothing would also need to be replaced, and Samuel, Enos, and Matt would need to buy new coveralls and equipment. The bill just ticking upward.

Thinking about it all saddened and overwhelmed Toni some days.

Samantha Havencroft walked in carrying a folding table. Toni pointed to the dining room.

"Take it there, dear, and thank you for helping us move back in," Toni said. It surprised her a bit to see Samantha in a plain work dress. The girl might be from a well-off family, but she wasn't afraid of hard work.

"It's my pleasure, Toni," Samantha said. "Once I see what you need, I can look around my house. I'm sure we have items we can donate to get the boarding house up and running again."

"There's no need for you to do that."

"I want to. I was worried you might not accept a donation, but Matt said you had collected a lot of items from people in town."

Toni laid a hand on Samantha's arm. Anything Samantha donated would probably become the best items in the house. "Thank you."

Samantha carried the table over to the dining room area and opened it up. It wouldn't be nearly large enough for the family to all eat meals together, especially once they had boarders again. It would have to do, though. Samuel said he would make a new table and chairs since he had plenty of time on his hands. They could stagger meal times until then, if needed.

Laura Spiker walked in carrying a box of kitchen utensils and headed toward the kitchen with it. She had seen the family moving into the new house and came to help. Jacob followed her, carrying a pot that looked almost as big as him.

Toni smiled and tussled his hair.

Matt had read in the newspaper this morning that the mining companies were trying to evict miners from company homes in Hagerstown, but the miners were refusing to leave because they had nowhere else to go.

The move in didn't take long since there was so little to move into the house. When everything was in place, Matt took Samantha back to show him his room on the first floor.

"You remember what it looked like when you visited me before?" Matt asked.

Samantha nodded. Matt opened the door. Inside, he had a small dresser propped up on one corner with a piece of wood because the leg was missing. A thick comforter folded on the floor would serve as his bed. That was it.

Samantha put her hand to her mouth. "Oh, Matt. You were better off in the hotel."

Matt walked into the room and sat down on his "bed." He patted the comforter beside him to get Samantha to sit.

"Believe it or not, I am happy to be back here, even though I've never lived here. As sparse as it is, this is my room. Even before the fire, I didn't have that. All the furniture in the room was Toni's. Now, I will be able to add things I want to have and make this my area."

What he didn't tell Samantha was that although Toni wouldn't accept his money to furnish the house, he could furnish his room however he wanted. He was still drawing pay from the Pinkertons.

"That's a nice way to think about, but it won't be comfortable sleeping on the floor," Samantha said. "You need to make a bed your first priority."

Matt slapped the wooden floor. "This? This is nothing. Remember, I was in the Marines. I slept on far worse than this when I was in Europe."

At the mention of Europe, Samantha reached up and lightly stroked the pink and white scar tissue on his neck that contrasted against his dark skin. It was his wound from the Great War. He'd been fighting Germans in France when he had been shot. Just as he had fallen to the ground, an artillery shell had exploded nearby, hitting him in the shoulder, neck, and chest. He had nearly bled out, but the corpsmen had stabilized him until his wounds could be closed. He had scars over much of his body, but the neck scar was the most apparent.

Matt reached up and held Samantha's hand in place. Then he leaned over and kissed her. He continued kissing her as he pulled her back onto the comforter. As he stretched out on the comforter, Samantha suddenly pulled away and stood up.

Blushing, she shook her head. "No, I can't do it. That is just too hard."

"Spoiled," Matt said with a smile.

"Not about everything, but there are certain luxuries I refuse to give up."

Matt put his hands behind his head and stretched out.

"It's like camping," he said.

Samantha frowned. "I hate camping. I'm going to see if your aunt needs anymore help."

She turned and left the room.

Matt stood up. He wouldn't admit it to Samantha, but he could use at least one more comforter to make his new "bed" passable. Otherwise, he wouldn't be able to sleep. He would definitely miss the feather mattress in the St. Cloud Hotel room. He would have to go shopping for a bed in Frostburg tomorrow. Tonight he could sleep outside in a grassy area where it would be softer.

Matt looked out the window at Eckhart. It surprised him to see Joey standing on the other side of the street, staring at the house. He was alone. He just stood and puffed on a cigar. Matt expected to see him walk across the street and come up to house. He figured Joey walked Laura and Jacob back to his house. Not that Joey would really be welcome here, but he had paid to have the house rebuilt. It was more of a face-saving gesture than anything else since David Lakehurst had burned the boarding house down while working for the coal companies.

Matt wondered what Joey would do if he ever found out Matt was also a Pinkerton Detective like Lakehurst had been. Matt didn't mind being a detective. He liked most of his assignments. The work was interesting and even exciting at times. This time, the situation was different. He was the one who had wrangled his way into this position to protect his family, but playing two roles—one for the Pinkertons and one for everyone else—was tiring.

He just wanted the strike to be finished. Of course, then he would have to leave Eckhart, and that presented its own problems. He had reconnected with his family and kindled a relationship with Samantha.

Perhaps his employer had the right idea not to send detectives to places where they had personal connections, but what choice did Matt have? He wanted to help his family. The coal companies could be ruthless when trying to keep out the union.

Not that Matt had given his family much help. They had lost their home because of him. Enos and Samuel were out of work because of the strike, and the family was nearly destitute.

Samantha walked back into the room. "Your aunt wants you in the dining room. She made cookies, and we have milk. She wants to celebrate moving into the new house."

Matt sighed and nodded. He glanced out the window again. Joey was gone. He leaned closer to the window and looked down the street. Joey was walking away alone.

Matt followed Samantha out of the room. His family and Jenny were standing around the small table that would serve as their dining room table until Samuel built something new. Laura walked in from the kitchen with Jacob, who was carrying a plate of warm sugar cookies. Toni followed them, holding a pitcher of milk.

"Grab a cookie and a glass of milk," Enos said.

Matt picked up a cookie and handed it to Samantha. Then he picked up one for himself. Toni handed him a glass of milk.

She raised her own glass. "To a new start in our new home," she said.

Everyone repeated her toast and took a drink of their milk.

Enos watched Laura Spiker raise her glass in the toast. Her hand shook, and he wondered if she would drop the glass. He watched her sniff at the milk before she sipped at it.

"It's just milk," he whispered to her.

"I know that," Laura said. Her tone was sharp. She was letting her agitation show through.

"I'm sure you do, but you wish it was something else, don't you?" He didn't like the way she looked. When he looked that way, he always slunk off to get a drink to calm his nerves. Laura might have a drink, but it wasn't what she wanted.

"Like what?" she asked.

Enos smirked. "Whiskey."

Laura's head snapped up. "Do you have any?"

There it was—that need, that desire—to let the alcohol burn away your worries and numb you to your problems. Enos still felt the pull of the bottle, but he could fight it better nowadays. Often, he would go out driving when he felt like drinking. It achieved the same goal for him, and he enjoyed it more.

Enos cocked his head to the side. "I'm not sure I'd tell you if I did."

Truth was, he had a jug in his room. He always had a jug in his room. He just didn't want to have to share it with anyone unless it was Jenny.

"Why not?" Laura asked, glaring at him.

"Because I know that look you're giving me right now. I've seen it in the mirror from time to time."

"So, you obviously don't have a problem with drinking."

"Oh, I do. I wouldn't tell my family because they already think I'm a drunk. I wouldn't want to confirm it for them. I don't think I drink as often as I used to, but when I do, I still drink as much."

Laura straightened up. "I'm not a drunk."

"That's good. Because you don't want to get like me. You have a little boy to look after. He's already lost his papa. He can't lose you, too."

Enos watched her look over at Jacob, who was playing patty-cake with Myrna. Then he noticed her hand steady, and she took a drink of the milk. She had her own version of driving to distract her from booze. He just hoped she could keep making the right choice.

Chapter 12

July 30, 1922

Paul Tomlinson paced his room in the Hotel Gunter. Stomping back and forth would be more accurate. The floorboard under the area rugs creaked loudly with each step. His white shirt was untucked and unbuttoned. The *Cumberland Evening Times* was wadded up on the floor.

Tomlinson wanted a drink, but he didn't dare go down to speakeasy in the basement in his foul mood. He couldn't chance any miners seeing him angry, perhaps out of control, and looking weak.

The railroad shopmen had accepted President Harding's plan. They had come to terms in a matter of weeks, and soon the railroads would start running regularly again. So much for solidarity among the unions.

Now, people were questioning why the United Mine Workers couldn't reach an agreement with the coal companies. The government and railroads had been willing to meet with the union and agree on a contract everyone could live with. So why couldn't the coal companies and UMW? The longer the coal strike lasted, the more the UMW's finances were drained. Money was going out, but it wasn't coming in from dues the working coal miners paid.

Even support among the miners for the strike was fading. They wanted to earn money again. Even if it was less than what they deserved, some was better than nothing. For the coal mines that were still operating, they were seeing record profits. The price of coal had risen from $5.50 a ton when the strike started to $7 a ton now. Unfortunately, none of the union companies and many of the non-union companies could take advantage of that. Businesses were importing coal from Great Britain, which could also be one reason the price was rising. Shipping costs were much higher.

The Maryland State fireman's convention was scheduled to come to town. Tomlinson would have to start his men working to disrupt that and keep them away if they could. The more business-es in the area shared the pain the miners were feeling because of the strike, the more those business owners and their patrons would pressure the mining companies to settle the strike.

Finally, he picked up the telegram laying on the table in his room and read it. *Can neither confirm nor deny that subject is a Pinkerton.*

Paul wadded up the paper and threw it off the side. For an answer like this, he had waited a month. What did it even mean? Someone had to know who Matt Ansaro worked for in Baltimore. He hadn't been unemployed all that time. More importantly, was that employer the Pinkertons? Certainly Tomlinson's contacts could find someone with the agency willing to talk.

He was going to have to take matters into his own hands.

He also needed to find out who had attacked Brian Purcell last month. Tomlinson had hoped he would have heard a rumor about it while he was waiting for word about Matt Ansaro. Neither approach had gotten him too far.

The person who attacked Brian could have been Matt. That would make matters simple. Tomlinson would only have one leak to worry about then. Then again, it could have been someone else, or Matt could be innocent entirely, and Tomlinson could just be looking for one person who had attacked the sniper.

He needed answers, and he wasn't getting any.

He took a deep breath and sat down at his desk. He pulled a piece of paper from the drawer and wrote Matt Ansaro's name at the top of it. Then he opened the top file on his desk and began reading through the reports he had been receiving about mining operations in the county and the backgrounds of different key miners. He searched for men who were newly arrived in the county, had no family, were not in the UMW, and perhaps, worked as a scab.

Of course, he realized Matt didn't fit the profile. He wondered again if Matt was entirely innocent.

Soon, he had added the name John Branard under Matt's. He set that file aside and picked up the next one. Once he had a list of names of potential undercover agents, he would have to decide what to do based on how long that list was. Judging by the size of the pile on his desk, he might be working all night.

Chapter 13

July 31, 1922

The Ansaros sat down to eat dinner around their small dining room table. The women got the prime seats around the table while the men sat on the floor with their plates in their laps.

The meal was only sandwiches and carrots because they were still didn't have their kitchenware replaced. Matt guessed they were lucky to have plates. Toni and Myrna were planning to go to Frostburg in the morning to start buying the things they needed for the house.

No one seemed to mind the light fare. They were talking and laughing at Enos's stories about moonshiners in the county when they heard shouts from the street.

Matt got to his feet and walked over to the front door to look outside. People were running past the house toward Angel Street. He could only catch snatches of conversation, but he heard one word that worried him. *Fire.*

"Something's on fire!" he called back to his family.

"Not again!" Myrna wailed.

Matt rushed outside and jumped off the porch. He went behind the house and grabbed a bucket off the back porch and followed the crowd up the street.

Smoke billowed into the evening sky. One of the miner houses was on fire. The older miner houses were built from stone and rarely had a problem with fires. The newer houses were wooden because they were cheaper for the company to build yet they still charged miners the same rent.

Matt saw a bucket brigade had formed, and he rushed to join them. The men in line pumped water into the buckets and passed them from man to man.

"Whose house is that?" Matt asked David Brown, who was next to him in the line.

"It was the Kettlemans, but I'm not sure if they were evicted or not. I used to see Ed Kettleman at the mine, but with the strike on…"

Matt took the bucket from him and passed it on to the next man.

Joey had started evicting miners again to make room for the strikebreakers Consolidation Coal was using, so the house might not be where the Kettlemans lived any longer.

Matt kept passing buckets down the line. A group of young boys ran the empty buckets from the fire back to the pump to be filled.

The rest of Matt's family joined the bucket line shortly after Matt. Samuel also brought another bucket. After an hour, one boy ran back and told the men at the pump the fire was out. Men who had been working the pump straightened up and shook out their tired arms.

Toni walked up to the still-smoking house. Men walked around inside, checking for any embers that could ignite and drowning them in water. The house looked like it might be salvageable. The windows were scorched as was some of the wood, but the roof and walls looked intact.

She saw Patrick Kennedy walk out of the house. His face was still soot covered, but she recognized him. She was used to recognizing faces covered in charcoal dust, and this was no different.

However, he was carrying a body too small to be an adult.

A woman yelled and ran forward. It was Ethel Kettleman. The woman clutched at the girl, who Toni realized was Mary Kettleman, but she was badly burned. Patrick passed the girl's body off to Ed Kettleman, who stood beside his wife.

Then Patrick turned away and hurried over to the front porch, where he sat down and buried his head in his hands.

Toni rushed over to the Kettlemans, but stopped before she reached them. She wanted to comfort them, but what could she say? The fire had just taken their daughter from them. Toni had nothing to compare that to. She had lost her parents, brother, and husband, but to lose a child? What must that be like?

She walked over to Patrick.

"Are you all right?" she asked.

The Irishman nodded and looked up. "I just need some fresh air."

"What happened in there?"

"I heard the woman screaming about her daughter and a fire, so I tried to help. I ran inside, and the little girl was on fire." He took a deep breath and sniffled. "The little girl was yelling and running around, and she caught other things in the house on fire."

"They are the Kettlemans. Don't you know them?"

"You should know that most miners won't speak to us."

"But you helped them."

Patrick nodded slowly. "They needed help, and I have a little sister. I tried to help, but the girl's clothes were on fire. I smothered the flames with a rug, but she was already…" He shook his head and sobbed.

Toni frowned. She didn't know what to say to Patrick either. He had rushed into a burning house to help people who probably would have spit on him if they passed him on the street.

Toni sat on the porch next to him. "You couldn't have done more than you did. It looks like you nearly died as well."

"Her flames caught other things on fire, but I couldn't carry her out until the flames on her were out." He let out a sob. "She screamed so much and cried. I tried. I tried to work fast. And then she was quiet." He shook his head. "That was the worst part. She was quiet, just as I got the flames out and I knew… I knew she was dead."

"I'm sorry." She kept saying that. She meant it, but it wasn't helping. She didn't know what else to say, though.

"I am, too," Patrick said.

"No, I'm sorry you had to go through that."

"Don't worry about me. Worry about them. That family will never be the same."

"I can worry about you both."

They fell into silence with both of them lost in their thoughts.

Ed Kettleman walked up to Patrick. Soot covered him from head to foot. His shoulders slumped and his head hung down.

"I wanted to thank you for what you did," Ed said.

Patrick shook his head. "Don't thank me. I wasn't able to get to your daughter in time."

"We... Ethel and me… we know you tried. You did more than we did. I was too shocked to move at first."

"What happened, Ed?" Toni asked.

"We had a fire going in the fireplace. We've been using more wood since the strike started. Ethel was cooking a stew, and one of the logs tumbled out of the fireplace. It caught the rug on fire. Mary tried to stomp it out, but it caught her dress on fire…" He took a deep breath and shook his head. "It all happened so fast."

A group of women walked by commiserating with Ethel. Toni wasn't sure what they had done with Mary's body. A group of men walked over to stand with Ed.

"The women are taking Ethel to the church," one man said.

Ed nodded. He stuck his hand out and shook Patrick's hand. "Thank you."

Ed walked off with the miners.

Patrick turned to Toni. "I'm going to write to my sister tonight. I know it's foolish, and she's all right, but I feel like I need to make sure. She's married with her own kids to look after, but I need to know she's all right."

"I don't think it's foolish. We all need our families."

Patrick nodded. "Thank you. I hope to run into you again in

better circumstances."

Then he turned and trudged slowly down the hill toward one of the miner houses.

Chapter 14

August 4, 1922

Matt walked next to Samantha down Main Street as he listened to her laugh about something funny that had happened at their dinner at Peter Jackson's diner. He enjoyed the sound of high-pitched laugh, and he realized he didn't hear enough of it.

What did that mean? A few months ago, he and Samantha had shared a lot of laughter. Nowadays, she seemed to get lost in thought more often and she didn't smile when that happened, let along laugh.

"Do you know what I'd like to do?" Samantha asked as she clung to his arm.

"What?"

"I want to go back to that lake we drove out to in Garrett County."

"For another picnic?"

Samantha shook her head. "No, I want to go swimming."

"Swimming?"

"You do know how to swim, don't you?"

Matt nodded. "I trained to be a Marine on an island next to the ocean. We were taught to swim as exercise. It was the first time I ever did it."

Swimming was the nicest part of his basic training at Parris Island in South Carolina. The rest had been learning hand-to-hand combat and marksmanship.

"Really?"

Matt waved his arm around. "You don't see any lakes here, do you? We used to play in some of the creeks when I was a kid, but they weren't deep enough to swim in."

"So, do you want to go?"

Matt cocked an eyebrow. "That water will be cold."

"Then let's hope the day is boiling."

Matt shrugged. "Okay. I need to stop at a store to buy a bathing suit. We boys usually went skinny dipping."

"Oooh, I bet that was a sight," Samantha said, blushing a bit.

Now it was Matt's turn to laugh.

"Hello, Matt."

Matt turned to see Paul Tomlinson crossing the street. He wore a white suit that Matt knew would start to look gray by the end of the day.

"Hello, Paul," Matt said.

"You two look like you were enjoying yourselves. Who is your lovely companion?" Tomlinson asked.

"This is Samantha Havencroft, my girlfriend."

"Really? You have excellent taste in women." Tomlinson turned and shook Samantha's hand. "I'm Brian Tomlinson, the United Mine Workers representative in this region."

"Nice to meet you."

"May I speak with your boyfriend privately for a minute? I promise I won't take long," Tomlinson said.

Samantha glanced at Matt, who raised his eyebrows, as if to say, I don't know what this is about. Then she stepped a half-dozen steps away.

"It's nice to see someone having a good time," Tomlinson said.

"Why shouldn't I be?"

"Well, the union in still on strike and our plans to scare the president went awry," Tomlinson said soft enough so Samantha wouldn't hear.

"What happened?"

"I don't know exactly, but someone stopped the man who was going to do the shooting."

Matt wasn't sure why Tomlinson was telling him this. Matt hadn't been in on the planning of that operation. Still, he had to keep from smiling.

"The UMW has decided to be more direct, and we're going to need all the miners helping," Tomlinson continued.

"Helping how?"

"Things are going to start developing soon. I am warning all the Eckhart miners to stay away from the company store."

"Not much worry about that. It's the company store. No miner wants to support the company right now."

"I mean, don't even go there to pay on your accounts. We are going to burn it down."

Matt's eyes widened. "That is bold. What if you are caught?"

"We won't use an Eckhart miner to do the job, so no one in town will recognize him. Afterwards, we'll see how well Consolidation Coal listens to the message."

"That sounds reckless and dangerous."

"Maybe, but this will start hitting them in the wallet like they have been hitting miners like you." He clapped Matt on the shoulder. "Just stay away from the store. You don't want to be seen."

Tomlinson tipped his hat to Samantha and said louder, "Good day to you, Miss Havencroft. Have a good day."

Matt walked over to Samantha, and she took his arm. They started walking toward her house.

"What was that all about?" she asked.

"Stupid decisions that are going to get someone hurt or worse."

"Worse? As in…"

"Killed."

Samantha stopped walking. "Really?" Matt nodded. "Then you have to do something."

"I know, but I have to decide what that is."

"Tell the police."

"That's easy to say, but the police need to have more to go on than my word. Besides, what if the union just changes the location where they want to attack?"

Matt and Samantha walked in silence back to her house. Matt kissed Samantha goodbye then went back to the boarding house and wrote a letter to William Singletary in Cumberland. Matt relayed what Tomlinson had said and when he expected miners to burn the Eckhart Company Store. He left it to Singletary to decide on what to do, though.

Tomlinson sat inside one of the miner houses in Eckhart looking out the window at the company store across the street. He had been in Pekin yesterday. Tomorrow, he would move on to the mine office for two of the mines in Lonaconing and then onto Westernport at the end of the week.

He had told six different people the same story he had told Matt Ansaro, although he had said the target and day of the attack was different each time. It was classic disinformation. If a miner had leaked the information, then something would happen when the attack took place.

Tomlinson hadn't lied to any of the suspected leaks. He would either discover a traitor to the UMW or he would take out a target. No one had stopped the pair of UMW miners in Pekin yesterday, and the UMW miners had burned the tipple.

The UMW won no matter what happened. Tomlinson almost hoped not to find the leaker so that he could take out six coal company properties.

Since it was dark out, he had to concentrate to see any movement in the shadows. He looked at his watch. It was time for his miners to move in and splash the company store with oil. He waited and watched and listened. He thought he heard liquid sloshing in a container, but he couldn't be sure. In a few more minutes, he would be able to see very clearly when the company store went up in flames.

Then he heard shouts. The shadows around the store shifted

unnaturally. Then he saw lanterns lit and people.

Tomlinson stood up and pulled deeper into the shadows of the house. Pinkerton agents rushed the two miners who had volunteered to help Tomlinson. They cuffed them and led them away from the company store.

Joseph McCord walked out onto the porch of the store. "I don't recognize them."

"They had two buckets of gasoline," one Pinkerton said.

"Take them to the county jail, and tell the deputies I'll be by in the morning to press charges."

"Yes, sir."

The agents dragged the miners away and Tomlinson sat back down, slowly shaking his head. Well, he had found his mole. Now what would he do about it?

Chapter 15

August 5, 1922

William Meese was one of a handful of miners who had given up and gone back to work at Potomac Mine near Barton. What choice did he have? The company owned his house, and he still owed money at a couple of stores in town. Even though the company didn't own the stores, the owners still wanted their payment. They were agreeable about letting his current debt go unpaid, but it was accumulating interest, and they wouldn't extend him additional credit until he started paying down his debt. He was living on vegetables from his garden and whatever his wife had canned. They also bartered some, but his diet since the strike began had been mighty light on meat. The company didn't force the issue with his house, but he didn't have enough to pay this month's rent.

So the superintendent gave him a choice: work or leave.

Not much of a choice. He had no car, and even if he did, he had nowhere to go. Even if he had somewhere to go, he had no money to pay rent somewhere else.

This was why there needed to be a strong union, so the mine companies couldn't treat the miners like this. Right now, though, the union wasn't doing much for the miners.

As he approached the mine, two masked men rushed out from behind trees. William stopped and looked around for help. No one was nearby.

One man held up a pistol. "It's your choice. If you cross us, scab, you'll die."

William had wondered how long it would be before the union came after him for crossing the picket line. His union friends in Barton had already started snubbing him, and union miners had already come after strikebreakers and beat them. They didn't understand that he needed to work. He had a family to support. He couldn't let them suffer because he wouldn't work.

"If I don't work, I'll starve."

"Let the union help."

"I tried that. They didn't."

The man holding the gun looked at the other masked man, who shrugged.

"Suit yourself," the man said, and fired.

William fell backward, momentarily stunned. Then he felt the pain and reached for his chest. He felt the wetness and lifted his hands. He saw blood covering them.

What else could he have done?

He was dead either way. At least this way wouldn't take so long.

Damn the mining company, and damn the union for that matter.

Matt was sitting on the front porch of the boarding house reading *Science Fiction & Fantasy Magazine* when a car pulled up and stopped. He was surprised to see Paul Tomlinson get out of the back seat. Two other men got out of the front seat.

Matt's stomach clenched at the sight of the men. It was out of place and that worried him. He had been feeling uneasy about Tomlinson since their conversation in Frostburg.

Matt stood up, suddenly wishing he had some sort of weapon. He started curling the magazine as tight as he could. It wouldn't do much good. It didn't have weight or a point, but he might be able to shove it into someone's face or throat if need be.

Tomlinson walked onto the porch while the other two men waited near the car, leaning on the hood with their arms crossed over their chests. They had the look of miners, but they were acting like bodyguards for Tomlinson. They even wore pistols on their hips.

"Good morning, Matt," Tomlinson said. He smiled, but it barely curled his lips and showed no emotion.

"Good morning. What brings you here?" Matt said.

"This is a sizable house you have here."

"I don't own it. It's a boarding house. I only live here."

"But your family owns it, and it's brand new, isn't it? The coal company built it for you."

"After their man burned it down."

Tomlinson nodded. "Funny about that. Why would David Lakehurst want to burn down the house of a fellow Pinkerton?" Matt tensed, expecting a fist to be thrown. "Was it a set up?"

Matt faked innocence. "What are you talking about? Fellow Pinkerton? I'm a miner."

"The two aren't exclusive. David Lakehurst hates you, you know."

Tomlinson sat down in the chair next to Matt.

"I can't say I'm fond of him either."

Tomlinson chuckled. He reached into his jacket pocket. Matt stepped forward and clenched the magazine. Tomlinson took out a folded piece of paper and handed it to Matt.

Matt opened the paper and read it. It was a letter outing Matt as a Pinkerton. It was from Lakehurst.

"And you believe this letter from a coal company man?" Matt said when he finished the letter. "He just wants the union to do what he couldn't. I beat him up and ran him out of town."

Tomlinson shook his head. "Of course not. I have other reasons." He lowered his voice. "Let's go for a drive. We have some things to talk about."

Matt glanced at the two men standing by the car. He wasn't sure what he and Tomlinson had to talk about, but he doubted he would like it.

"I don't think so. I don't like what you're insinuating," Matt said.

"I'm not insinuating anything, Matt. I'm saying it outright. You're a Pinkerton working for the coal companies. Now, who I say that to depends on whether you get in the car with me. Nothing will happen to you. I promise. But we need to talk, and we can do it privately in the car."

Whether Tomlinson had any real proof against Matt didn't matter. He had enough to act on and enough to turn the miners in the county against him. Matt's time in Allegany County was over. What more was there to say? He had to wonder why the man hadn't come with a mob of miners to drive him out of town, or worse.

"Fine, let's go," Matt said.

They walked to the car and climbed into the back seat. Tomlinson settled back and lit a cigarette. The guards waited until Tomlinson settled in before climbing into the front seats.

"Head toward Westernport," Tomlinson told the driver.

The man started the car, turned it around, and headed back to the National Road. At the top of the mountain, he took a left on the Westernport Road.

"First things first," Tomlinson said. "You work for me now."

"How do you figure that?"

"Your secret will stay a secret only as long as you do what I say. You've been spying on the unions for the Pinkertons. Now, you are going to spy on the Pinkertons for the union. You are going to tell me what the coal companies are planning to do against the union."

Matt gave up playing innocent. It wasn't working. Better to face things head on. "I'm not told that type of information. I'm a field agent. I send information. I don't receive it."

"You get some."

"I can count on two fingers the times I've been contacted with information about what will be happening."

"What you get you relay to us."

"And if I don't?"

Tomlinson chuckled. "It should be obvious. I will let every

miner in this county know about you. You might get away, but I doubt your family will. They will be held just as much to blame as you are."

"They don't know about me."

Tomlinson shrugged. "Who will believe that?"

"It's the truth."

"Then you betrayed them and every other miner in Eckhart."

Matt couldn't argue with that. How many times had he felt that way? He had come to Eckhart wanting to help his family, but things hadn't worked out that way. His uncles had lost their jobs, and Lakehurst had burned the boarding house down.

"In addition to you relaying any information you receive to us, we will also give you information that we want you to relay to your bosses."

"Like what?"

Tomlinson shrugged. "It will be information that helps the union in some way. You may actually become the hero the miners think you are."

Tomlinson tapped the shoulder of the driver. "Pull over, Mike."

Mike pulled the car off to the side of the road and let it idle.

"It's time for you to get out," Tomlinson said, waving a hand dismissively toward the side of the road.

"Out? We're in the middle of nowhere."

Tomlinson shrugged. "Then you can walk back or wait for the trolley to pick you up."

Matt climbed out of the car.

Tomlinson said, "You'll be hearing from us unless you hear from the Pinkertons first."

The car headed back down the road, throwing dust and pebbled into the air. Matt choked on the dust as he tried to duck from being hit by the pebbles.

Matt started heading north again.

He was in a fix now. The UMW had him trapped. Tomlinson was right. It would be easy enough for Matt to leave, but his family had nowhere to go. Eckhart Mines was the only home they knew.

If Matt relayed bad information to Pinkertons, his job with them wouldn't last long. Then he would be even more at the mercy of Tomlinson.

It was not looking good.

Chapter 16

August 6, 1922

The blonde-haired woman stepped off the Cumberland and Westernport trolley and brushed the dust from her dress. She supposed the cars were open at this time of year to keep them from getting too hot inside—but the dust! The dress had cost $40 in Baltimore.

The trolley moved on toward the east, stirring up more dust. The woman coughed and waved a hand in front of her face.

She looked across the street at the small town, if you could call it that. Eckhart Mines was even smaller than Frostburg, and she considered Frostburg a small town. She walked down the street toward the cluster of homes and businesses.

Well, one thing was certain, it shouldn't be too hard to find Matt here.

She saw the building off the left with a sign over the porch that read: Eckhart Mines Store. That looked like as good a place as any to start.

She walked through the front door and heard the bell over the door jingle. It wasn't anything she would call a store. Hutzler's on Saratoga Street in Baltimore, where she liked to shop for her everyday clothes, had five floors, multiple departments, and who knows how many salespeople ready to help her. This room had wall shelves fronted by a U-shaped counter and a few tables full of merchandise in the open areas. It seemed to have a little of everything: clothing, food, household goods, tools, seeds, and more.

The clerk was an older man with graying hair and a large bald patch from his receding hairline. He wore round, wire-frame glasses and sat behind the counter reading a newspaper. He had looked up when she walked in, but he hadn't bothered to stand or ask if he could help her. Customer service had a lot to be desired in a small town.

She saw an open door and wondered if it led into another room where someone would actually help her. She headed in that direction.

"You can't go in there," the clerk said.

"And why not?"

"It's the mining office."

"Mining office? The sign outside said store."

The clerk closed his newspaper and stood up. "This is the store. That room's the mining office. Do you want something?"

She drew her shoulders back. "My name is Priscilla Bankert. I am looking for someone. I thought someone here might know him, and since you are the only one here, I'll ask you."

Silence fell between them. Finally, the clerk said, "So, are you going to tell me this man's name or what?"

"Oh, yes, his name is Matt Ansaro. You would recognize him. He has a large scar on his neck. He was a war hero and wounded in the war in Europe."

The clerk shook his head. "Sorry, I don't know him. The only Matt Ansaro I know with a large scar on his neck was no war hero."

Priscilla frowned, which she didn't enjoy doing because it formed lines on her face. "You are very rude and pompous to be a store clerk."

"Look who's talking about being pompous. That dress cost more than some people here make in a month."

Priscilla turned to leave. There had to be an easier way to find Matt than to stand around and let this man whom she wouldn't hire to walk her dog insult her.

A large man came to the door of the mining office. He was

well dressed and not a bad-looking man, if a bit overweight, which from her short time in this area was unusual to see.

"Excuse me, ma'am. My name is Joseph McCord, the superintendent of these mines. Did you say your name was Priscilla Bankert?"

"Yes, I came all the way from Baltimore looking for Matt Ansaro only to be treated as filth by this man." She waved a hand at Harry Portnoy.

"Is your family the Baltimore Bankerts who own Baltimore International Shipping?"

Priscilla smiled. At least someone in this backwater village recognized her.

"Why, yes, they are," she said.

Joseph laughed. "Portnoy, you are a fool. This woman could buy this store a dozen times over easily."

"She's welcome to it," Portnoy said.

He opened his newspaper and saw back down.

"I believe I heard you ask about Matt Ansaro," Joseph said.

"Yes. I know him from Baltimore."

"Well, Matt works for me, at least when he works. The miners are on strike."

"So, can you tell me where I might find him?"

"I don't know if he's home right now, but he lives in the new house up the hill. I recently had my employees built it for Matt's family. It's the sixth house on the left. Would you like me to escort you?"

Priscilla smiled. "No, thank you, Mr. McCord, but it is nice to meet a gentleman."

"Well, if you need anything, feel free to come visit me. My office is in here, and there's an outside entrance so you don't have to deal with Portnoy."

"That's kind of you. Thank you."

"My pleasure, ma'am."

Priscilla turned and left.

It was easy enough to follow Joseph's direction. She found the house and paused outside to stare at it. It did look newer than the other houses around it. Those houses were gray from coal dust. This house still appeared white.

She walked up onto the porch and knocked on the door. A middle-aged woman with dark hair answered it. She had to be related to Matt. They shared similar features.

"Hello," Priscilla said. "I'm looking for Matt Ansaro."

"He's not here right now. May I help you?"

"Will he be home soon? I came all the way from Baltimore to see him."

"Really? I don't know when he'll be home. He didn't say." Priscilla's shoulders sagged. She had come so close to finding him. "Would you like me to give him a message?"

"You can tell him Priscilla came by and that I'm staying in the Hotel Gunter and that I'd like to see him."

Toni nodded. "I will do that."

Priscilla turned away. She thought she might cry for a moment, but then she took a deep breath and headed back to the trolley stop. It wouldn't be long now.

After Priscilla Bankert left the store, Joseph walked to the door and looked out the window to watch her walk away. A beautiful woman, and a very wealthy one. What business could she have with Matteo?

"What was that all about?" Portnoy asked.

Joseph lit a cigar and puffed on the end of it. "That was about the future."

He had heard the woman while he had been sitting in his office. He had been more than willing to ignore her, but then he heard her name. Her family was one of the wealthiest in Baltimore. Her father owned a shipping line that brought goods from all over the world into Baltimore's harbor.

"What are you talking about?" Portnoy asked.

"Her family is wealthy."

"So? You aren't related."

"That remains to be seen."

If he could secure a job with Baltimore International Shipping, Joseph would be able to get out from under his father's shadow. He just needed a woman like Priscilla Bankert to help him get ahead.

Chapter 17

August 6, 1922

Samantha walked down the path from Old Main and saw Matt sitting under a maple tree in the shade. He leaned back against the tree and relaxed. His hands were behind his head, and his eyes were closed.

"You look like you're ready to sleep," she said.

He opened his eyes. "Just enjoying the warmth and sunlight. How was your class?"

She rocked back and forth on her feet. "All right. Busy. I've got a lot of work to do and think about."

Matt stood up and dusted off the seat of his pants. "Like what?"

She shrugged and started walking. "It's just that things are winding down. This is my last class of my last semester. I'll be going to the model school soon to put everything I've learned into practice."

The model school was a public school that the Frostburg Normal School ran in cooperation with the Allegany County Board of Education. The normal school provided the teachers who taught classes under the supervision of college instructors. It allowed normal school students to get valuable real-world experience before they actually had a teaching job.

"That should be a good thing," Matt said.

"It is, but things will change when I graduate."

"They always do."

Samantha shook her head. "You just don't understand, Matt."

"If I don't understand, it's because you're not explaining it to me."

She really didn't want to have to talk about this today. She had too much on her mind to be thinking about him, too.

"I will probably get a job teaching somewhere other than Frostburg or Allegany County," Samantha said. "It depends on where the teaching jobs are. New teachers aren't usually put in a school by themselves. I will probably wind up in a larger school in a city."

Matt stood up, brushed his jeans off, and took Samantha's books. They started walking toward Frostburg.

"You knew that would happen."

"Yes, but that time always seemed so far away. Now, it's here."

Matt said nothing as they walked, and Samantha was almost grateful for the silence.

"Something else happened, didn't it?" he asked.

"What? What do you mean?"

"You've known for some time that you would be graduating, and yet, you've never seemed that upset and distracted by it."

"It all just hit me."

"Yes, but why did it hit you? Something changed to make everything seem that much more real to you."

How was it he could read her so well? He knew her better than she knew herself.

"You got a job offer, didn't you?" he asked.

Samantha stopped and stared at him. "How could you know that?"

Matt grinned. "I guess I'm a bit of a detective."

"More than a bit."

"So, is it a good job?"

Samantha shrugged. "I suppose so. It's in Annapolis."

"Well, I know it's not at the Naval Academy."

She rolled her eyes. "Matt It's in a small school in the city. I would be teaching the younger students in the school."

"Don't you want to?"

"I'd love doing that, but I'd have to leave here. I'd be on my own, which I don't mind, but what about us?"

"You want to be a teacher. So if this is a job you want to do, you should do it." He seemed so nonchalant about her leaving. Did he not care about them?

It wasn't necessarily her dream job, but it was one of the few schools that was still looking for teachers to fill positions. Most new teachers had been hired in June. This job offer came with the conditional understanding that she would graduate at the end of the month.

"Aren't you upset?" she asked.

"Do you want me to be? Yes, I am not thrilled about things, but I am happy for you. Besides, one of us should be working the job he or she likes. It's not me. I'm not even working right now. I have my own decision to make. I enjoy being home with my family, but I may have to leave to find work myself."

"Where would you go?"

"Back to Baltimore probably, or maybe to Annapolis."

"Could you be happy there?"

He shrugged. "I've visited there before. It's a pretty town. I like the waterfront. Maybe I could get a job on one of the fishing boats."

"That would be wonderful." She hugged him.

"What would be wonderful?"

Samantha turned and saw Professor Williamson walking up to her and Matt.

"Oh, Professor, I didn't see you. How are you?" she asked.

"I'm done my classes for the day, so I'm walking into Frostburg for lunch before I head home."

Matt held out his hand. "We haven't met. I'm Matt Ansaro."

The professor shook Matt's hand. "You must be Samantha's

miner friend."

Matt glanced at Samantha and she looked away.

"So what were you talking about that is so wonderful?" the professor asked.

"Annapolis," Matt said.

"Really? That's my hometown."

"I got a job offer to teach at a school there," Samantha said.

Professor Williamson smiled. "Excellent. I was wondering if they would offer you a position."

"You knew about this?" Samantha asked.

The professor nodded. "Yes, the school superintendent for Anne Arundel County knows me. He also knows I got a job here. He contacted me wondering about any promising teaching graduates because they had a teacher who got married and quit."

"So, you got me the job?"

Williamson shook his head. "Nothing of the sort. As I said, I didn't even know the superintendent made the offer. I just recommended you to him."

Samantha wasn't sure what to think. She had wanted to accomplish her goals based on her ability, not who she knew.

"Why?"

"Why not? You are a bright student. Annapolis will be lucky to have you. Since my family lives there, I visit fairly often. I'll stop in to see how you are doing."

Samantha smiled. She noticed Matt off to the side. He seemed far away. Had he stepped back?

She said goodbye to Professor Williamson and started walking toward her home. Matt shook Williamson's hand and followed her. As they got closer, Matt said, "Look at the time. I need to hurry if I'm going to catch the trolley as it swings through town."

"I thought we were going to do something this afternoon," she said.

"So did I, but I need to catch the ride back to the boarding house."

She knew he was lying. Matt routinely walked the mile and a half between Frostburg and Eckhart. He only used the trolley if he was going to Cumberland or down to one of the towns along the Creek. He probably did even more walking since he had had his leg cast removed.

"Congratulations on the job," he said before turning and walking away fast.

Despite what he had said, Matt didn't ride the trolley. Oh, he was on time to board it. He saw it moving through town. He just would rather walk. It helped clear his mind, and he was in no particular rush to get back to the boarding house. He hadn't been thrilled to hear the professor talking with Samantha in a way that seemed more familiar than a professor should, but what did Matt know? He hadn't graduated high school, let alone college. It was just another reminder that Samantha was not in his social class. She was more like Priscilla in this way than in their physical similarities. Given how things had turned out with Priscilla, this wasn't a good sign.

He also thought about what he could do about Tomlinson and the problems he was creating for both the union miners and the coal companies. Tomlinson was just as much a thug as David Lakehurst had been, except Tomlinson dressed better.

Matt needed to deal with Tomlinson in a way that wouldn't make things worse for his family. He wondered if he could convince them to work in a non-union mine in Pennsylvania. He doubted Toni would leave Eckhart, though. She had stayed here even after her husband had been killed in the mines.

He walked into the boarding house, and suddenly a mass of blonde hair was in his arms. For a moment, he thought Samantha had rushed at him. Then he realized this woman felt different. He pushed her away from him so he could see her.

"Priscilla?"

It couldn't be. He had just been thinking about her earlier, and now she was here? Was he daydreaming?

"Matt, oh, Matt." She kissed him before he could say anything.

He pushed her back and held her at arm's length. She looked as beautiful as ever. Despite not wanting to, he still found himself attracted to her.

"What are you doing here?" he asked.

"Isn't it obvious? I came to see you. I missed you."

Matt looked over her shoulder and saw Toni and Myrna looking at him with wide eyes.

"She showed up a little while ago, looking for you," Toni said. "She said she was your fiancée."

Matt glanced back and forth between Toni and Priscilla. "She was until she called off the wedding." He looked at Priscilla. "What are you doing here? The last I heard, you were back to being the grand prize for Baltimore society men."

"I missed you," she said.

"Well, you made your choice and without talking to me about it, as I recall."

"Matt, please, can we talk?"

What should he do? Throw her out? A part of him wanted to do that, but a part of him also wanted to take her in his arms. He motioned to the sofa, and she sat down. He sat down in the rocking chair across from the sofa. He didn't trust himself sitting next to her.

"Can we speak privately?" Priscilla asked. She glanced over at Toni and Myrna.

Myrna said, "Come on, Toni. We've got dinner to prepare."

They turned and walked into the kitchen.

"I'm not sure if I could say what I need to say in front of strangers," Priscilla said.

"You know, they are listening from the kitchen, don't you?" Matt said.

Priscilla looked around nervously.

"And what do you need to say?" Matt asked.

She pressed her lips together and looked around the room. Finally, she muttered, "I'm sorry."

Matt nearly laughed. "That actually looked like it hurt you to say."

"Just my pride."

"So what brought about this change of heart?"

"I was scared, Matt. My parents and friends kept telling me I was making a mistake marrying you, that we were from two different classes. It all finally got to me, and I called off the wedding. My parents sent me to the ocean to relax and clear my head."

"Meanwhile, I was left not knowing what happened."

"I wrote you a letter…"

"I never received it."

"I know. I left it with my parents to give to you when they sent me away. I always assumed they did. I only learned recently they burned it."

Matt rolled his eyes. "Of course they would."

"Don't blame them."

"Who should I blame?" Matt snapped. "Did someone else burn the letter?"

"Blame me. I shouldn't have written a letter in the first place. I should have spoken with you. That's why I'm here."

That calmed him down, although he was still upset.

"There's nothing to talk about any longer. I've moved on, and so have you."

"When I came back from the ocean, my head was clear, and I realized I wanted to marry you. I had gotten cold feet like many brides, but in my case, my family's feelings made it worse. When I found out you were gone, I thought I was too late, and you had moved on."

"I have."

She reached over and laid a hand on his arm. "Well, I haven't. I tried. Men my parents approve of wanted to date me. They are from the right families, and some of them are quite handsome, but none of them make me happy. I don't laugh with them. I don't enjoy taking a rowboat into the harbor and laying back to look at the stars with them. Not that any of them have suggested it. One evening before a date, as I was getting ready, I looked in the mirror and realized I wasn't smiling. I was getting ready to go to the theater with an eligible man, and it wasn't bringing me joy. I used to always smile, getting ready for our dates. Sometimes, I even hummed." She paused and looked at her hands. "Things started to clarify for me with that realization. Not right away, but over the next few days."

"And how did they clarify?" Matt asked, truly curious.

"I love my parents. They're my parents. I want them to be happy and proud of me, but their happiness, in this instance, is going to make me miserable. To whom do I owe my allegiance? I need to be happy, Matt, and you make me happy. That's what I want."

Matt shook his head. "It's too late, Priscilla. I moved on. It was hard, but I had to move on. Now, I'm finally happy. I'm even seeing someone."

"But why did you come here? You had a good job in Baltimore."

Matt hoped she wouldn't mention the Pinkertons. Matt had no doubt his aunts were listening from the kitchen, especially since he didn't hear any cooking sounds. Toni knew the truth, but not Myrna.

"I couldn't stay in Baltimore any longer. I needed a change of scenery," he said.

"But here?"

Matt nodded. "It was just what I needed. My family was here. They helped me move on."

"But you are working as a coal miner. You can do so much more."

"It's not the best job, I admit, and I don't know if I'll stay here. I definitely don't want to stay a coal miner. But right now, it's the right place for me."

She reached out and laid a hand on his knee. He felt his muscles stiffen.

"Come back to Baltimore. My father can get you a good job. You could be in charge of security at our shipyards."

Matt stood up. "How can you ask me to do that after what you just finished telling me your parents did? Do you actually think he would help me, or I could accept his help?"

"Then find another job."

Matt shook his head. "I'm happy here, and this is where I want to be now."

Priscilla stood up next to him. "Matt, I love you."

He closed his eyes and took a deep breath. When he opened them, he said, "Go home, Priscilla."

She stared at him saying nothing. Finally, she stood up. "This isn't over, Matt. I know I surprised you, but I'll give you some time to think things over. I'm staying in room 210 in the Hotel Gunter."

She kissed him on the cheek and then turned and left. Matt sunk down into the chair and buried his face in his hands.

Chapter 18

August 6, 1922

Deciding that his family needed to know the truth about what he was doing was easy for Matt. He had never been comfortable keeping the secret that he was Pinkerton from them. It had been necessary. Now it was necessary to tell them the truth, but he didn't know how to do that. He had been living a lie for months now. What would they think of him?

Then there was the question of what he would do after Priscilla left and the strike ended. His worlds were colliding, and secrets couldn't stay secret much longer.

The walk from the trolley stop to the boarding house had never seemed longer.

Myrna and Toni were in the kitchen cooking, as usual. They smiled when they saw him.

"Are Samuel and Enos home?" Matt asked.

"Samuel is out back and Enos is sleeping," Myrna said.

"I need to talk to everyone. Can you get Samuel? I'll get Enos."

"What's this all about, Matt?" Toni asked.

Matt frowned. "I want to wait until everyone's here because I would rather not have to say this more than once."

"Is it about that woman?" She crossed her arms over her chest and glared at Matt.

"Not really," Matt said.

"Your *fiancée.*"

Another secret that needed to be dealt with.

Matt shook his head. "It is long over with."

"She doesn't think so." Toni stared at him as if daring him to deny it.

Matt headed upstairs to the third floor and knocked on Enos's door until Enos mumbled, "Come in."

Matt opened the door. "Enos, you need to get dressed and come downstairs."

Enos threw his pillow at him. "Go away. I need to work tonight."

"Enos, I need you downstairs for a family meeting."

"About what?"

"You'll find out downstairs. Hurry up."

Matt walked back to the living room. He paced back and forth as his family gathered. Enos was the last one to come downstairs. He sat down next to Toni and leaned against her, still half asleep.

"So why did you need us all together?" Toni asked.

Matt kept pacing. How to start?

"Toni, you know what I need to tell everyone, at least part of it."

Toni straightened up. Matt could tell she knew what he was going to say.

"When I came back to Eckhart, it wasn't to become a coal miner," Matt said.

"Who wants to be a coal miner?" Enos mumbled. Toni shrugged her shoulder to knock his head around.

"I already had a job when I came here. I am a Pinkerton Detective."

"What!" Samuel said.

Enos's eyes opened wide. "No way!"

"I was working in Baltimore when I heard the agency was sending undercover agents in the field to find out who the union members were and report on union activities for the coal companies. I was worried you two might be fired." Matt pointed to Matt and Enos. "So, I told my boss I came from a coal town, and I could fit in. I told him I came from Garrett County, otherwise he wouldn't have sent me here. I picked a place close to Allegany but far enough away nobody would supposedly know me."

"I can't believe you lied to us and spied on us!" Samuel shouted, pointing a finger at him.

"I didn't spy on you. I spied on others."

"You're mincing words. You spied on people you know."

"I was trying to help you and make sure the coal companies didn't think you were a union member."

"But I am union, and you were there when Enos joined the union."

"I know."

Myrna tugged on Samuel's arm, trying to get her husband to sit down again.

"I can't believe you did this to us," Samuel said as he finally sat down, glaring at Matt.

"I was trying to help you."

"Well, a hell of a lot of good you did. Both Enos and I got fired."

Matt nodded. "I know. Things have gotten out of control."

"We could have died when Lakehurst burned down the house!"

"Calm down, Samuel," Enos said as he pushed himself to a seated position.

"Why aren't you upset?" Samuel asked.

"Because this is Matt. Do you think he was really trying to do something to hurt us?" Enos asked.

Samuel stopped and took a deep breath. He shook his head. "No."

"Okay, then. What are you so upset about?"

"I feel betrayed."

"But he didn't betray us. He just handled things badly." Enos turned to Matt. "You really did a bad job of protecting us."

Matt nodded.

Toni said, "So why are you telling us this now?"

"This is the part you don't know, Toni. Paul Tomlinson, the union organizer, found out about me. Lakehurst apparently told him as his final revenge."

Like too many of union's organizers, Tomlinson was a fanatic. He enjoyed the perks of rising in the ranks of union leadership, and that power grew as more miners joined the union. He was the UMW's version of Joey McCord; Low-level leaders who enjoyed power too much. Their only difference was one's power came from miners, and the other's came from the coal the miners dug.

"So he's going to expose you to everyone," Samuel said.

"Not yet. He's blackmailing me. Either I help him, or he exposes me and also makes it look like you all knew what I was doing."

"The miners would run us out of town."

Matt nodded. "That's my problem. He knows if I just had to worry about me, I could leave town. No problem. For you all, it wouldn't be that simple, and even if you left, you wouldn't be able to work as union miners."

"I can't believe he would do that," Samuel said. "He would be hurting innocent people."

"Look around you, Samuel. Innocent people are getting hurt on both sides. I know you know about it. I read the stories in the newspaper, and you read the same paper. You can't think the union is innocent in all this."

"So what are you going to do, Matt?" Myrna asked.

"Right now, I'm stalling. Tomlinson thinks he has me over a barrel. I'm hoping he doesn't. He really wants to use me to spread disinformation, though, or he would have already exposed me."

Enos threw a pillow at Matt. "I've got enough people coming after me, Matt. I don't need any more."

"What do you have to worry about?" Samuel asked Enos as Matt batted the pillow into a corner.

"The miners and coal company men aren't the only ones fighting. The moonshiners are fighting over territory. Nobody is satisfied with what they have and they want what isn't theirs," Enos said.

"I told you moonshining was dangerous," Toni said.

"So is mining right now, but at least moonshining pays well," Enos said.

"What are you going to do, Matt?" Myrna asked again.

His shoulders slumped. "I haven't decided. That's why I wanted to talk to you all. I'm sorry, but you're part of this now. Anything I do might impact you all. Do you have any suggestions?"

"You should have asked that question months ago," Samuel said.

"I thought I could keep it from impacting you then. That's why I came back."

"My life is here. I don't want to leave," Samuel said.

"I couldn't care less where I live. If I'm not going to mine any more, I could move to Frostburg or Cumberland," Enos said.

Samuel turned quickly in Enos's direction. "You're giving up mining?"

"Yes," Enos said. "It doesn't matter how this strike turns out. I'm saving for a car, and when I have one, I will start running a taxi service."

"What about you, Toni?" Matt asked.

"If you are found out, Matt, and we leave, we would have to leave this house behind. It's all we have. And Samuel is right. Our lives are in this town."

By Matt's count, that was three people saying he needed to make things right with the miners, and one saying he didn't care. He ran his hand over his face.

Matt nodded slowly. "Okay, I need to think this over."

He walked back to his room and lay down on his quilt bed. It felt harder than usual, if that was even possible. Well, good. Hard decisions deserved a hard bed. He wouldn't sleep well whether it was because of the bed or the things he needed to figure out.

After a few minutes, Samuel walked back and knocked on his open door.

"I haven't figured out anything, Samuel. I need to sleep on it."

His uncle stood there with his arms crossed over his broad chest.

"It's a big decision and a hard one. Listen, for what it's worth, even though I'm angry at what you did, you're still family. We've talked. And we trust that you will make the best choice you can for everyone."

"I'll try, but there doesn't seem to be a good choice."

"I didn't say a good choice. I said the best choice. Sometimes, they are not the same."

Matt nodded. "Thank you."

"Let us know what you're going to do."

"I will."

"No more secrets," Samuel said.

Matt nodded. "No more secrets."

Chapter 19

August 7, 1922

Joseph paused in front of room 210 in the Hotel Gunter. He smoothed out his suit and straightened his fedora. He ran through a scenario in his head and then knocked on the door.

After a few moments, Priscilla opened it. She was dressed casually in a middy blouse and a pleated skirt. Even so, she was still a stunning woman. How had Matteo captured her heart?

"Good afternoon, Miss Bankert."

"Good afternoon, Mr. … McCord, isn't it?"

He smiled in a way he considered his most charming. "Yes, ma'am."

"What can I do for you?"

"Well, ma'am, after you left the store the other day, I realized that our families are business partners of a sort."

"How is that?"

"Both our families own stock in the Baltimore and Ohio Railroad."

Joseph's father didn't have significant holdings in the railroad, but Joseph had wanted to find any connection that would make him appear of a higher social standing. She had seen him in the small company store when she was used to being in large Baltimore department stores. Being a mine superintendent was fine for Allegany County, but it would take more than that to impress a woman of Baltimore society.

"What is your father's name? My father also sits on the railroad board of directors. He knows many of the large shareholders in the company. I may have even met him."

"His name is Winston McCord. However, I did not come here to talk about business or our families."

Priscilla smiled. "Oh, do you have some news about Matt?"

Joseph's stomach churned. What hold did Matteo have over this woman? She was a Baltimore socialite, and Matteo was a coal miner.

"No," Joseph said. "I have a Renault GS, and I thought you might like a tour of the countryside and, perhaps, lunch in Cumberland. We could dine at the Fort Cumberland Hotel. President Harding ate there last month."

Her smile turned into a frown. "Mr. McCord, I have no interest in being courted by you. I came to this country town looking for Matt Ansaro. I want to convince him to return to Baltimore with me. Can you help me with that?"

Joseph's mind scrambled to rescue the situation. He had thought Priscilla would appreciate some upscale treatment with the dinner and ride in a nice automobile. It would certainly be better than anything Matteo could offer her.

"I wouldn't presume such a thing, Miss Bankert. I offered because I thought I might provide some insights about the Ansaro family and Matt in particular. I have known him since we were children together. Although I must admit, I heard your reunion did not go well. I can't say why he would rebuff you for this life."

Priscilla smirked. "Yes, I can't either. We were to be married, and now he seems happy here."

"Perhaps, though, if we combine what we both know of him, we can come up with some answers that can help you?"

Joseph couldn't care less about helping her attract Matteo. He wanted to spend time with her so she could see how much better an option he was than a coal miner.

"You might offer me some insights at that, Mr. McCord."

He bowed his head slightly. "Call me Joseph, please."

"Then you must call me Priscilla. You said you have a car?" Joseph nodded. "Well, perhaps some fresh air would clear my head and help me think better."

Joseph smiled. "It certainly couldn't hurt."

She went and got her purse, and Joseph led her out to the street where he had parked his Renault.

Joseph might be living with Laura now, but that didn't have to be a permanent arrangement. After all, they weren't married. He hadn't even told her he was coming to see a potential rival for his affections, although it wouldn't be much of a rivalry. Things certainly hadn't been going the way he had imagined them going with her. She was unenthusiastic in bed and drank far too much. Plus, he never imagined a life with him raising someone else's brat.

Priscilla, on the other hand, could offer him not only the pleasures of the bed but the advantages of wealth and society. It was a wonderful mix—a perfect one. It was certainly one Matteo could not appreciate.

Joseph smiled. One more advantage would be that he could steal another woman away from Matteo. That would settle once and for all who the better man was.

Matt sat on the front porch for an hour staring at nothing before he finally got up and started walking up and down the streets in Eckhart. Priscilla was still around. He could almost feel her presence like a feathery weight on his shoulders. Why did she have to return when he finally got his life straightened out or, rather, almost got his life straightened out?

Did Matt still love her? He didn't know. Did Priscilla still love him? She seemed to think so, but he wondered if she really knew what she felt. She led a sheltered life and was not used to resistance. If Priscilla's father and mother protested about her renewing her relationship with Matt, would she give in again? Could he risk it?

Should he risk it? After all, he had Samantha. Well, he had

Samantha for a few more weeks until she moved to Annapolis. Who knew what would happen then?

Maybe he wasn't destined to have a wife, at least not as long as the Pinkertons used him for long-term undercover work. One thing he knew was that he couldn't risk telling Samantha the truth. Best to let her continue thinking him a coal miner until she left Frostburg. He might not be far behind her, given the way things were going.

As he walked up the National Road toward Frostburg, he saw Laura squatting on the front porch playing catch with a rubber ball with Jacob. They bounced it back and forth to each other.

When Jacob saw Matt, he climbed off the porch and ran over to Matt, hands raised.

"Matt!"

Matt scooped the boy up and tossed him into the air and caught him. Jacob laughed with delight.

"Again!" he called.

Matt repeated it. When he put Jacob down, Matt said, "You must be eating well, little man. I think you are heavier."

Laura walked over. Her eyes were clear and focused today.

"Are you heading into Frostburg?" she asked.

"I don't know. I just needed to walk and clear my head."

"Is something bothering you?"

Matt hesitated, but perhaps he needed a woman's perspective on the situation, and he wasn't sure he wanted to talk to Samantha about it. It would give her another reason to want to leave Frostburg.

Matt nodded. "You know, I could probably use a woman's thoughts."

"Do you want me to walk with you, or would you like to sit on the porch?"

"Is Joey home?"

Laura shook her head. "He's in Cumberland meeting with his father."

"Let's sit then."

Matt walked over and sat on the edge of the porch with his legs hanging off the side. Laura sat down next to him while Jacob started throwing his ball around the front yard.

"So what has got you bothered?"

He sighed. "I have never mentioned this to you, but I was engaged to be married last year."

"Really? I guess something went wrong since you are in Eckhart without a wife."

Matt nodded. "She called it off."

"She did?"

"Yes, and I thought I had gotten over her and moved on. I'm with Samantha now."

"But…"

"But I came home yesterday, and she was waiting for me in the living room of the boarding house."

"That must have been a shock. I can guess why she came to see you."

He drew back in surprise. "Really?"

"There would only be one reason why she would come out here herself. She wants to get back together with you."

"Yes!"

"So what happened?"

"I told her I had moved on just like she had done."

"She obviously hasn't."

"Yes, she has. She has been dating back in Baltimore. She told me it was with no one serious. She has been dating, though, so that means she had moved on."

Laura shrugged. "Maybe, but she came here and told you she wasn't over you. Don't you think that also shows something?"

Matt sighed. "I suppose."

"So what she's probably thinking is you think she moved on and she hasn't. So if you think you have moved on, maybe you haven't."

Matt shook his head. "That doesn't make sense."

"To her, it does. She is looking for a sign that you still love her."

"Why? She doesn't love me."

"Matt, when you saw me kissing those other guys at the school dance, you thought I was done with you, didn't you?"

"Yes," he said cautiously, expecting to be caught in a trap.

She laid a hand on his arm. "I wasn't. I was confused. I was angry. I was hurt. All that combined to make me do something I shouldn't have, because it made things worse. We broke up, and you left Eckhart."

"Okay," he said hesitantly.

"Don't you see the similarity? When Priscilla called off the wedding, she must have been confused and torn between you and her parents. Then you leave Baltimore and get on with your life. She tried to prove to herself she could, too. It doesn't mean she did. She may have just made bad choices like I did."

Matt didn't think he would ever understand a female's mind. They saw the world differently than he did.

"So what should I do?" he asked.

"Do you love her?"

Matt shook her head. "No. I'll care for her. I always will, but I don't love her. She was a step toward me finding the right person, but I'm not sure we would have worked well together as a couple. The social gap is too wide."

"Then you have a problem. She's going to take that care you have for her as love."

"What? Are you saying I shouldn't care about her?"

"No. I'm saying you're making things harder for her to move on. You've got to push her away while caring for her."

"How do you know this? It's got my head spinning."

"I told you. I felt the same way for a long time."

"But you got over it."

Laura nodded. "I moved on like you did. When Priscilla finally moves on, she'll be all right, too, but you can't make her move on. The best you can do is distance yourself from her so it's harder for her to keep holding onto you."

Matt sighed and leaned his head forward into his hands.

Chapter 20

August 8, 1922

Because of all the violence associated with the coal strike in Allegany County, the state's attorney called a special grand jury to consider how to deal with the attacks and fighting. It had even moved beyond fighting. Union miners had killed William Meese simply because he wanted to work and support his family. If anything had shown the county commissioners and states attorney that something needed to be done to curb the violence, it was that murder. The grand jury ordered the county commissioners to form a special police force. This force would operate throughout the county, even in towns that had their own police, but their jurisdiction would be over incidents concerning the coal companies and their employees. This included both mine workers and strikebreakers.

However, even when extra deputies were hired, they couldn't be everywhere. The violence might have slowed down, but it didn't end.

Perry Nelson and John Hagenbuch walked about the road from Mt. Savage to the Union Mine on an overcast morning that threatened rain. The Union Mine wasn't a coal mine. It was a clay mine for the clay used to make Mount Savage's famous fire bricks. Half the states in the country used bricks made from clay that came from Savage Mountain. The clay was mined using the room-and-pillar method that coal miners used. It was a method that mined as much material as possible, creating rooms where the ceiling was supported by pillars of earth. When the section was mined as much as could be, the miners pulled back, removing the pillars and any last bit of clay or coal. With all the pillars removed in such a large area, it was unstable and would eventually collapse on its own. The only catch was getting the clay down off the mountain. It currently used six cars on a three-rail incline that operated in counterbalance. As three loaded cars descended, they would raise three empty cars for a mile and a quarter.

On an average day, 100 tons of clay could be mined, but the clay miners had walked out to support their coal-mining brothers. Perry's and John's fellow miners weren't too happy when the pair went back to work after the national strike ended. The United Mine Workers hadn't forced the local mines to accept the union and were unlikely to now without the weight of a national strike forcing the coal companies to bargain. Consolidation Coal's operations in other states were running now and relieving the financial pressure on the company in Maryland. Perry and John believed the local coal miners were fighting a losing battle.

"How's your wife?" Perry asked as they trudged along.

"She's still sick," John answered. "It's nice that we can use the mine doctor again, but he hasn't been much help. He keeps trying different medicines, but nothing seems to work."

Cloris had started feeling listless a couple months ago. They had chalked it up to her not being used to have nothing to do because of the strike. Then she had started having aches and pains all over her body. Her headaches got to be so bad she was afraid to move her head. Dr. Kellerman was at a loss as to the cause. None of his powders, tablets, and syrups did much to stop the symptoms, let alone the illness.

"I came back to work partly so Cloris could start seeing the doctor, but it's not helping," John said.

Perry clapped his friend on the shoulder. "Eileen will bring over some food for you and the kids."

"I appreciate it, but you can't keep doing that."

"We have to look out for each other, John. No one else will. Not the union. Not the company."

The company kept them working as close to slaves as they could be because they were always in debt to the company store. The United Mine Workers just wanted its dues without offering its members much in return.

When the national strike ended and the Allegany County miners stayed out, that didn't sit right with some miners. The county miners weren't union to start with, so why should they continue to strike when miners in other states weren't? The county miners were going deeper into debt as their accounts at the company stores and even other businesses were accruing interest. The coal companies had offered to pay better wages, but they wouldn't recognize the union. Many miners were happy with the offer, but the UMW wanted the mines unionized.

A small group of miners in the county had returned to work. They needed to feed their families and they couldn't do that if they weren't working.

John and Perry heard the rumble of a truck moving down the road from Mount Savage. The two men moved off to the side of the dirt road so the truck would have room to pass.

"He's being downright rude," Perry said. "He can see us standing here. Why doesn't he slow down so he doesn't stir up so much dust?"

"Probably the mine owner or some big wig from Cumberland. I doubt they even realize how much trouble they're causing us."

"Or care."

John wondered what it would be like to drive a car and go anywhere he wanted. It wasn't ever likely to happen with what little money he made. Besides, if he had the money, he'd spend it on a good doctor for his wife. He's much rather have her get better than have a fancy car to ride in.

The truck came closer, picking up speed. John pulled a kerchief from his pocket and held it up to nose to filter out as much dust as he could.

As the truck passed them, someone sitting in the bed threw something at John and Perry.

"Scab!" the men in the truck yelled as the truck flew past.

John noticed the flame first; then, he saw the bottle.

"Get down!" he shouted as he dove on Perry.

The Molotov cocktail exploded, showering the two men with splinters of glass. John felt the sting as some of them went through his shirt and into his back and legs.

John rolled off Perry and looked around. The gas in the bottle had caught the grass on fire.

"Are you all right?" he asked.

"Yeah, yeah. Thanks."

John stood up and reached a hand down to help Perry up. Instead, Perry pointed at him. "John, you're smoking."

It was just about then that John felt the heat on his back as something ignited his flannel shirt. He yelled and dropped to ground and rolled around, trying to extinguish the flames. Although he managed it, all the rolling also drove some of the glass splinters deeper into his back. He winced as he sat up. He could feel moisture and knew some of them must be bleeding.

He shook his head. At least he could use the mine doctor.

Paul Tomlinson sat in a rocking chair on the second-floor porch of the Hotel Gunter. He sipped occasionally from the glass of beer on the small table next to the chair. He looked out over the traffic on the National Road and marveled that a tunnel actually ran under the road between the Hotel Gunter and the building across the street.

The tunnel allowed the hotel to bring in coal directly to its furnaces without having the dust dirty the halls of the hotel. Of course, that was only if Paul allowed it. He also believed that moonshiners probably snuck a lot of their product into the hotel through the tunnel. That he allowed.

He wondered if the hotel was under the control of the United Mine Workers because of the tunnel. He guessed a case could be made for it since coal was transported through the tunnel. Paul wouldn't make an issue of it, as long as the hotel didn't cater to scabs and bring in coal. Of course, now that the national strike had ended, they could always say that it was coal purchased in Pennsylvania or West Virginia.

It was confusing having the strike continue in Maryland while the rest of the country had reached a settlement. He needed to bring the coal companies in Maryland to heel and get them back in line with the rest of the country.

A young bellhop stepped onto the porch and handed Paul a folded sheet of paper. He tossed the boy a nickel. The bellhop smiled.

"Thank you," he said and then left.

Paul unfolded that paper. *No one working at the Union Mine today*. Paul smiled. The message was unsigned, but he knew who had sent it and he knew what it meant. A message had been sent to the men of the Union Mine. Miners stuck together, whether they were union members or coal miners. Those who didn't stick with the other miners were not real miners and there was a price to be paid.

Now, if he could bring Matt Ansaro to heel. He hadn't heard from the Pinkerton in two days. Paul needed to encourage Matt to make the right decision. Paul was tempted to tell everyone that Matt was an undercover agent, but he didn't want to waste a source. He had to find another way to set Matt on the proper path to redemption.

Toni cracked open the door to her room and listened. She didn't hear anyone in the parlor, although someone might be in there alone reading. Myrna was probably in the kitchen still cleaning up, but Toni could avoid her.

Toni opened the door wider and stepped into the hallway. She slowly walked down the hallway, trying not to make any of the oak strips in the floor creak. She sighed when she saw it was empty.

She eased open the front door and stepped onto the front porch, closing the door as quietly as she could.

She shook her head. "What has gotten into you, Toni?" she

whispered to herself. "You are acting like a foolish schoolgirl, and you being fifty years old."

Toni knew what had gotten into her. She had realized how lonely she had become. She had family around her, but no husband, no special man. Michael had died in the mines two years ago, and there had been no one since then.

She walked down Store Hill to the Gem Theater. It wasn't as crowded as it usually was when the miners had cash coming in and their families could afford a night out to watch a movie. Lately, the crowd had been primarily strikebreakers and a few women. They were usually from Frostburg and weren't from mining families.

She passed some people from town as she walked. She waved to them, but didn't engage them in conversation. Some of them obviously wanted to talk when they saw Toni was dressed up like she was going to church. That had probably been a mistake on her part, but Toni wanted to look her best.

She purchased a ticket and went inside the dark theater. She stood in the doorway, waiting for her eyes to adjust. Then she began scanning the people in the theater. She saw Patrick Kennedy after a few moments.

He saw her and stood up. He walked up to her and extended his arm. She took it and walked with him back to their seats. His attention made her realize how lonely she had grown. She had surprised herself, though, when he had asked her out and she agreed to see a movie with him.

"You look lovely, Toni," Patrick said.

She felt herself blush. How long had it been since a man had complimented her like that? "Thank you."

"I'm thinkin' you might be embarrassed to be seen with me, though."

Now she felt herself blush for a different reason. She laid a hand on his arm and said, "I'm not embarrassed. Really. But if the wrong people see us together, it could cause problems for my family, and we have enough right now."

"I'm sorry to hear that."

"It's not your fault, at least not directly."

"I want you to know that I have started looking for other work. The problem is there's not a lot of work to be had because of the business slowdown, and what work there is has been taken up by miners who can't work in the mines because of the strike. Also, there's the issue of finding time to get out of town and look around."

"I can keep my eyes open for jobs. What are you looking for?"

Patrick shrugged. "I'd love to do carpentry again, but I am willing to do anything. I applied at the Kelly plant in Cumberland. It looks promising."

"Really?"

The Kelly-Springfield Tire Company had manufactured tires in Ohio but had started work on a new plant in Cumberland in 1916. The city had offered a lot of incentives to get the new factory, including eighty-one acres of land, $750,000 toward construction, and infrastructure improvements. In return, the company provided around 3,000 jobs to area residents, and many of them paid better than mining. Tires had been manufactured at the new plant since last April.

"As promising as anything else, but at least they are hiring. I told you I was willing to find other work. Coal mining isn't in my blood, so if giving it up will help things work between the two of us, I am willing to do that."

Toni smiled at him.

The movie started. It was *Blood and Sand* starring Rudolf Valentino, and the story about a poor boy becoming a famous matador soon took their minds off work and whoever might be watching them.

After the movie, they took the trolley up to Frostburg to eat dinner. Toni didn't worry about being seen with Patrick there either. They walked along the street to an Italian restaurant. Following their meal, they walked back to Eckhart in the dark because the trolley had stopped running.

"We should split up," Toni said as they neared the town.

Patrick nodded. "You go on up ahead. I'll lag behind to keep an eye on you and make sure there's no trouble."

She hesitated and then kissed him on the cheek. "Thank you for a lovely evening."

"The first of many, I hope."

She smiled. "I do, too."

"You know if I get that job at the Kelly plant, I would have to move closer to Cumberland."

Toni nodded. "That wouldn't be too bad. I could take the trolley to see you and you, me.

She started down the hill and found it comforting to know that Patrick was somewhere behind her, making sure she didn't run into any problems from strikebreakers, animals, or even tripping.

It didn't mean that she could be seen with him in Eckhart, at least not while he worked for the coal company. If that happened, people would treat her as badly as poor Laura Spiker, whom they considered a traitor to coal miners. Someday, though. Hopefully, someday soon.

Chapter 21

August 9, 1922

Samuel sat on the hill beside the entrance to the No. 10 Mine. He was in the shade of a tree, so he didn't have to worry about sunburn once the sun came up over the ridge.

He looked at the pile of rotten food he had set in front of the mine entrance. He was a dozen or more feet away from the spoiled fruit and chicken entrails. Unfortunately, the breeze was carrying the smell toward him. It made his eyes water, but he stayed where he was. His position offered him a direct view of the mine entrance.

He watched as a rat crept from the shadows toward the food. It was gray and as large as a five-month-old cat. Too bad he wasn't paid by how much each rat weighed.

He raised his rifle and sighted along the barrel. The rat moved closer. Samuel fired. The rat jumped in the air and fell dead.

Too bad the mining companies couldn't be taken care of so easily. But that was the problem, wasn't it? The mining companies looked at the miners like they were rats, and the UMW looked at the strikebreakers like they were rats. When that happened, some-one was bound to get shot.

Samuel walked forward and picked it up by the tail. It was a large one about a foot long. He dropped it in the burlap bag with the other two rats.

He told himself that he had to make sure to never see the strikebreakers as rats, nor the Pinkertons like Matt. Sure, some might be bad apples like Lakehurst. Samuel doubted Matt would disagree with that, but some strikebreakers were just men trying to earn a living. They had just happened to have fallen further down the economic success pole than miners. Even Toni admitted that some of them were nice men, although she was also quick to point out that some of them were pigs.

He walked back and sat down to wait some more. Coal mines were notorious for the number of rats that lived in the shafts, and the miners didn't help matters by bringing food into the mines and tossing aside scraps they couldn't eat. The industriousness of the rats was one reason the miners carried their lunches in metal pails rather than paper bags.

Now, without the miners underground, the rats lost a food source. They had started coming to the surface, spreading into homes, ravaging gardens, and even attacking chickens. Farmers were reporting chickens with parts of their wings and feet missing, and many young chicks fared even worse.

The mine rats were becoming such a nuisance and health risk that the county was offering a twenty-five cent bounty on each rat killed.

He walked back and sat down to wait some more. Coal mines were notorious for the number of rats that lived in the shafts. They stole miners' unguarded lunches. When mine mules had been kept in the mines, the rats had also stolen their grain. The industriousness of the rats was one reason the miners carried their lunches in metal pails rather than paper bags. However, some rats were also clever enough to figure out how to get into the pails.

The problem with the rats arose with the coal strike. Since many mines weren't operating, miners weren't underground, providing the rats with a food source. The rats had started coming to the surface and spreading into homes in their search for food. People were reporting thousands of rats in Eckhart, Barton, Hoffman, and many sections along Georges Creek. Farmers and gardeners in the coal region complained that rats were ravaging their gardens and chickens. The rats ate corn, cabbage, tomatoes, and young chickens. Other farmers reported their chickens had parts of their wings and feet missing, which was attributed to attacks from mine rats.

It was becoming such a nuisance and health risk the county was offering a twenty-five cent bounty on each rat killed.

Samuel had taken up hunting rats in the mornings to add to his meager income. He stayed at the mine until the sun was well up and then carried his bag of rats to the mine office, which had been set up as a bounty checkpoint. Each morning, Samuel thought he would come home empty-handed, that there couldn't be a rat left in the mine. Yet, each day, he showed up at the office with a bag.

He walked down Porter Road to the mining company office with his bag of six rats slung over his shoulder. He saw Portnoy looking out the front window. When the storekeeper saw him, he walked out onto the porch and stood in front of the door with his arms crossed over his chest.

"You know the rule, Ansaro," Portnoy said. "No rats in the store."

Samuel stopped in front of him and held up the bag. "Are you sure these are rats?"

Samuel opened the bag and pulled out one of the dead rats by the tail. Portnoy frowned and and pushed Samuel's arm back into the bag.

"What's the matter, Portnoy? Afraid people will think you're getting more meat for your sausage?" Samuel asked.

"I do not use rat!" He noticed a woman walking down the street. "I do not use rat in my sausage. I use quality pork," he said loud enough for the woman to hear.

He pushed Samuel toward the side of the building. "Use the office door."

Samuel smiled and walked away. In addition to picking up a little additional money each day, Samuel enjoyed walking into the mining office and dropping the bag of dead rats on the counter. It seemed à propos when dealing with the mining company. He enjoyed it even more when the blood soaked through the burlap and onto the counter.

Samuel walked into the office and let the bag slide off his shoulder onto the counter.

Joey looked up from his work when he heard the sound. "More rats?"

"You should know," Samuel said with a smile.

Joey set the cigar he was smoking in an ashtray. "Yes, I should know, but somehow, no matter how much policing I do, rats always work their way back into the mines. I blame the miners."

Samuel hesitated. Joey wasn't usually so talkative when Samuel dropped off his bounty. "I've got six rats that won't be going back into the mine."

"I wish my rat problem was as simple as shooting them. I have to wait until I get these." Joey picked up a couple of sheets of paper off his desk and shook them.

Samuel knew Joey wanted him to ask what the papers said, but he didn't want to play along. He suddenly felt like Joey knew something that Samuel would not like, and Joey wanted to savor the moment.

"I believe you owe me a dollar and a half," Samuel said.

"Six rats is a good haul, but you're going to have to kill more than that to make a living as a rat catcher."

"I just pass the time in the mornings doing it. When the strike is over, I'll go back to the mines."

Joey cocked his head to the side and raised an eyebrow. "That's where you're wrong, Samuel. Like you, I am also a rat catcher of sorts. When I find them, I want to make sure they don't get back in the mine." He held up the papers again. "This is a report from the Pinkertons listing all of the miners in this area they have identified as union members. Your name is on this list, Samuel, and Enos's, too. Do you know what all the people on this list share? They are all ex-coal miners now. When the mines reopen, they won't be going back underground."

Samuel wanted to shout at Joey, but he knew it wouldn't do any good. Mines were free to hire and fire whomever they chose, and even though Samuel was a member of the United Mine Workers, it could offer him no protection right now since they were on strike and the county mines didn't even recognize the union. Samuel had known it was a risk to join the UMW, but he had believed in their goals for miners. He had hoped that enough of the county miners would join the union that they couldn't be ignored.

Joey took a silver dollar and a 50-cent piece from his pocket and tossed them on the counter.

"Here's your bounty. I guess I'll see you tomorrow, although I doubt it will be this early. You'll want to stay later and collect more rats."

Samuel took a deep breath. He wanted to throttle Joey. He thought of something else.

"Don't you want to count them and make sure I'm not lying?"

Joey shook his head, but Samuel opened the mouth of the bag, grabbed the corners of the bag, and flipped the rats at Joey. He yelped when one of the dead rats hit him and jumped backward.

"I'll see you tomorrow," Samuel said. Then he walked out of the office.

He headed up to the house, wondering what he could do to make up his lost mining wages. He was already trying to do anything he could to make money, but he always saw it as a way to hold out until he could start coal mining again. Now, it looked like that would not happen. He needed to find a full-time job so he could keep contributing to the family's expenses. He'd also have to tell Enos that he wouldn't be going back into the mines. Enos probably wouldn't mind, though. He seemed happy enough delivering moonshine. He could keep doing that and make better money than he would in the mine.

This wasn't Matt's fault, at least not directly. Maybe his nephew was right, and it was time to move.

He might find some short-term work in Frostburg. All the businesses were making plans for the annual Elks' convention, complete with a large fireworks display. The owners were looking for additional help to handle all the additional people who would be in town. That work could at least take him through the next couple of weeks until he figured out what to do.

Samuel walked into the house and headed for the kitchen. He wanted a cup of coffee and perhaps a biscuit and butter.

Myrna and Toni were in the kitchen slicing warm bread for sandwiches. Since they only had one boarder currently, they didn't have to lay out large spreads. But even a small lunch took some prep work.

Myrna saw Samuel and walked over to kiss him on the cheek.

"Any luck this morning?" she asked.

Samuel hugged her and said, "Yes and no."

"What's that mean?"

Samuel walked over and poured himself a cup of coffee. He looked around for the biscuits left over from breakfast.

"Do we have any biscuits?" he asked.

Toni put her hands on her hips. "We are going to eat lunch in fifteen minutes. You can wait."

Samuel rolled his eyes and sipped his coffee.

"So what's got you worried?" Myrna asked.

"Who says I'm worried?"

"Samuel, we've been married long enough that I can almost read your mind."

He sighed and set his coffee cup down.

"Joey McCord found out Enos and I are union members. He fired us."

Myrna stiffed. "Both of you?"

Samuel nodded.

"Does Enos know?" Toni asked.

"I don't know."

"Just when I thought things had turned around for us," Myrna said.

"Just when I was beginning to think Joey might actually be a human being with feelings and not a company puppet," Samuel said. Joey had paid for the new house, after all.

She hugged him. "Well, at least things are no different now than they were."

"What do you mean?"

"You weren't working before. You're not working now. If anything, Joey firing you probably helped things."

"You and me have different definitions of help."

"No, he did. Now you won't be looking for work just to get by until the strike ends. You know you won't be going back. You can look for permanent work. We can even move somewhere else if we have to."

"I might go back if the union wins," Samuel said.

"Joey fired you. He won't rehire you."

Samuel nodded. "I'll check the brick factory in Mount Savage and the tire factory in Cumberland tomorrow."

Myra was right. Things didn't feel so bad now that he had some options that might be better than coal mining. He might even check in with some of the hotels. If he wanted to open his own hotel someday, he had better start learning the trade.

He wondered why Joseph hadn't gone ahead and fired Matt, too. Of course, he had tried that once before and been forced to rehire him. Now Samuel understood why. Matt couldn't very well spy on the miners if he wasn't working as a miner.

Matt was lying on his mattress when Toni came to his door.

"Priscilla is back." She paused. "She seems like a nice girl. You could have a life with her and be far away from all this."

"There are a couple of problems with that. One, I wouldn't leave you all in the lurch, and two, she doesn't love me, at least not enough to go against her family."

Matt sat up and buttoned his shirt. Then he walked out to the living room where Priscilla sat on the sofa. She stood up when she saw Matt and came forward to give him a kiss on the cheek, as if everything was fine between them. He held her back.

"What are you doing here, Priscilla?"

"I told you, Matt, I want to give us another try."

"And I told you, it's over. You moved on last year, and I finally moved on. I'm happy."

"Working in a coal mine?"

"I'm happy not because of the job, but because I'm back with my family, and I have Samantha."

Priscilla nodded. "Yes, I've heard about your pretty co-ed. Do you really think she'll want to stay around here when she graduates?"

That was something Matt worried about all the time, not that he would admit it to Priscilla or anyone. "Her father lives here. She could teach at the college." He knew that wasn't happening, but he didn't want to admit that Samantha would probably leave the county.

Priscilla put her hands on her hips. "Really? Your Samantha considers herself a modern woman. She doesn't want to depend on her father."

"Unlike you," Matt interrupted.

Priscilla nodded. "Yes, I can see how you might think that, but I'm here, aren't I?"

"Yes, you are. That surprises me and makes me wonder why."

"I told you why. Come back to Baltimore with me."

"I'm needed here to help my family. I just found out my uncles lost their jobs because of the coal strike that's going on."

"Then bring your family to Baltimore. I can get them work for twice what they are making here."

It was a tempting solution. He could move his family away from here, where they would be despised if the truth ever came out about Matt. They would even have work. He doubted Toni and Samuel would want to live in a big city, though. They were uncomfortable in Cumberland, and that was far smaller than Baltimore.

"They're miners," Matt said finally.

"They need work. I'm offering it."

Matt sighed.

"Matt, let's take a walk. I don't want to argue. I want to talk."

Matt looked around. He knew Toni and Myrna were probably listening in the kitchen and staying out of sight.

"Okay, fine, let's take a walk." He motioned toward the front door.

Priscilla smiled and stood up. Matt held open the door for her. He noticed the high heels she wore and wondered how long this walk would last. They headed along Store Hill into town. Priscilla wobbled a bit, walking on the uneven surface. How had she walked from the trolley stop at Kelly's Pump?

Priscilla talked about their dates in Baltimore when they had walked along the waterfront or one of the streets of the city. She had admired the architecture of the row homes and houses, although she preferred her family's mansion in the city's Federal Hill area.

Matt saw Laura walking out of the ice cream shop with Jacob. He slowed his walk, hoping she wouldn't notice him.

She didn't. Jacob did.

The little boy ran over to Matt and hugged his leg. Matt patted his head. "How are you doing, Jacob?"

"I got ice cream." He held up the small cone. The ice cream was already melting in his hand from the hot August heat.

Then Laura reached them. "Hello, Matt." She glanced at Priscilla.

"Hello. Laura, this is Priscilla Bankert. She is visiting from Baltimore."

"Priscilla…" She lifted her chin a bit and said, "Ohhh…"

Matt smelled alcohol on her breath. Two thoughts flashed through his mind. Where had she gotten it, and why had she been drinking already? She didn't seem drunk, but her eyes were a bit red.

"Pleased to meet you," Priscilla said, holding out her hand for Laura to shake. "Are you Matt's girlfriend from when he was a boy?"

Laura blushed. "Yes, I guess that would be me. That was a long time ago."

"They say first loves are the hardest to get over."

Laura shrugged. "But we both did. Get over each other, that is." She patted Jacob's head.

"I see, and is your son's father a coal miner?"

Laura frowned. "He was. He died in a cave-in."

Pete Spiker and Rico Moretti had died in a cave-in that had trapped four other miners, including Matt. Pete had died on the verge of being rescued when a rock fell from the ceiling and hit him in the back of the head. The mine foreman had told Matt that miners shouldn't have been in that tunnel. It was too unsafe, but Joey had insisted on using it. Matt doubted Joey had even been in that tunnel to examine it. Joey thought going underground was beneath his position as mine superintendent.

Priscilla put a hand to her mouth. "Oh, I'm so sorry."

"As am I. Well, I will let you and Matt continue your walk." She took Jacob's hand.

"Bye, Matt," the boy said.

"Bye, Jacob. Better finish that ice cream before it melts."

Laura and Jacob headed up the hill toward Joey's house while Matt and Priscilla started walking in the opposite direction.

"So that was your precious Laura."

"Precious?"

"I never heard you say an ill word about her, but it seems like she's not much more than a drunk."

Matt stiffened. "She's not a drunk. She drinks, but she's a good person and a good mother."

"See what I mean? Not a bad word."

Matt shook his head. "She's no more a drunk than you. I've seen you swill plenty of fancy drinks at your social gatherings."

"Not anymore."

"Really?" Matt doubted that.

Priscilla nodded. "I gave it up after you left. I realized I was too dependent on it, and it had cost me some of my willpower that I used to be so proud of. So I stopped drinking. It was actually harder than you would think given that liquor has been outlawed. I couldn't rely on my father to help me, but I had a few friends who did. I'm surprised that they are still my friends, though, the way I treated them during my dark times."

"Dark times?"

"The liquor didn't want to let go. It made me… act crazy."

"But you're all right now?"

Priscilla shrugged. "I'm better, but I have to be careful not to slip up and take a drink. It might put me back where I was when I knew you."

Matt paused. "So are you saying booze made you want to marry me?"

Priscilla shook her head. "No, booze made me too weak to stand up to my father and marry you. You were a good decision I made, but when I lost my willpower, I couldn't be myself. I got rid of the liquor, and my willpower is slowly returning."

Matt nodded but said nothing as they walked.

Could Laura be an alcoholic? She'd never been in the past, but he had to admit he smelled alcohol on her breath a lot more since Pete died. He wasn't even sure he would recognize the signs. He hadn't with Priscilla, and he had been about to marry her.

"I've changed, Matt. Can't you see that?"

"Honestly, no, but I'm willing to give you the benefit of a doubt. If you have changed, if alcohol was the problem, and you've gotten past it, then I think that's wonderful. But I've changed, too. I'm not the same person you knew in Baltimore. I'm not even the same person who came back here. I thought I knew what I wanted and what I was doing, but I don't. My roots here go deeper than I thought and now that I'm back, I can feel that. I have obligations here that I have to fulfill before I can decide what I will do next."

"I understand, but am I one of the options for what you might do next?"

He thought. Was she? Had he totally ruled out returning to Baltimore? "Yes, I suppose you are."

Chapter 22

August 10, 1922

Enos cruised south on the Westernport Road, enjoying the warm night air. The moon was full and bright. He could almost see the road without his headlights. Nights like this gave moonshine its name because bootleggers worked at night under the moonshine rather than the sunshine.

Enos had one last delivery for the evening in Lonaconing. Then he could head back home with a few more dollars to add to his growing savings in the cigar box he kept under his dresser. The amount had grown so much that he had gone to the bank last week to trade in the smaller denomination bills for larger ones. He even had two one-hundred-dollar bills in his collection. Sometimes, he took them out just to stare at them. Each one represented nearly three months of what he could earn as a coal miner. He had earned this in a month. He had barely managed to save them when David Lakehurst had set the boarding house on fire. Enos had had to make a decision, and he had lost a jug of his best moonshine in order to save his money.

He'd meant what he'd told Matt. He was willing to leave Eckhart if he needed to. In fact, living in Cumberland would probably be better for the taxi business he was planning to start. More people meant more rides were needed.

He didn't envy Matt's choice, though. Both sides in the coal strike had proved willing to be violent. Matt was trying to walk a line between the two that was getting thinner every day. At some point, he would fall off and anger one side or the other.

A car coming north on the road turned suddenly, blocking the road. Enos reacted instinctively and swerved to the right, hoping he could go around the car. The car slid off the road, bouncing hard. Enos tried to turn it back to the left, but with half the tires off the road, he was only partially successful. The car slipped to the side and smashed up against a tree.

The impact threw Enos to the right and his thigh smashed painfully against the steering wheel.

When he pushed himself back into a sitting position, he saw two men walking toward the car. For a moment, he thought they were coming to help him, but then he saw they carried shotguns.

One man opened the driver's side door and yanked him out. Enos fell to his knees and held his hands up.

"Who are you?" Enos said.

The man smashed the shotgun butt into Enos's chest and he fell over, clutching at his chest. The man kicked Enos in the side.

"Be quiet and you'll go home," the man said.

The other man opened the back door of the Duesenberg and rooted around. Enos guessed he was searching for the hidden latch to release the back seat. It surprised Enos when the man found it. Either he had gotten lucky or he was familiar with hidden latches in cars. The man lifted the back seat and tossed out the last three gallons of moonshine Enos had been on his way to deliver.

The man who had kicked him turned and fired twice, shattering the jugs while the other man took out a knife and stabbed the driver's side tires on the Duesenberg.

"Where's the money you collected tonight?" the first man asked.

"What money?"

The man raised the shotgun and pointed it at Enos's face. Enos raised his hands and cowered.

"If I have to, I will shoot you in the face. That way, I won't risk shredding any of the money, but your family won't be able to identify you then."

Enos wondered if the man would really kill him over one night's receipts. He decided not to take the chance since he had a feeling these were the same men who had shot at him along the National Road a couple of weeks ago.

Enos reached into his pocket and pulled out the roll of money from his deliveries. The man reached down and took it. The other man hit Enos in the head from behind. His vision blurred, and he fell over unconscious.

When he woke, he was alone next to his car. He wasn't sure of the time or how long he had been unconscious, but it was still night out.

He swayed unsteadily as he stood up. He felt the back of his head where it throbbed and his fingers came away bloody.

Enos looked at the car. He wasn't going anywhere in it with two flat tires. He only had one spare. What was Vincent going to say when he saw the wreck? This car cost more than Enos earned in a year of mining coal.

He walked to the road and headed north. Hopefully, he would find someone to give him a ride back to Eckhart, but it was still too early enough in the morning for traffic and he was about four miles south of Frostburg.

His head throbbed with every step he took.

What was going on with these attacks? Had the competition between moonshiners truly grown so desperate they were attacking each other? They were doing the revenuers' jobs, although with a lot less care about who got hurt.

Enos lucked out when a man driving his truck to Frostburg for an early morning pickup of goods at the railroad station stopped to pick him up. He hesitated when he saw Enos's head.

"Do you need me to take you to the hospital?" the man asked.

"It's worse than it looks," Enos told him. "Can you drop me off in Eckhart? That's where I live."

The man nodded and Enos climbed in the truck. After the man

dropped him off near the company store, Enos hiked up to the mountain to Vincent Gambrill's hidden still rather than heading home. He tried to think of a way he could break the news about the car to Vincent without the man firing him.

Vincent was tapping cork plugs into the jugs of the night's batch of moonshine when Enos walked into the clearing. Vincent gave him a quick glance. "What happened to you?"

Enos explained while Vincent inspected Enos's head. Enos winced as his boss prodded the wound. He wondered how it looked if it felt this bad.

"You should have gone to the hospital, Enos," Vincent said.

"I thought you would want to know what happened."

Vincent nodded. "I do, but I also don't want you falling over from blood loss or something worse. You're my best driver. The police have never caught you on the road."

"It is that bad?"

"It's bad enough. Get in my car. I'll take you to the hospital."

That worried him. Vincent drove his Renault, which he had purchased in Baltimore. He let Enos drive occasionally, although not on his delivery runs. Given what happened to Enos tonight, that was probably a good idea.

"This fighting over territory is getting out of hand," Vincent said as they drove through Frostburg. "We're going to start taking some precautions."

"Like what?" Enos asked.

"For one, two men will make all deliveries from now on, and both of them will be armed. If Jack Pickett's men start getting shot at, they won't be so daring in their attacks."

"Jack Pickett?"

"Yea, that's the guy running the operation in Pennsylvania, although he has put together a set up somewhere near here. I'll post some more men around the stills and start offering a reward for information that stops these attacks. I need to find out where their operations are and shut them down."

Enos wasn't sure whether those things would help or make matters worse. It was bad enough that coal miners and company men were at each other's throats with shootings, beatings, and destruction. Now the moonshiners would be shooting each other, but something needed to be done. Enos just hoped Western Maryland didn't start looking like the Old West.

They drove to the north end of Frostburg where the doctor on duty at Miner's Hospital stitched the gash on the back of Enos's head closed. Although the hospital served everyone, it was established to try to keep injured miners from becoming fatalities. The doctor said it wasn't bad, but he would have a bald spot there until the hair grew back.

"Just as long as my cap can cover it," Enos told him.

"This won't go unanswered, Enos," Vincent said when they were back in the car. "I am going to find where those sons of bitches have their stills and shut them down."

"What if they're in Garrett County or Pennsylvania?"

"I'll still find them. It may take a little longer. Maybe I'll take their territory away from them and see how they like it when someone else plays rough."

"People are going to get hurt or killed."

Vincent nodded. "The more money's on the table, the more risk people are willing to take, but I don't intend for it to be my people who get hurt."

Enos knew there was no way to guarantee that. Vincent's competitors were probably thinking the same thing.

It was nearly dawn when Vincent drove him back to the boarding house and dropped him off out front.

"We'll talk more about this tonight after I think about it some more," Vincent told him before he drove away.

When Enos walked inside, he saw Jenny sitting on the couch in the living room with a book in her lap.

"What are you doing up?" he asked.

"I got worried when you didn't come home," she said. "I've been hearing stories about how dangerous it is getting to be for moonshiners around here."

He shouldn't have told her the stories about the bootleggers in the area. He hadn't meant to scare her. He had just wanted to entertain her.

"That sounds about right."

Jenny saw the bandage on his head. "What happened?"

So Enos explained the story a third time. Jenny already knew he was a moonshiner, so he didn't have to pretend that he had been in a car accident.

"So you'll be alright?" she asked when he finished.

He nodded. "They wouldn't have let me leave the hospital if I wasn't." Of course, he didn't mention his head still throbbed and so did his legs where the steering wheel had hit him. His chest was bruised, and it hurt if he breathed too deeply. The doctors had given him some pills for the pain. He would have to take one before he went to bed, otherwise, he doubted he would get to sleep.

"Goodnight, Jenny. I'll see you later this morning."

He walked over to the stairs and started up. He moved slowly because every time he lifted his leg, he felt pain shoot across the top his thigh. Jenny moved up next to him, slid under his arm, and grabbed him around the waist.

"Let me help you," she said.

"I can make it."

"Yes, but by the time you do, it will be breakfast time, and you'll have to come down again."

Enos gave a short laugh and winced from pain across his chest. "Not so sure about that."

He also knew he probably wouldn't want to get out of bed when he woke up in the morning. He needed to make sure he kept the bottle of pills close.

With Jenny's help, he made it to his room in a reasonable amount of time. Jenny kissed him on the cheek.

"Goodnight, Enos. Feel better."

"That certainly helped," he said with a smile.

Chapter 23

August 12, 1922

Samantha sat on a bench near Old Main. Of all the benches on the grounds of the Frostburg Normal School, this one was her favorite in spring and fall. She enjoyed the warmth of the sun as it fought off the slightly cool temperatures in the air. On summer days, it could grow hot quickly as the sun and temperature worked together. Still, she smiled as she closed her eyes and tilted her face toward the sun.

"Are you asleep?"

Samantha opened her eyes and saw Professor Williamson standing next to her. He wore a straw boater to keep the sun off his head and held half a dozen books tucked under his arm.

"Hello, Professor. I came over to make sure everything was in order for my teaching semester, and I thought I would enjoy the day."

"It is a beautiful one."

"You haven't been here for a winter yet. The wind across the mountain will chill you through the heaviest coat."

"Not something to look forward to then, I take it?"

Samantha shook her head. "On the contrary. You will appreciate the warmth of a roaring fire in the fireplace and look forward to the first leaves of spring."

A quiet fell between them, and Professor Williamson shifted the books to his other arm.

"I've been meaning to ask you, Samantha, if you accepted the teaching position in Annapolis."

Samantha straightened up and smiled. "Yes, I'm looking forward to it, but I need to finish my teaching semester at the model school here first."

Because she had taken classes year round, her graduation fell in the middle of a typical school year.

"I don't see that as being a problem for you."

She shook her head. "It's not. It just delays when I can start there. I really appreciate you recommending me for the job, Professor."

He smiled. Samantha thought it made him look like a boy. It brought out his dimples.

"Call me Cliff. I am sure you will excel as a teacher."

"I hope so."

He shuffled back and forth. Finally, he seemed to straighten himself up and ask, "Would you like to get something to eat?"

"I had lunch before I came here."

"Well… we could go to dinner. I am quite fond of the restaurant in the Hotel Gunter."

Samantha paused. She had been about to say yes, but something felt off. The professor seemed too nervous about a casual meal.

"Prof..." She started again.… "Cliff. Are you asking me out? On a date?"

"Yes. You are no longer my student and won't even be in the college any longer, so I see no problem with it."

Samantha raised her eyebrows. "Except I have a boyfriend."

"That doesn't mean you can't see other men. It's not as if you are married."

She drew back a bit at that. "Matt and I have had some miscommunications on just where our relationship is, but one thing we both agree on is that we aren't seeing other people."

"Are things that serious between the two of you? It could

cause you problems with your job."

Samantha realized that. Too many schools expected their teachers to be unmarried. If they married, they were removed from the classroom. It was an archaic rule that she hoped to change when she moved into a power of authority in a school system.

"I realize that."

"And you are still pursuing a serious relationship with him?"

"I wouldn't say pursuing. It just happened. I wasn't looking for a relationship. Matt and I just stumbled into each other… quite literally." Matt had caught her when she had fallen off an apple crate while passing out pamphlets promoting women's equality. Then he had helped her when two drunk miners had harassed her.

"And what happens after next semester?" Professor Williamson asked.

Samantha shrugged. "I don't know. We may not be together then. That would make things easy."

Cliff stepped back. "I'm sorry. I just thought if started we seeing each other now, it would make things easier in Annapolis."

"Easier?" Things started clicking into place and she jumped to her feet. "Professor, I appreciate what you did for me with the job, but I'm going to be a teacher, not someone you can date when you're in town."

His face turned red. "I'm sorry if I misunderstood. I just thought we got along so well that it only made sense that we might see each other when I visited Annapolis."

She pondered what to say next. "We do get along well."

"I find you fascinating."

"I consider us friends. I've got one more relationship than I need right now. I sincerely hope he doesn't want to marry me. I want to be a teacher, and I can't do that right now if I am also a wife."

"What about Matt? Does he know that?"

Samantha frowned. "He knows it, but we avoid talking about it."

"You can't avoid it forever."

She nodded slowly. "No, no we can't."

Chapter 24

August 14, 1922

Joseph walked into the house and saw Laura slumped on the sofa while Jacob played on the floor with a set of wooden blocks. He shook his head. *Drunk again.* He walked back to the bedroom.

He started undressing because he had to get ready for his date with Priscilla Bankert. He needed this to go well. She was his way out of Eckhart, Western Maryland, and coal mining. With her support, Joseph could get out from under his father's thumb and be the successful businessman he was destined to be.

He tossed his clothes onto the end of the bed and started looking through his closet for a crisp white shirt.

Laura walked in and sat down in the chair in the corner of the room.

"You didn't say 'hello' when you came in," she said.

"I thought you were asleep."

"Are you redressing?" she asked as he removed a suit from the closet and looked it over.

"Yes, I need to get ready for dinner."

Laura stood up suddenly. "Really? Are we going somewhere nice to eat?"

Joseph turned to stare at her. "*We* are not going anywhere. I have a dinner engagement with Priscilla Bankert."

"Matt's Priscilla?"

Joseph rolled his eyes. "No, not Matt's Priscilla. Priscilla Bankert of the Baltimore Bankerts."

"But I met her this afternoon with Matt. She was quite nice. Can I come with you? It's been weeks since you've taken me out."

Joseph held up a finger. "No. This is business."

Laura cowered a bit. "I don't think she would mind."

"She is from one of the wealthiest families in the state, and you are a single mother and a widow. What on earth do you think you would have in common?"

Laura frowned and looked at her feet.

"Stay here and play with Jacob," Joseph said. "Get drunk if you want. You seem to like that lately, although don't get too drunk. I'll expect you ready and eager in bed when I get home."

She nodded and walked out of the room.

Joseph finished dressing and added a bit of cologne for good measure. He left without saying goodbye to Laura and drove his Renault up to the Hotel Gunter.

He checked himself in the lobby mirror before he headed upstairs to the second floor. When Priscilla answered the door, she looked lovely, but not as dressed up as Joseph. She wore a light-blue silk dress that seemed to hang loosely and yet stretch over her figure at the same time. He smiled at her appearance and escorted her downstairs, where he had reserved a table in the hotel restaurant. The restaurant was considered one of the nicer eateries in Frostburg, although Cumberland had larger and fancier places.

The President had eaten at the Fort Cumberland Hotel Restaurant. Joseph could have taken Priscilla to Cumberland, but he wanted people to see him with her. Let them imagine what was happening and then start gossiping about it. It would only help his prospects.

A candle sitting in a centerpiece lit the table. The waiter held Priscilla's chair as she sat. As she settled into her chair, Joseph said, "Please bring us your best Pinot Noir."

"But, sir, the law," the waiter said, as if Joseph didn't know the hotel's wine cellar was still stocked. He held up a twenty-dollar bill. The waiter smiled and took the money. "Yes, sir."

"I'll just have a cup of tea," Priscilla said.

"I thought you would enjoy a nice glass of wine with dinner," Joseph said.

Priscilla shook her head. "I don't drink alcohol anymore."

"Did you give it up along with most of the country?"

She shook her head. "No, it was something more recent. I didn't like what it did to me. It cost me Matt."

Joseph frowned. He had been hoping alcohol would smooth his wooing of Priscilla. That's what had helped finally win him Laura, although she had taken the drinking too far lately.

The waiter left with their drink orders, and Laura picked up the menu. "What do you recommend?"

"I usually get a sirloin."

She held up a hand. "That's too heavy for me. I think I am in the mood for ravioli tonight."

The waiter came back with their drinks and Joseph ordered dinners for the two of them. When he left, Priscilla said, "So you said you could tell me things about Matt that would help me win him back."

This was moving too fast. Joseph needed to slow things down so Priscilla could get to know him.

"I didn't think we would be discussing him over dinner."

"What did you think we would do?" She stared directly at Joseph with her pale blue eyes. They seemed to look right through him and expose the truth of his plans.

"I thought… I thought we could talk about us."

"Us?"

"Yes, get to know each other and discover how we might help each other."

"I don't need to get to know you, Mr. McCord, for you to help me. You already told me you knew things that I am interested in. Was that a lie?"

This was not going at all how he had planned. Joseph had to regain control.

He shook his head. "No, of course not. I am just trying to understand why you are so interested, Matteo. He is a poor coal miner, and you are a woman of wealth and breeding."

Priscilla grinned. "If you only see Matt as a poor coal miner, you don't know him at all. He is one of the best people I know."

"I find that hard to believe. People think he is a war hero, but he only ran off to join the Marines because he cheated on his girlfriend."

"That would be Laura Henshaw, although now she's Laura Spiker."

That caught Joseph off guard. He hadn't expected Priscilla to know about Laura. "Yes."

"Matt told me about her when we were dating, although you left out the part about her kissing several boys at the dance where she thought he was cheating on her. They were children. Besides, Matt said he joined the Marines because he didn't want to be drafted into the Army. He wanted to choose how he served."

"Perhaps," Joseph admitted. He certainly would not argue with a woman who could get him out of Eckhart.

"Is he seeing someone here?"

Joseph's eyebrows arched. "I believe he is seeing Samantha Havencroft. She is the daughter of the president of the state normal school. Come to think of it, she looks a bit like you. Perhaps Matteo has a preference for well-to-do blondes, although I must say, Samantha is not nearly as attractive as you."

Priscilla ignored the compliment and asked, "Are things serious between them?"

"That is hard to say. From what I have heard, her father is not happy with the pairing. Also, she is a student at the school. Once she graduates, she will probably move to teach at some little country school."

"When does she graduate?"

"I don't know. Soon, I suppose."

"Then it is not too late for me."

Joseph cocked his head to the side. "There is another woman he has been seen frequently with and who now lives the family.

Her name is Jenny Washington. Some say she is a prostitute, but she seems to have formed an attachment to Matteo and he to her."

"A prostitute? That doesn't sound like Matt."

Joseph shrugged. "I can't say for certain. I don't need to pay for such services. It is only something I heard mentioned among some of the men in Frostburg."

Priscilla frowned.

Let her stew on that tidbit about her precious Matteo.

The waiter returned with their meals and conversation trailed off while they ate. Joseph wasn't sure whether it was because he had planted some doubt in Priscilla against Matteo or she was just concentrating on eating.

When they finished the meal, Priscilla declined dessert and said she wanted to return to her room. Joseph paid the bill and escorted her back to her room on the second floor.

"Thank you for dinner, Mr. McCord."

Not thinking, Joseph leaned in and kissed her goodnight. Priscilla pulled back and slapped him across the face. He stepped back and put his hand on his cheek. He only just managed to keep his anger in check.

"I just thought…"

"I said dinner, nothing else."

She turned and went into her room, slamming the door shut. Joseph shook his head slowly, seeing his vision of a new life in Baltimore fade.

When Joseph walked down to the lobby of the hotel, he saw his father sitting in a chair next to the dead fireplace. He was tempted to act like he hadn't seen the man and walk out, but Joseph would only pay for the affront later.

He walked over and sat down in the chair on the other side of the fireplace.

"What are you doing here?" Joseph asked.

"Waiting for you," Winston McCord said.

"How did you know I was here?"

"I went by your house and your whore told me."

Joseph winced to hear his father call Laura that, but then she was living with him without being married. His father would think that.

"So now you've set your sights on Priscilla Bankert. My guess is she sent you packing. She probably considers you much the same that I consider Laura Spiker."

Joseph was surprised his father even knew Laura's name.

"It might surprise you she doesn't. She was even engaged to a coal miner once." Joseph was stretching the truth. Matteo hadn't been a coal miner when he and Priscilla had been engaged.

"Engaged, not married. She came to her senses."

"You think you know everything, Father, but you really don't."

Winston chuckled. "I never claimed or thought I knew everything. If it seems that way to you, it must be because you are so lacking."

Joseph pushed himself to his feet. "I don't have to sit here for this," he said sharply.

"Not for this, maybe, but it's not why I came to see you. So sit down. We need to talk about the mine."

"What about it? It's operating. I've got the strikebreakers working."

"It's barely operating. The strike is over. Why aren't your miners back to work?"

"The union here is keeping them out. The UMW wants to be recognized. They took advantage of the national strike and the financial pressure it put on the company to get more members. While we were hiring strikebreakers, the UMW was feeding the striking miners and giving them money. We offered the stick while the UMW held out the carrots. I haven't given in, nor have most of the other mine operations, so they don't feel like they can walk away now. It would hurt their credibility among the miners here, since they are going to be the ones hurt if the union loses this fight."

"They won't be the only ones to lose. With the national strike over, mining is getting back to its normal levels everywhere but Maryland. If Consolidation Coal can't fill its contracts because of the Maryland mines, it will sell them off or shut them down entirely to cut operating losses here."

"I can't make the miners come back to work. That's not my job."

"You're wrong there, Joseph, because if the miners don't come back or those mines don't increase their production, it will be your job." Winston stood up. "Stop trying to marry above your station, Joseph, and worry about the work at hand."

Then he walked out, leaving Joseph sitting next to the fireplace.

Chapter 25

August 14, 1922

Matt walked up the stairs from the lobby of the Hotel Gunter and down the hall until he found Priscilla's room number. He stopped in front of the door and took a deep breath. Then he knocked on the door.

"Who is it?" Priscilla said from inside.

"It's Matt."

The door opened. Priscilla stood in front of him wearing a light-blue day dress that brought out the color in her eyes. He wondered why she looked so much shorter until he noticed she wasn't wearing high-heeled shoes. It was the most casual Matt had seen her dressed since she had arrived in Frostburg.

"I didn't expect you," she said.

"I'm sorry I didn't send word, but I thought we needed to talk. I think you might have taken more from our last conversation than I meant."

Actually, he had told Laura about his talk with Priscilla, and she had warned him that Priscilla might have thought he was leaving open the possibility of Priscilla and Matt getting back together.

Her eyebrows raised slightly. "Oh."

She stepped back. "Would you like to come in?"

"Are you sure? We can talk downstairs." He would have preferred that. It was less likely they would get into a shouting match if they were in a public place.

"Matt, I know I can trust you, and there aren't any society gossips to worry about seeing us together in my room."

Matt hesitated a moment and then walked inside. Priscilla shut the door.

"I had a pot of tea brought up a little while ago. It's still warm. I can pour you a cup," she offered.

"No, thank you."

She waved to a chair next to the small table. "Sit. I've been in Frostburg a while now, and I have to say, it has it charms. It reminds me of Baltimore."

Matt's eyes widened. "You're joking."

Priscilla shook her head. "I said it reminds me of Baltimore. Frostburg is like Baltimore in miniature. They both have workers and shopkeepers. They both have an industry that life revolves around. In Baltimore, it's the harbor. Here, it's coal mining. They both have the railroad and colleges. Why, if you consider the size of the college here compared to the size of the town, it would be larger than anything in Baltimore."

Matt noticed she was speaking quickly, which was unlike her. She probably wanted to keep him from saying what he had come here to say.

"Priscilla."

She kept right on going. "I do find the name of this town interesting. I thought it was named Frostburg because of the cold winters, but it is actually named after a family called Frost."

"Priscilla," Matt said louder and bit more sharply than he had intended. She stopped speaking. "About everything you told me before, I agree. You have changed."

The corners of her mouth turned up with the beginnings of a smile. "I'm glad you noticed, but I did tell you."

Matt nodded. "Yes, you did. It's not that I didn't believe you, but I guess I had to see it for myself and have it sink in. I can see it now, and I think it is definitely a change for the better." Her beginnings of the smile became a full smile. "I've changed, too, though, and you won't acknowledge that."

"I don't see that you have."

"Because you are treating what I'm telling you like I treated what you told me. You're not looking to see the change. When I came back to Eckhart, it was for my Pinkerton work. When I left five years ago, I didn't think I'd ever come back, but when I knocked on the door to the boarding house and saw my aunt, I knew it was right. And for reasons other than my work. Oh, there are still issues that need to be dealt with, but on the whole, I'm happy here."

"You can be happy in other places," Priscilla said. "People move around all the time, trying to find the place where they'll be happiest."

"Yes, but that's not going to be Baltimore. It might not even be here. I just know that war changed how I look at this place and the people here. I'm happier here than I was in Baltimore."

"Is that because of me?"

Matt shook his head. He reached out and patted her hand. "I'll admit you were the reason I was happy to leave Baltimore, but you're not the reason for me knowing the city is not the place for me. Actually, when I look back on my happy memories of the city, you are in many of them."

"That's nice."

"It's the truth. I can look back on my time in Baltimore now and smile." It was as much a surprise to Matt as to Priscilla. It had crept up on him until one morning a couple weeks ago. He realized he was smiling as he remembered walking through Lexington Market in the city.

"I am sorry I put you through the bad things, though," Priscilla said. "It wasn't fair. You didn't deserve it."

"I believe you. That doesn't mean I want to get back together. It's like the memories. I'm happy for the time we had together. I learned a lot about myself and being in a relationship. I got to see qualities in you that I liked and didn't like. It helped me figure out what I'm looking for in a wife."

"And it's not me, even though we were going to be married?"

Matt nodded slowly. "No, it not you… at least not all of you. You have some wonderful qualities, but in the end, I don't think we would have worked out. You may not have thought leaving me before the wedding was a wise decision, and looking back, it probably was. I think you may have seen then what I am only seeing now."

Priscilla chuckled. "I wish I could take credit for being that wise, but it's like I told you. I was weak. I couldn't take the pressure my family was putting on me."

"You will find someone who will make you very happy, Priscilla, because you're moving through the same process as I am."

"I think I will, too."

"I know so, and he will be the right guy for you. Better than me. Back then, I think I was picturing you with some rich society guy who would marry you for your family connections or money."

She cocked her head to the side and said, "I almost did that after you."

"He wouldn't have loved you, and he probably would have cheated on you. I don't think you would pick someone like that now. He may still be a rich, society guy, but he will love you completely because you are learning who you want."

Priscilla stared at Matt for a few moments and then started nodding. "Okay, I see it now."

"What?"

"I see what you were talking about earlier. You are different. You are more comfortable with who you are. You used to be a little jealous when men paid attention to me, and you were self-conscious about not being from the same social class as me. I don't see that in you now."

"Maybe I have moved forward. I hope I have. I'm not the person I can be yet, but I hope I'm getting closer."

Priscilla leaned across the table. She touched his scar with her fingertips, and then ran them over her cheek. Matt's skin still tingled at her touch. He couldn't help it. Priscilla grinned as if she could read his mind and sat back.

"So, this girl, Samantha, is she the one for you?"

Matt sighed. "At one point, I thought she might be. She has a lot of wonderful qualities like you do. You share some of those qualities, but there are other ones that don't match well. I think one of them will be what pulls us apart."

"I'm sorry, Matt." He believed her.

"One of the things I've learned is to appreciate the good things life brings you when you can because you never know what will happen in the next moment. The war taught me that. I'm think she'll be leaving soon. I'll be sad, but like our relationship, I won't regret it. She's looking for her own qualities in a man, and while I have some of them, I don't have enough of them or the right ones."

He and Priscilla talked for another half hour, and when Matt finally left, he felt things had finally been settled between the two of them. She gave him a hug and a kiss on the cheek. He promised to talk her to the train station when she decided to return to Baltimore. They had come together for a time, and it had been wonderful, but now they had both moved on. Her life was in Baltimore society, and his life, for now, was in Eckhart Mines.

Enos stopped the Duesenberg in front of the cabin near Mount Savage. The flat tires had been repaired. Although it was still dented on the side that had slammed against the tree, it still ran.

He had been told to arrive here by 8 p.m., and apparently he wasn't the only one who had received the message. He saw four other cars around the cabin, including a Renault.

A man with a rifle opened the cabin door and stared at him. Enos turned off the engine.

"Vincent Gambrill told me to be here," Enos said.

The man nodded. "He's inside."

Enos got out of his car. He walked over to the Renault and looked it over. It had to be Vincent's. Few people in the county had one.

"C'mon, I'm not going to stand here all night," the man at the door said.

Enos walked over and the man stepped aside. Enos walked into the one-room cabin and saw six men, including three who held rifles.

"Hi, fellows," he said, waving.

"Good, you're the last person we were waiting for," Vincent said.

He sat at a round table with a map of Garrett County spread across it. His shirt sleeves were rolled up to his elbows, and he was smoking.

"You all know we've been having trouble with Jack Pickett and his men. All of you here have had run-ins with his crew. He is trying to move in on our business along Frostburg and the Creek. Now, I don't mind competition… too much. As long as everyone plays nice, I feel like there's plenty of business to go around for now. Jack Pickett is no longer playing nice."

Vincent tapped on the map. "It turns out that Pickett's operation isn't even in Allegany County, which we suspected. He has his still hidden near Avilton. He can operate from Garrett and sell in Allegany, which makes it harder for the law to catch him since his men are always moving around making deliveries over here."

"How did you find that out?" someone asked. He was a lanky man. Enos thought his head might hit the top of the cabin.

"For the last week, I've had men following my men making deliveries. They went after Jason Pitzer two nights ago and almost ran him off the road. The car following Jason switched to following Pickett's men and followed the car back to their still. Now that we know where they are, we're going to do something about it."

"What can we do? They are in Garrett," Enos said.

"It would have been easier if they were in our county. I could have sent the law after them. I could try that in Garrett, but I have no idea who is on Pickett's payroll. If I tell the wrong person, he would tip Pickett off, so we are going to shut down his operation ourselves."

"Won't he just start a new still somewhere else? For that matter, what if he has a second or third operation? You do."

Vincent nodded. "That's good thinking, Enos, and both those

things are possible unless we do one thing."

"What's that?" Gerard Mueller, one of the moonshiners around the table, asked.

"We have to eliminate Pickett. Without him, the operation will be thrown into turmoil. His lieutenants will try to take over, and if we're lucky, it will split the operation. Even if they survive and continue, what's left will be smaller and easier to deal with. Also, what happens to Pickett will serve as a lesson to the others to stay in their own county."

Enos straightened up. He didn't like how this sounded. They were declaring war on the other moonshiners for doing something Vincent was doing, which was to expand outside their county.

"This won't end well," Enos said.

"Why's that?" Vincent asked.

"You're starting a war."

Vincent straightened up. "A war that I will win."

"Yes, but as long as this county is an attractive market for moonshine, moonshiners will come. Some may even grow large enough inside the county to challenge you."

"So? We will give them more of the same."

"Right now, Pickett's men aren't expecting us. I'm sure we will win this fight, but everyone who comes after will be ready for a fight."

Vincent chuckled. "You worry too much, Enos. This will be a quick fight to destroy the stills, steal what they have made, and take out Pickett."

Enos didn't like the term "take out." Vincent was being vague. Did he mean to kill Jack Pickett or just turn him over to the police? He remembered Samuel telling him about the violence across the country associated with bootleggers. Enos needed to get Vincent to stop.

"Jeremiah, Duke, bring over the box," Vincent said, waving toward the corner of the cabin.

Two men walked over to a footlocker left over from the war. Each man grabbed a leather strap on the end, carried to box to the table, and sat it on the ground beside Vincent. He flipped open the top and revealed rifles and pistols.

Vincent smiled. "Take one of each, men, and plenty of ammo. We're going hunting."

Enos knew he should leave now. This was going too far. However, he wasn't sure he wanted to cross a room of armed men.

He reached into the box and pulled out a Browning 1922. He shoved the pistol into his waistband. Vincent handed him a box of ammunition for the weapon.

"OK, we are going to drive to the stills. Once we hit Avilton, we'll drive without lights. Follow me. Stay close once you turn off your lights."

The men loaded their weapons and headed out to their vehicles. There were seven men among the five vehicles.

Enos noticed his hands shaking as he started his car. He wished he could take a drink, but he never drove and drank. If they were going to be driving without lights for any distance, he would need to have his wits about him, not to mention if there was going to be shooting.

Vincent led the small convoy from the cabin south of Frostburg. They drove to Lonaconing and then headed west on Douglas Hill Road as it went over the mountains and into Garrett County. The road swung to the north. When it crossed the Little Savage River, the cars switched off their headlights. Anyone listening could still hear the car engines, but they wouldn't be able to see the cars.

Enos just wished he could have talked to someone about this. It made little sense. Things were going to get just as bad for moonshiners around here as they were for miners. The violence wasn't working for the miners, and it wouldn't work for bootleggers. It was making life in the county miserable for Enos because he didn't know his enemies were.

Vincent's car rolled to a stop. The other cars pulled off to the side of the road and parked. He got out and walked back to the other cars.

"Most of us have to go on foot from here. Duke and Charles will drive down the road to the turnoff to the still. We'll come in from behind and scatter anyone there. When the shooting starts, Duke and Charles will come up the road after the guards. They'll be driving the truck so we can load it with whatever we can carry off," Vincent explained.

Enos and the others climbed out of their cars and checked their weapons. Enos kept taking deep breaths to calm himself. He didn't want to be here. He didn't sign on with Vincent to be a mercenary. He wanted to drink moonshine at night and drive fast cars during the day. This wasn't supposed to be a dangerous job other than the chance of getting arrested.

The men moved quietly through the trees. Luckily this area was steep, like the hill above Eckhart. They moved slowly so they wouldn't twist an ankle or make too much noise. It seemed like it took them forever, but the still probably had to be far enough from the road so it wasn't obvious to anyone who drove by.

Enos saw a bright area ahead of him, probably illuminated by a fire. Vincent stopped and looked back at his men.

"We'll go in shooting. The men around the still probably won't be armed, but watch out in case the shooting brings in any guards they have watching the paths to the still." He took a deep breath. "Let's go and be careful."

The men charged into the clearing, yelling and shooting. Enos made sure to fire over the heads of the men in the clearing, but at least one worker was hit. Enos saw him grab his arm as he ran into the woods.

The still workers scattered into the woods. Vincent kept looking around. He went up to one man who was lying on the ground, too afraid to run, and shouted, "Where's Pickett?"

"I… I don't know. Home, I guess. He's never out here this late," the frightened man said.

Vincent kicked him in the side and he screamed.

The truck barreled into the clearing and stopped. Duke and Charles jumped out.

"Everyone load up as much as you can! What we can't take with us destroy," Vincent ordered.

Enos and the others grabbed at any equipment they could use

to build a new still. However, the mash vats were too heavy to move. Duke took an axe from the truck bed and chopped at them until they were kindling. The porridge-like liquid poured onto the ground. The liquid soaked in, leaving only the grain used in making the moonshine on the ground.

Once the equipment was loaded, any finished moonshine that had been bottled was added. Anything else was dumped or broken.

Duke and Charles climbed back into the truck while Enos and the others jumped onto the running boards and held on as the truck sped down the dirt path to the road. Once it neared the other cars, the men jumped off.

"Good work tonight," Vincent said. "I'll make sure you all get a bonus."

"You didn't get Pickett," Harry Grove, another of the moonshiners, said.

Vincent shrugged. "No, but I sent him a message he'll remember."

Enos climbed in his car and drove toward the intersection with the Frostburg Road. He didn't feel like celebrating. This felt wrong. It felt worse than a raid by revenuers. Someone could have been killed tonight.

This was not the job he had signed up for.

Chapter 26

August 15, 1922

Jenny walked downstairs from her room and saw Enos sitting on the couch, looking out the front window. He was usually either asleep or working on his car at this hour of the morning.

"Hello, Enos," she said. He didn't look over. "Enos," she repeated.

He turned his head and blinked. "Oh, hello, Jenny."

"You look like you're in another world, and it's not a happy one."

He sighed. "Maybe, I am. Just when I thought I had things figured out, everything changed on me."

"Like what?"

"Do you really want to hear? You might not like it," he said.

She walked over and sat next to him on the couch. "Just tell me what has you so sad all of a sudden."

He rubbed his whisker-stubbled chin. "You know things have been rough with my job lately." Jenny nodded. "Well, it's just gotten worse."

"Are the police after you?"

Enos shook his head. "Not only the police. Now other moonshiners are going after each other."

"And that's worse than being shot at?" Jenny asked.

Enos nodded. "Much. My boss attacked the rival moonshiners last night. He took me with him. There was a gunfight. We were lucky no one was killed."

"Oh, Enos."

His head drooped. "I hated the whole thing. I know I should hate those men for what they did to me, but what we did seemed just as wrong. As much as I like to drink, it's not worth shooting someone over."

"Then you should stop delivering moonshine again. You shouldn't have to get into shootouts when you are only a driver."

"I didn't want to do it, but Vincent Gambrill told me to, and I was one of the men we were avenging."

"Do you think it will happen again?"

He looked into Jenny's eyes. "I would bet on it. Jack Pickett wasn't at the still, but it was his operation. So he is fine, except now he's mad. He can't let that attack stand, or it will hurt his reputation. Others will try to take over his territory. That's why Vincent attacked. Pickett was already trying to take over this area. Vincent couldn't let it stand."

Jenny sighed. "So, you think Pickett will do something against Vincent, and it will go back and forth."

Enos nodded. "And probably get worse because each side will want to end things finally and decisively. Someone will get killed."

"And you can't say no?"

Enos shrugged. "I can, but Vincent will then let me go. He will need fighting men soon more than just drivers. I can't be one without being the other."

It touched Jenny that Enos was trusting her enough to ask her opinion. She needed to give him sound advice to show he hadn't misplaced his trust.

"Then quit. You don't have to do it right now. You can keep driving and see how things go, but if it comes to the point you have to choose to attack Pickett or quit driving, quit driving."

"But I enjoy driving."

Jenny laid a hand on his back. "You do, but you don't like this fighting more. You said yourself, it's going to get worse." Enos nodded. "So you need to make a choice. You need to make the change you want. The time hasn't come to make a choice yet, so keep driving and save your money. Then, if and when you have to make a choice, you can quit. You will either have money to live on or you can buy yourself a car."

Enos smiled. "You're right. It's hard because I have liked this job up until now. Why do things have to change?"

Jenny patted his arm. She heard an axe hitting wood.

"Is your brother back to chopping wood?" she asked.

"No, this time it's Matt."

Jenny stood up and started toward the back door.

"Jenny." She stopped and turned back to Enos. "Thank you."

"Any time, Enos."

"Want another driving lesson later?"

She laughed. "Yes. Definitely."

"We'll head down Georges Creek this time. Maybe you can race the streetcar."

She smiled and walked into the kitchen. She opened the back door and stepped out onto the small porch. Matt wore his under-shirt and jeans. The white shirt was soaked with sweat as he swung the axe over and over.

He finally noticed her and stopped his work.

"Did you need something?" he asked as he wiped his forehead with the back of his arm.

"Can you teach me to fight?" she asked.

She had been thinking about this for some time, and had finally just decided to take the chance.

"Excuse me?"

Jenny held up her fists and tried to imitate a boxer. "Fight. I want to learn how to fight."

"Isn't that sort of the opposite of what you are usually trying to do?"

She frowned. "That's why I need to learn. What if I meet another David Lakehurst?"

Matt swung the axe and sunk it into a log he had split. He

walked over and stood next to Jenny.

"I understand why you want to learn or think you do, but even if you had known how to fight, it wouldn't have helped with Lakehurst. He was twice your size and he enjoyed hurting people." Matt leaned in closer. "The more you fought back, the more excited he would have become."

"Then what would you have me do? He beat me when I put up no resistance, and you say he would have beat me if I had fought back."

Matt sighed. He understood her dilemma. When he had a cast on his leg, he had been no match for Lakehurst. It hadn't mattered to Lakehurst that it had been an unfair fight. That was the way he liked his fights.

"Had Lakehurst been an ordinary person, you might have been able to fight him off. It probably wouldn't have even happened in the first place."

"So what do I do? Hope for the best?"

"When I was in the Marines, they taught me not to charge headfirst into enemy fire if I could flank the enemy and take them out with much less danger to myself."

"But there are times you do have to charge into enemy fire; times when there's no other choice, like with Lakehurst... for you and for me."

Matt held up his hands in surrender. "Fine. I will teach you what I can, but I will teach you how to best defend yourself, not to go on the offensive against everyone who wrongs you."

Jenny hugged him and kissed him on the cheek. "Thank you, Matt."

"So, you've got me teaching you to fight and Enos teaching you to drive. What are you going to have Samuel do?"

Jenny tapped her chin and looked toward the sky as if thinking. "He could teach me to shoot. He shoots rats all the time. That could come in handy," she joked.

"How often do you see a rat?"

She arched an eyebrow. "Oh, there's more than one type of rat."

She stood up.

"I want to tell you something, Matt, but I'm not sure how you'll take it. I'm afraid you'll get angry at me."

"Is it something you did?"

Jenny shook her head.

"Then why would you think I would get angry with you?"

"I've found that when men get angry, they take it out on whoever is close. It doesn't matter if I had anything to do with it." She was remembering how Lakewood beat her up and left her in the alley in Frostburg.

He held up a hand. "I promise not to take it out on you. If I do need to get rid of my anger, I'll just chop some more firewood."

"I saw Joseph McCord and Priscilla eating dinner in the restaurant in the Hotel Gunter when I was working the other night."

Matt took a deep breath and didn't blink.

"Maybe they had business."

"What business?"

He hefted the axe. "I don't know."

Jenny shook her head. "I know men, Matt. He wanted more from her than conversation and dinner." She paused, then added. "I'm sorry."

Matt shrugged. "He's welcome to try. I just don't want Laura hurt."

"What about Priscilla? You used to be engaged to her."

"Joey is closer to her social class. If she falls for him, then it only reinforces that I wasn't right for her."

"You said you didn't want Laura hurt."

Matt closed eyes and rubbed them. "What else have you seen?"

"I've seen Laura drunk in the speakeasies around Frostburg."

Matt shook his head. "No, she wouldn't go there."

"She did, and although she didn't dress like I do when I go, I heard some men talking. They thought she was a prostitute."

Matt waved a finger at her. "No! Remember who you're talking about."

Jenny stepped back. "I'm sorry. Now I didn't see her go off

with anyone, but if the men are thinking about her that way, they are going to start asking."

"She can say no."

"Yes, but if she's drunk, she might not be thinking straight enough to do that. That's how I got started in the business. If she's at that point in her life, I can tell you it's not a happy place."

"What's she got to worry about? Her bills are paid. She lives in a fine house now and doesn't have to worry about where her next meal is coming from."

Jenny cocked her head to the side. "She has to live with Joseph."

"She chose him, though, and she has seemed happy enough when I see them together," Matt said.

Jenny shrugged. "I can only tell you what I've seen. I'm sorry."

Matt nodded. He gritted his teeth and his face reddened. Then he turned and walked over to the wood pile and picked up the axe. He set a chunk of wood on top of a larger section of wood. Then he swung the axe. The chunk of wood split in half and the two pieces flew off in opposite directions.

Jenny lowered her head and started walking toward the back door of the boarding house.

"Jenny," Matt said.

"Yes."

"Thank you for telling me all that. I know you were scared. I'm mad, but not at you. You're a good friend."

She sighed and walked into the house.

Later that day, word began circulating that an agreement had been reached to end the coal strike after more than four months. President Harding had agreed to form a federal commission to look into the miners' grievances if the miners returned to work.

It didn't change anything from what it had been before the strike. It also didn't help the Western Maryland coal miners. Once again, the union had left them holding the bag because the mining companies didn't have to recognize the unions.

That same night, the United Mine Workers locals met throughout Allegany County. Paul Tomlinson and the local presidents discussed the options with the miners. The miners wanted to return to work, unionized or not. They had bills to pay and families to feed. Tomlinson made even bigger promises of support if the miners stayed out, saying that with the national strike ended, the UMW could concentrate its resources to supporting Western Maryland with more food and strike pay. Few miners believed him because they knew the union had spent most of its money supporting the national strike.

The miners also knew that if they gave in once again under pressure from the coal companies, they would always remain there. The coal companies were hurting just as much as the miners. The UMW was willing to help the miners continue the fight. It was unlikely other coal companies would support their business rivals if they didn't have to.

The miners voted to stay on strike until the coal companies recognized the unions. The UMW kept their food commissary open and sent financial aid to help support the miners.

However, the coal companies didn't sit back and take it. More strikebreakers arrived from Pittsburgh, Cleveland, and West Virginia. Miners who had managed to keep their company homes through the strike lost them. Matt saw some of the uniformed Pinkertons armed with submachine guns protecting groups of strikebreakers. More of the miners started walking around armed as well.

Neither side planned on giving in. Western Maryland was last battlefront to fight back the UMW.

Chapter 27

August 16, 1922

Matt met Jenny in the backyard of the boarding house. He had been thinking about what he could teach her that would best allow her to defend herself. She had neither the size nor the need to fight like a Marine.

She was a small woman who would be going up against larger men. However, she had a few advantages. Those men would often be drunk, they would be focused on having sex with her, and she would probably be wearing high heels.

Jenny walked out of the house onto the back porch, and Matt had to put his hand over his mouth to keep from laughing.

"What?" she said, as she spread her hands wide and looked at herself.

She was wearing a loose, white blouse and a black skirt that ended above her knees. She also had on white stockings and canvas shoes.

"I think you solved your problem," Matt said.

"How?"

"If someone sees you dressed like that, they won't attack you. They'll laugh."

Jenny stuck her tongue out at him. "For your information, I

called Samantha and asked her what the girls at the college wore for their physical education classes."

"And she told you to wear that?"

"Yes, I did."

Matt turned and saw Samantha walk around the side of the house wearing an identical outfit. A couple of curious onlookers trailed behind her. They were miners from town who had nothing better to do with the strike still one. Samantha walked over and kissed Matt on the cheek. Then she slapped him lightly for laughing.

"What are you doing here and dressed like that?" he asked.

"Well, Jenny said you were going to teach her how to defend herself, and I thought that would be something useful to know, especially if I am going to be living on my own in Annapolis."

"And you actually wear that outfit to exercise at the college?"

Samantha nodded. "You don't expect me exercise in a dress and heels do you?"

"Heels might not be practical to exercise in, but they would be useful for what I am showing you."

"How could we exercise in heels?"

Matt had Samantha sit next to Jenny on the porch and tried to ignore the spectators standing at the corner of the house. He explained to them that he was going to show them some things they could do to protect themselves if they were ever attacked. He would not teach them to fight like men because they weren't men.

"Is that why you wanted us to wear heels?" Samantha asked.

Matt took her hand and pulled her to him. Then he turned her so she was facing away from him.

"So let's say a man attacks you on the street from behind." Matt grabbed her in a bear hug. "What do you do?"

Samantha thrashed around, but Matt held her tight with her arms pinned against her sides. Matt nuzzled her neck.

"You're having fun doing this," Samantha said.

"You wanted to learn. Now stomp on my toes. Gently, please, I don't want more broken bones," Matt said.

She did, perhaps, a little too hard. He grunted and let her go.

"Now, it won't always be that easy, but if you are wearing

heels at the time, the force of your stomp will get focused down to the end of the heel and have some power. Now if your attacker is wearing boots, this won't be too effective. It also works best if he grabs you from behind."

"You made it easy for her. That won't help at all," heckled one spectator who had followed Samantha to the back. Matt didn't recognize the man. He was probably a strikebreaker. He was overweight with a long brown beard that probably took him an hour to wash the coal dust from each evening.

"You think so?" Matt asked.

"I know so," the man said. "No stomp on the toes would make me let go of a pretty little thing like that."

Matt sighed. He waved Jenny over and whispered, "I want to let this guy try to grab you. He's going to expect you to stomp his foot, so he'll try to keep them away or maybe lift you off the ground. So before you stomp his foot, either elbow him in the gut or make a fist and swing it backwards to hit him in the groin. Either of those should distract him enough to stomp on his foot and let go. Are you okay with that?" Jenny nodded.

Matt said to the group. "Jenny has agreed to help with a real demonstration. Since this man thinks I made it too easy on her, would you like to play the part of the attacker and see if you can hold onto this 'pretty little thing'?"

The man grinned and stepped forward. "I certainly would."

"Now, I just want you to grab her from behind, and we'll see if she can get free," Matt said.

He positioned himself close in case Jenny got into trouble. The man came up behind her and wrapped his arms around her. He grabbed her high, so his hands could cup her breasts, but it left her lower arms free. Then, like Matt had guessed, the man lifted Jenny off the ground so she couldn't stomp on his foot.

Jenny quickly balled her right fist and swung it backward into the man's groin which was an easy target since he had lifted her up. The man yelled as he dropped her and doubled over. She landed and promptly stomped her heel on his foot, although he had already let her go.

Samantha applauded her, bouncing up and down on her toes.

The man straightened up. "That wasn't fair, you bitch."

Matt stepped in front of the man. "No one asked you back here, and no one made you take part. I saw how you grabbed her. You're just the sort of guy she wants to protect herself from."

"I didn't hurt her. She punched my balls."

"And that's with one lesson. Imagine what she'll be able to do when she learns more. You had better be careful about what women you try and go too far with."

The man glared at Matt and looked like he might try to him. Matt just stared at him. The man glanced at the scar on Matt's neck.

"I'll just remind you I've had more than one lesson," Matt said.

The man nodded. "I saw you take down Lakehurst."

"Why don't you go home? These ladies and I have some work to do."

The man glanced at the women, then once more at Matt, and walked off saying nothing.

Matt turned to the two other people watching. "You need to go, too."

"Why?" one man asked. "We didn't say anything."

"These women are here to work. They don't need you watching them get handled roughly. Plus, this is private property, and I'm asking nicely."

The two other men grumbled, but they left.

Matt turned back to Jenny and Samantha. "So, you can see a bit of what you might be up against. Jenny, you handled yourself well."

Samantha put a hand on her arm. "You really did. I was impressed."

"I was scared when he lifted me off the ground," Jenny said. "I'm glad Matt warned me. How did you know?"

"It was a guess… an educated one, but a guess. He had seen the move that we practiced, so he tried to figure out a way around it. Lifting you up was the easiest solution, which brings me to the next lesson. You have to think on your feet. You have to figure out which of the things I teach will work in a given situation. When Jenny couldn't stomp her foot down, she used her fist."

"I think I'll call that move the nutcracker," Jenny said.

Samantha laughed. "Jenny!"

"One thing to keep in mind is that your punches won't be as powerful as a man's, so you need to get the most out of them. That means aim for the soft spots: the groin, the nose, the eyes, the throat."

He taught and demonstrated various defensive moves he could think of. He also explained the rationale behind them so they could keep it in mind when they had to execute the moves themselves. He kept them working for an hour.

"Okay, that's enough for today," Matt finally said. "I want you both to practice your moves for the next couple days with a willing partner. Go easy on them and don't try to injure them, especially if I am the one helping you."

They thanked him and went into the house for lemonade while Matt stood on the back porch.

Samuel walked up beside him. "Do you really think that will help them, Matt?"

"You saw them practicing. What do you think, then?"

"It might be helpful, but it might make them overconfident, too."

"Not Jenny. Samantha, maybe, but she's naturally overconfident. I'm not indulging them, Samuel. The things I'm teaching them will work against most people. Not too many men are thinking about assaulting a woman if she has just kicked their balls up to their stomach."

Samuel chuckled. "Then maybe you should teach Myrna and Toni, too."

"Are you worried about them being attacked?"

Samuel nodded. "A little. Look around, Matt. This isn't the Eckhart we know any more. The men on the street aren't the same ones we used to work with. These are strangers who are being protected by men like David Lakehurst. They are men who want the love of a woman but are being scorned by any woman from a coal mining family. On top of that, tensions are ratcheting up every day the strike continues. Things have already happened, and they are going to keep happening."

Samuel didn't mention the looming threat of Matt's exposure. It hung over Matt like a weight on the verge of falling. Something would have to be done about Tomlinson. Matt had hoped the strike being settled would mean Tomlinson was leaving the area. Instead, the union organizer had convinced the local miners to stay out. Tomlinson would be more desperate than ever to get a favorable settlement before the miners lost confidence in him.

Matt looked up and down the street. Samuel was right. Things had changed. It wasn't a small town any longer. It was a battle-field. Few women were outdoors. The men walked in groups, except for the Pinkertons.

"If they want to learn, I'm willing to teach them," Matt said.

Chapter 28

August 17, 1922

Matt walked Priscilla to the Cumberland and Pennsylvania Railroad Depot in Frostburg. She held her arms around his arm as they walked. Her pleated blue skirt swished around her legs.

"You can still change your mind," she said.

Matt patted her hand. "I can, but I won't. I need to be here. People here need me, especially right now. You don't need me."

"But I want you."

"Thank you for saying that."

"Well, if you're going to stay, you need to watch out for Joseph McCord," Priscilla said. "He hates you."

Matt smiled. "I know. The feeling is mutual."

"Are you happy here, Matt?"

"I'm needed."

"That's not the same thing."

He nodded. "Yes, I'm happy here, which is surprising, because five years ago, I had been anxious to leave."

"Are you staying because of Samantha?"

Matt sighed. "No. Things are not settled between us, and I learned not to plan my future on something that's not settled."

He glanced sideways at Priscilla. She saw him and said, "Yes,

I know you're referring to me."

"Samantha is a lot like you. She may need the big city like you do. I've seen the big cities. I've seen how they can be destroyed. I want to build something and start here."

He wondered if he was attracted to that type of woman. If so, it didn't match up well to his personality.

"Things are pretty tense around here. I can't see much building getting done," Priscilla said.

He nodded. "It's the strike. You're seeing things at their worst right now. The strike has stopped everything, and nothing will move forward until it ends. But it will end."

The train whistle blew, and he led her to the door to her car in first-class. She kissed him on the cheek and stepped aboard. The train would take her to Cumberland, where she could switch to the B&O to Baltimore.

"Take care of yourself, Matt. If you want, you can write to me occasionally."

He smirked. "And you me."

She waved and walked into the car to find her seat. Matt watched her get settled through the windows, and then he turned and walked back to Eckhart.

Joseph, Laura, and Jacob sat at the dining room table eating pork roast, mashed potatoes, and asparagus. No one was saying much, although Jacob pushed the asparagus around on his plate and frowned.

Laura leaned over and cut the asparagus into small pieces and mixed it into the mashed potatoes with plenty of butter. Jacob loved mashed potatoes, and it would help cover the taste of asparagus.

"The mine seems more active today," Laura said.

Joseph nodded. "I was able to bring in a half a dozen miners who got tired of being out of work. They are being taunted by people in town, though. They might not last. And they don't enjoy working with the strikebreakers."

"I'm sorry."

Joseph waved away her sympathy. He cut another piece of

pork roast and ate it. Laura went back to eating her meal. She watched Jacob and encouraged him to eat his mashed potatoes, which he did with some reluctance.

When he finished, Jacob asked, "Can I go play outside?"

Laura nodded. "But you have to stay in the yard and don't go near the road."

"Yes, Mama."

He tossed his linen napkin on the table, slid off the chair, and ran to the front door. He was outside in a flash.

Laura took a deep breath and stared at her meal. She had eaten little. Her stomach was in knots and not just because she had had nothing to drink for two days. Still, her head was clear, and if she was going to broach the subject, it needed to be now.

"Joey," she said.

He looked up but said nothing.

"There's something I wanted to talk to you about. When I first moved in with you, you talked about marrying me when I was over my mourning for Pete." She paused, expecting him to say something or acknowledge that he remembered. He said nothing.

"I'm ready now, Joey. I'm ready to get married again and be your wife."

She wasn't sure if she truly was ready or not, but she knew she needed more stability in her life. She wasn't a miner's wife any longer, but she wasn't Joey's wife either. If she had been, people would not have treated her as badly as they were.

Joey stared at her for a few moments and then laughed. That had not been the reaction she expected. She thought he would be excited about the prospect of marrying, given how much he had talked about it.

"What's so funny?" she asked, trying not to worry.

He pointed his fork at her. "You."

"Why?"

"You think I would marry you."

"But you said…"

"I said what I needed to get you into my bed. Yes, I was at-tracted to you and even had feelings for you. I might have even meant what I said at some point, but you have been a disappointment, Laura. You whored yourself out to me and who knows who else. You wouldn't fit in my world, and you don't bring any benefit that would help me advance. Marry you? You're lucky I allow you to stay here."

Laura felt herself start to lose control. She knew she would cry at any moment. Luckily, Joey wiped his mouth off and left the table. She sat with her hands in her lap, staring at her plate.

She had gambled her future on Joey, and it hadn't paid off. She had ruined her reputation and trapped herself in this house with a man who only wanted her around for sex. The worst part was she couldn't do anything about it. She couldn't leave. She had no place to go, and she couldn't tell Joey "no" for the same reason. He would throw her and Jacob out with no place to go.

She heard a snigger and looked up. Mrs. Middleton was in the kitchen doorway smiling like the Cheshire Cat in *Alice's Adventures in Wonderland*. She had heard the entire exchange between Laura and Joey.

Laura stood up and hurried outside to the front porch. She sat on a rocking chair and watched Jacob playing with his wooden soldiers in the grass.

What had she done? What had she been thinking?

She had traded one worry for another, one problem for another, and there was no fixing this one. She had wanted not to worry about where she would find money for food and rent so much that she hadn't seen the catches in Joey's offer to move in. Sure, she had plenty of food to eat and a fine house to live in, but that had created new problems for her. The people of Eckhart hated her. They considered her a traitor to the miners and a whore.

And truth be told, Laura did, too.

"Hello, Laura."

Laura wiped the tears from her eyes and looked up. She saw Matt walking down the hill from Frostburg. Jacob saw him, too, and ran over to greet him. Matt picked him up and swung him around. Then he set him down and walked over to Laura.

"How are you?" he asked.

"I've been better," she admitted.

"What's the matter?"

She shook her head. "It's not important."

"Of course it is if it upset you."

"What were you doing in Frostburg?" she asked, trying to change the subject.

"I was seeing Priscilla off at the train station. She realized it was time for her to move on and go home."

"Are you sad to see her go?"

He shrugged. "A little, maybe. She was an important part of my life for a while, but I hope she is happy."

"I was an important part of your life for a while, too."

Matt grinned. "You still are."

She shook her head. "Not really. Not like I used to be." Things had been so simple then, but she hadn't realized it at the time. She had ruined it all, just like she had ruined her life now. Why did she make such poor choices?

"We aren't teenagers anymore," Matt said.

"I know, but things were so much easier back then."

"They didn't feel like it at the time. What's bothering you, Laura? I know you've been feeling isolated from everyone in town, but you have friends in the boarding house."

"Don't try to help me, Matt. I don't deserve it."

She stood up and walked into the house.

Chapter 29

August 20, 1922

Laura swung back the picture that hid Joey's bar. The space behind it held only empty glasses. The bottle of vodka and the bottle of bourbon were gone. They hadn't been empty. Why would Joey move them?

She swung the picture back into place and walked over to the basement door. Joey kept most of his stash of pre-Prohibition liquor in the basement, anyway. She would have a better selection. Not that she was picky. As long as the alcohol dulled her pain, she didn't mind what it was.

She turned the knob and pulled. The door was locked.

It had never been locked before. She could go into any room in the house. Joey has said so.

She rattled the knob, thinking the door might be stuck. It wasn't. It was locked.

Mrs. Middleton walked around the corner from the kitchen to see what the racket was. When she saw Laura pulling at the door, she grinned.

"Mr. McCord locked that," she said.

"I can see that. Where's the key?"

"I don't know."

"I need to get down there."

"Then I guess you'll have to find Mr. McCord," Mrs. Middleton said. Grinning, she turned and walked back into the kitchen.

Laura turned and leaned against the basement door. Why would Joey lock the basement?

She went into her bedroom and dressed. Then she combed her hair and applied some make-up. When she was finished, she walked into the kitchen and told Mrs. Middleton that she was going into town and the housekeeper would need to watch Jacob until she got back.

She walked down the hill to the mine office, where she found Joey sitting behind his desk. She hadn't seen him much the past week. On the one hand, she didn't mind because she wasn't having to have sex with him every night. On the other hand, if he lost interest in her, she and Jacob might find themselves without a place to live. It was one of the reasons she had dressed up to come see him. After Joey's refusal to talk about marriage, she needed to smooth things over between them.

Joey looked up when she walked into the office. He was sitting at his desk at the back of the room, reading the newspaper. He looked her over and smiled. "Laura, what are you doing here?"

"I was trying to go down into the basement, but the door is locked," Laura said. "I wanted to come get the key."

"No," Joey said, frowning.

"No?"

"You heard me."

"Why not?"

"Because you have gone through more of my stock in a month than I did in a year."

"You can afford more."

"Maybe, but I shouldn't need to buy more for a long time, although that is looking less and less likely."

"But Joey…"

"No, Laura. Find something to do other than drink. Now I have work to do. I'm trying to keep a mine running with men who barely know what they're doing."

Things hadn't gone the way she had hoped. She had been too direct. She should have flirted with him more.

Joey lowered his head to concentrate on the papers on his desk. Laura stared at him for a few moments and then stomped out of the room. She wanted to scream at him, but she knew it would only make matters worse. This made her want a drink even more.

She felt at her small clutch purse she carried with her. She had little money in it. Joey rarely gave her any, but then, she didn't need much. Joey paid for her food, housing, and clothing.

Laura walked up Store Hill to Beer Alley. It was the alley where the saloons, and now the speakeasies, were located. Although the saloons had been shut down because of Prohibition, she knew of one place that still operated in the basement of a house. It only sold moonshine, so she hadn't visited it before because she always had access to better liquor in Joey's house.

She identified the non-descript house by the stones laid out in a square near the road. She walked up to the back door and knocked.

A white-haired woman answered. She wasn't old, but her hair had already turned white.

"What do you want?" the woman asked.

"A drink."

The woman stared at her for a moment and shook her head. "My husband, brothers, and father are all miners and pro-union."

"My husband was a miner," Laura said.

The woman nodded. "I know. He was a good man. You aren't. We don't serve company whores."

She shut the door in Laura's face. Laura knocked again, but the woman didn't answer.

Was the woman right? Would Pete be ashamed of whom Laura had become? A company whore? No, but certainly Joey's. He didn't love her. That much was obvious now. Had it always been that way, even when he had been courting her? Had she been too stupid to realize what Joey wanted? Matt and others had tried to warn her about Joey, but she had never seen that hard side of Joey that others had seen. Even when she had been married and Joey didn't have a chance with her, he had still been kind. What had changed between them?

She walked down the street and saw the Cumberland and Westernport trolley from Cumberland rolling up the National Road toward Frostburg. She went to Kelly's Pump and waited. The car stopped and Laura climbed on board, paying the fare before she sat down.

She got off the trolley in Frostburg and looked around. She tried to remember where she had heard people talking about getting a drink in town back when they still talked to her.

She saw a pool hall across the street called Frostburg Billiards. The name rang a bell, and she crossed the street and went into the establishment. Despite the large front windows, the interior was dim except for the lights that hung over the four pool tables.

Men played games at two of the tables. They stopped when Laura entered and smiled. She wondered if they were striking miners. Working men certainly wouldn't be in here during the day.

There was a bar at the back of the room. The shelves behind it that usually held bottles of liquor were empty.

Well, what did she expect? They couldn't openly display liquor. That would be too blatant a violation of the law.

Laura walked back to the bar, but there was no bartender, since he wouldn't have any work to do.

A man sitting on a stool asked, "Can I help you, ma'am?"

"I thought I could get a drink in here," she answered.

The man shrugged. "Not here. We'd rather not be arrested and shut down."

She hesitated. "Oh, well I guess I didn't mean in here, but I heard there was another place."

The man looked her up and down. "I'm sure I don't know what you're talking about."

"Do you know where I can find a place, then? I could really use a drink right now."

"I don't know you, ma'am. I could get someone in trouble if I said the wrong thing."

"My name is Laura Spiker. I live in Eckhart."

"A miner's wife?"

"Not anymore. He was killed in the cave-in in March." Tears welled up in her eyes, but she wasn't sure if she was missing Pete or upset at not being able to get a drink.

The man nodded. "I remember that. I'm sorry."

"Me, too."

The man sighed and stood up. He waved for Laura to follow him. Then he walked behind the bar to a backroom. He pulled on a set of empty shelves. They were attached to the wall and both the shelves and wall panel swung open.

He looked her directly in the eyes. "I'm trusting you, Mrs. Spiker."

Laura nodded and started down the staircase that was hidden behind the wall. She could hear people talking, but they fell silent when she walked into the room.

It was a bar hidden in the basement. The bar ran along the far wall. The room also had half a dozen tables in it. Four men stood at the bar and two of the tables were occupied with both women and men. Everyone went back to talking and drinking when they saw Laura wasn't a threat to them.

Laura took a deep breath and walked to the bar. This one had a bartender who approached her.

"What can I get you?" he asked.

"What do you have?"

"Nothing fine, I promise you. All our stock is locally brewed. We may call it scotch or rye or whatever, but it tastes the same. It is all hooch."

"Then I'll take a glass of your best hooch."

The bartender chuckled. He pulled a glass from beneath the bar and set it in front of Laura. Then he poured three fingers worth in it.

"Fifty cents."

Laura pulled out her purse and removed a dollar. "Make it a double."

"Don't you want to try it first?"

"If it's all you've got, it doesn't make a difference."

The bartender shrugged and took the dollar. Then he added more moonshine to the glass. Laura picked up the glass and smelled the liquor. Then she took a sip. It burned like it had been brewed with hot peppers. It wasn't as smooth as Joey's pre-Prohibition liquor. Why would anyone drink this?

The bartender chuckled. "I warned you."

Laura nodded. "I think I need to sit down while I drink this or it may knock me down."

She took her glass and walked over to an empty table. She sat down and took another sip. She wanted to take a larger mouthful, but she worried it might scald her throat. She managed to finish the moonshine fairly quickly in small sips. Then she ordered another double. By then, either her throat was numb or her head was because the liquor wasn't burning her throat any longer. The second drink went down much easier.

She looked around the speakeasy. It wasn't crowded, but it was still early evening and a weeknight. It would probably fill up a bit more before the place finally closed. It had mostly men in it. She was one of only three women.

She felt better after she finished the second drink. She knew she was getting drunk, but she would just sit here until she felt sober enough to go outside and walk home. Then the fresh air would help clear her head. The air down here was filled with the smell of sweat, cigarette smoke, and alcohol.

Still, she didn't mind it. It was peaceful. She wasn't known here, so people didn't hate her and talk behind her back and frown when they looked at her. She enjoyed being able to blend in.

She ordered another drink. She would sober up later.

A blond man brought her drink over and set it on the table. She took out a dollar from her purse. The man waved it away.

"Don't worry. I paid for this one," the man said.

"Thank you."

"Can I sit with you?"

"Why not?"

The man pulled out the chair and sat down.

"I haven't seen you in here before," the man said.

Laura nodded. "I've never been. It's my first time here. I like it."

"You certainly brighten up the place."

"I do?"

"Look around. You're the most beautiful woman in here."

Laura smiled. How long had it been since someone complimented her? This place might become her favorite place.

Calista had been working the speakeasy for about fifteen minutes when Laura Spiker walked in. Laura might not have been dressed to attract men's attention, but her looks did that for her.

Calista carried on a conversation with her prospect for the evening, stroking his arm and kissing him to give him a preview of things to come. Meanwhile, she kept an eye on Laura.

What was she doing here? If she recognized Calista as Jenny, Laura could ruin everything. Jenny had a wonderful place to live now. She didn't want the Ansaros to kick her out of the boarding house.

She saw Laura sit down at a table and start drinking alone. That was never a good sign. It meant that Laura had come to drink and not socialize. It wouldn't take much booze for a petite woman like Laura to get drunk.

Calista had hoped once she told Matt about Laura, he would find a way to keep her out of places like this. The woman might be an adult, but she wasn't used to way things worked in a speakeasy.

The man Calista was with laid a hand on her thigh and stroked it. She let him and even moaned lightly to make him think she was excited.

"There's only so much we can do here, Handsome," she whispered in his ear.

"Then let's get out of here."

He started to rise out of his seat, but she pulled him back down. "Not so fast. I'm not free."

"Can't we talk about that later?"

Calista watched a man named Chuck Anders bring Laura a

drink and sit down. Calista knew Chuck. She had been with him more than once. He was a pig. He knew it and didn't care because he was willing to pay for sex, so he didn't have to be charming or sincere.

She also recognized his opening move in trying to get sex. She was watching it play out now.

Calista realized the man with her said something. She took a deep breath and said, "Sorry, I was thinking about what we're getting ready to do."

The man grinned. "I said, how much do you want?"

Calista saw Chuck brush a hand along Laura's cheek. Wasn't she supposed to be with Joey McCord? What would he think if he found out about this? Matt had been doubtful Laura would be in a place like this, but here she was. He might be in a relationship with Samantha Havencroft, but he still considered Laura a friend.

She patted the man's arm. "I need a minute, Handsome. I see someone I need to talk to."

"What? But…"

"I promise I'll be back soon."

Calista stood up and walked over to the table. Chuck saw her coming and pulled back.

Calista said, "Hello, Laura."

Laura looked at her, her eyes unfocused. Calista knew she was already drunk. She wouldn't be making good decisions.

"I didn't see you over here," Calista said. "You look like you could use a ride home."

"I'm not sure."

"Isn't your son waiting for you at home?"

"Jacob? Yes, he's at the house with Mrs. Middleton."

"I'm sure he's missing you. He's a sweet boy." Calista had seen Jacob Spiker at the Ansaro boarding house from time to time. Myrna and Toni doted on him. Calista had wanted children once, but that didn't seem likely now.

"Why don't you leave us alone, Calista?" Chuck said. "We are close to reaching an agreement here. When we're finished, then Laura can go home."

"Agreement?" Laura said, slurring her e's.

"Yes, you've spent a few dollars on drinks here this evening, and I've spent some on you, too. I thought you might want to get that money back and have a little fun," Chuck said.

"Laura, you're drunk. You're in no condition to be making decisions like that," Calista said. From what Matt had said about Laura, she would not be considering this if she wasn't drunk. Of course, he said he had never seen her drunk before.

"I like fun," Laura said. "I haven't had much fun lately."

"You heard the woman, Calista. She wants to have some fun. Don't worry, I've got plenty of money right now. If you want your turn, I'll be back in a little while." Chuck stood up and took Laura by the arm. Then he led her to the staircase and out of the speakeasy.

Calista wanted to do something. She felt like she needed to or Laura wouldn't be the only one regretting this night tomorrow. She couldn't, though. It was Laura's decision, right or wrong. Chuck was no David Lakehurst, but he was certainly no gentle lover either.

Calista shook her head and walked back to the man she was going to leave with. He stood up and passed her the money.

"Are you ready to leave?" he asked.

"Yes, I am, Handsome. Where are we going?"

"Well, I can't take you back to the bunkhouse where I'm living, but the alley is dark enough for us to be alone."

Calista rolled her eyes and wondered if she needed help as much as Laura.

Jenny came into the boarding house late. She washed the scent of the man, sex, and garbage off her. Then she slipped on her nightgown and climbed into bed.

She was just getting drowsy when she heard something thump on the stairs and someone cursed. She sat up and pulled on a robe. Then she went to the door of her room. She cracked it open and looked into the hallway. She saw a head sticking up above the stairs and realized Enos was lying on the stairs.

She stepped out into the hall and whispered, "Enos?"

Enos raised himself up on his forearms. "Hi, Jenny."

"Went drinking after work, did you?"

He nodded in wide arcs.

She walked over to him, grabbed him by the arm, and pulled him to his feet. "Let me help you to your room."

He managed to stand up, but he wobbled unsteadily.

"I quit, Jenny."

"Certainly not drinking."

He shook his head. "No, this was my last hurrah. Vincent said he found out where Jack Pickett lived and wanted to raid the man's house. I said I couldn't do that. I didn't think it was right. I quit, and then I spent my last pay on a jug of moonshine."

"And apparently drank it all yourself."

Enos laughed, and Jenny's eyes watered from the smell of alcohol on his breath.

"Not quite all, but I made a good accounting of myself," he said.

She helped him up the stairs to the third floor attic where his room and Samuel and Myrna's room were. She checked the door to his room and found it unlocked. She staggered into the room and dumped Enos onto his bed.

"Wheee!" he shouted.

"Quiet down, Enos," Jenny warned him. "People are trying to sleep."

"I don't want to sleep." He held out his hands toward her. "Come here, Jenny, or should I say Calista?"

"I don't think so," she said.

Enos patted the bed next to him. "C'mon. Let's have some fun. I won't tell anyone. I promise."

"No, Enos. You need to sleep."

"What's the problem? I can pay you. I have money left over."

That's what it always came down to, didn't it? Men just expected her to lift her skirts if they flashed some money, whether or not she was working. She had thought Enos was different. He was kind and funny. When it came down to it, though, he was just like every other man.

She turned and walked out of the room leaving lying Enos half on the bed.

Chapter 30

August 22, 1922

Laura woke in the morning with her head throbbing and her body aching. It hurt to even lift her arm and drape it over eyes to keep out the light.

She felt someone stir beside her, and she sat up suddenly. She saw flashes of something happening with a man she didn't know, but when she looked over, it was only Joey in bed beside her.

She looked around. How had she gotten here? She remembered going to Frostburg yesterday and finding the speakeasy. She couldn't remember anything after the second shot of moonshine.

The room started spinning, and she felt like she might fall back into bed. Instead, she forced herself to slide off the mattress and stand up. She was naked, not even wearing her nightgown. She pulled on a robe and went out into the hall and into the bathroom. She drew herself a warm bath and slipped into the tub. The warmth of the water helped ease some of the aching.

She lay back in the tub and closed her eyes. It brought her no peace. She saw flashes of an alley. She was bent over with her hands against a brick wall. Behind her, a man she didn't know was thrusting into her.

She gasped and opened her eyes. She grabbed the soap from

the dish and scrubbed her body. She starting thinking she would rub her skin raw, but she didn't feel any cleaner.

What had happened yesterday in Frostburg? Was that where the alley had been? Not many of the buildings in Eckhart were brick.

And who was that man?

What had she done?

She prayed it was a bad dream, but she knew differently. She could feel it. It might have been Joey she felt, but she didn't think so. It was that man… that stranger.

Her stomach clenched up. She pulled herself out of the tub just in time to lean over the toilet and vomit. She stayed there on her knees, heaving and crying.

Finally, she stood up and dried herself off. Then she slid back into her robe. She brushed her teeth to get rid of the taste of vomit.

She walked back to the bedroom and sat down on the edge of the bed. What had she done? What had she become?

"Where were you last night?" Joey asked.

That was the question that needed answering, wasn't it? Where had she been?

"I… I was in Frostburg," Laura answered.

"Why did you go there?"

Laura sighed. "I needed a drink."

Joey snorted. "Of course you did."

He rolled to his side and sat up. Then he walked over to his closet and pulled out a white shirt and tweed pants to wear.

"What's that mean?" Laura asked.

"It means you're a lush."

She felt tears well up in her eye. He was right, but she hated that he was right. "Maybe I have reason to be."

"And what reason would that be? You have a good life here. What makes you want to throw away all sense of decorum so you can have a drink?"

Laura shook her head but said nothing. He didn't love her. He used her. She got up and walked across the hall to Jacob's room. He was still asleep, curled into a tight ball.

She sat down on the bed beside him and stroked his hair. He was looking more like his father every day. They even had the same cowlick, and Jacob was all Laura had left of her husband. Then she thought how ashamed Pete would be of her and the way she had been acting lately.

She was ashamed of herself.

Joey was right. She was a lush. All she had wanted to do was forget about having no control over her life, and she had only wound up making things worse for herself.

Jacob stirred under her touch and opened his eyes.

"Mommy."

Why wasn't his smile enough for her? She loved him so much. Why couldn't she be the mother he deserved?

"Good morning, Angel."

He laughed and rolled over and hugged her. Laura felt a warmth spread through her body as if she was standing in front of a fire.

Jacob sat up, and she picked out an outfit for him to wear and helped him get dressed. Once he was dressed, they played with a set of wooden blocks, seeing which one of them could build the tallest town.

When she heard Joey leave, she ventured out of the room with Jacob to eat breakfast in the dining room. Laura looked away from Mrs. Middleton. The woman's stare seemed to tell Laura that she knew exactly what Laura had been up to.

Laura wasn't hungry, so she only ate a piece of buttered toast and drank a cup of coffee. Jacob wolfed down a bowl of oatmeal with brown sugar.

After breakfast, Laura went back to her room to dress for the day. She found her plainest dress, a pale yellow one with white lace fringe. It was out of style, but it had been her everyday dress when she had been living in the miner's house with Pete. Not only did the dress remind her of happier times, she doubted it would catch anyone's eye.

She was just finishing up when she heard a knock at the door. Mrs. Middleton answered it. Laura supposed it wasn't important because the woman didn't come back to tell her anything.

Laura walked into the parlor.

"Who was at the door?" Laura called to the housekeeper.

"No one."

Laura looked out the front window and saw Matt pacing the front porch. Laura hurried to the door and opened it.

"Matt, I'm sorry. Mrs. Middleton didn't tell me you were waiting."

Matt stopped pacing. "I guess she doesn't like me much either."

"Do you want to come inside?"

Matt hesitated and then said, "Can we sit outside? I'd rather not have to worry about Mrs. Middleton listening in or telling Joey I was in his house."

Laura waved to one of the rocking chairs on the porch. "Have a seat."

They sat in the chairs, so that they were turned in each other's direction but not facing each other directly. She watched Matt shift uncomfortably in the rocking chair. She knew him well enough to know she wouldn't like what he was about to say.

"Just say it, Matt, and stop polishing the seat of the chair," Laura said.

He took a deep breath and said, "I'm worried about you, Laura."

"Didn't we already have this conversation?"

"Yes, and I guess this is still a continuation of that. When I asked you the question then, it was because you had had too much to drink. I could smell it on your breath. Since then, I heard about you being in a speakeasy and leaving with a man."

"So? You've been in speakeasies."

Matt nodded. "From what I was told, the man you had left with bought you a lot to drink, and then you and he… went into the alley and…" Matt couldn't finish.

Laura felt her face turning red with shame. She had been seen. Someone had recognized her and the story was already spreading. She jumped to her feet.

"Matt! No, it didn't happen. How could you think that?"

Matt stood up and put his hands on her shoulders. "Laura, calm down. I came here to talk, not accuse you."

He eased her back into her rocking chair. Laura couldn't look at him. She sobbed into her hands.

"How could you say something like that, Matt?"

"First off, I didn't say anything bad. You jumped to that conclusion, which pretty much confirms what I was told. Second, I will not say anything about it, and the person who told me only did so because she knew we are friends and she was worried about you. She won't say anything."

It didn't matter. Matt knew. He knew she had whored herself to someone. But he had already known that, didn't he? She had done the same thing with Joey. She had gotten drunk, and he had seduced her. At least she knew him, but then everyone knew she was living with Joey as his mistress. That was why they hated her.

"Laura, look at me."

She slowly raised her head. Matt reached out and took her hands in his.

"I want to help. I know what happened, but why did it happen? It's not like you," Matt said.

She slowly shook her head. She had considered the question herself many times, and the only question she came up with was, "It helps me."

"Helps you how?"

"Forget. It helps me forget Pete is dead. It helps me forget about the way people treat me."

"But getting drunk is leading you to make some poor decisions."

Laura wasn't sure if it was the liquor that was leading her to make bad decisions. She had been known to do that sober, like the time at the school dance when she thought Matt was cheating on her. He hadn't been, but she thought so. She tried to get back at him by kissing a lot of the boys at the dance. Afterward, she had found out she was wrong, but it was too late. She and Matt broke up.

"I want to forget, Matt."

"Laura, you left with a man who got you drunk."

She shook her head. "I didn't."

"People saw you."

"Well, nothing happened."

"People saw you."

Laura gasped. Someone had watched her having sex in the alley? She didn't remember seeing anyone, but then, she barely remembered the alley.

"You think this is just me acting like I did in high school, don't you?" she snapped.

"No, I came because I was worried. Not just because of what you're doing, but I'm worried you might be an addicted to alcohol."

"You mean you think I'm a drunk."

"No."

Laura pulled her hands away from Matt's. "Yes, you do, but I'm fine. I'm not making bad decisions. I have everything I ever wanted. A child. A nice home. I don't have to worry about money. Maybe I should be worried about you. You're an out-of-work coal miner who has to live with your aunts and uncles."

Matt stared at her for a few moments and then stood up.

Laura wanted to stop, but she couldn't. She just kept spewing mean things. She didn't feel anger at Matt. It was Joey she was mad at, but he wasn't here for her to vent her anger.

"I'm sorry to interrupt your perfect life," he said.

"I am not your responsibility, Matt, just because Pete asked you to look after Jacob and me. I am a grown woman. I can take care of myself."

"Then why don't you?" Matt barked. "Why do you stay with Joey if you can take care of yourself?"

He turned and walked off the porch and headed to the road. Laura buried her face in her hands and just cried.

Enos walked into the boarding house and went upstairs to the second floor. He been sitting with a group of striking miners on the front porch of Chabot's Store. He had squirmed uncomfortably as they had made comments about some of the women who went into or out of the store. He might share some of the same thoughts, but he didn't voice them, at least not where the women could hear him. He had realized how those women felt because he kept seeing Jenny's expression when he had offered her money. It was his one vivid memory from that evening. On the one hand, he wished it could be lost in the haziness of his moonshine memories, but on the other hand, he needed to remember it because he needed to fix things. Jenny hadn't spoken to him in days. She even avoided meals, so she wouldn't have to sit at the table with him.

Enos rapped lightly on Jenny's closed door. After a few moments, she opened it. He noticed she wore a high-necked dress and had her hair tied back in a bun. She looked a lot like a school teacher.

"What do you want?" she asked coldly.

Enos couldn't meet her stare. "I wanted to apologize. I was very drunk last night and don't remember how I even got home. Apparently, I was very loud, though. Samuel said he looked out his door and saw you helping me because I was too drunk to stand. Then he told me I said some very inappropriate things to you, particularly since you were helping me."

Jenny shook her head. "No, you were right. I am a prostitute. Men pay me for sex."

Enos wasn't sure what to say to that. Instead, he held out the bouquet of wildflowers he had picked.

"I'm sorry," he said. "I wasn't trying to excuse my behavior." He shook his head. "I just wanted to explain what had happened."

"I know what happened. I was there."

"I wish I could take it back. I wish I didn't prove my family right at times. I don't think of you like that, Jenny."

"You do. You are just too polite to say it. The booze just lowered your resistance."

"No," he said firmly. "I don't think of you that way, particularly since I've gotten to know you. I think of you as a speed demon, as someone who has a sharp sense of humor, as a survivor, as a beautiful woman, but not what came out of me last night. That was the booze talking, and when it talks, it doesn't have anything nice to say."

He held the flowers up higher. She reached out and took them.

"Thank you," she said.

"There's something else I want to show you. May I come in? I need to go to your window."

She looked over her shoulder at the window. "My window? Why?"

"It won't take long. I promise."

She hesitated and then stepped back, probably curious what he would do. Enos stepped inside the room and she saw the moonshine jug in his hand.

"I don't want to drink, Enos."

He nodded. "Neither do I."

He walked over to the open window. He lifted the jug out of the opening and turned it over. What moonshine was left in it poured out and onto the porch roof below. When the jug was empty, he brought it inside and set it on the night stand.

"Use it as a vase to remind you of the promise I'm making to you," Enos said.

"That was a lot of money you just poured out," Jenny said.

"No, it was a lot of bad things I would do or say that I threw away. That is what was left over from the jug I bought last night. After Samuel talked to me this morning, I looked at that jug and saw it as something evil. It made me hurt someone whom I care about. It made me say some vile things that I didn't mean. How could I want to chance that happening again?"

"So? What? Are you a teetotaler now?"

Enos frowned. "Lord, I hope not, but I may have to be if I can't handle my booze."

Her eyes widened. "You're serious."

He nodded. "I hurt you, and that's the last thing I would want to do. If the choice is the booze or not hurting people I care about, then I choose the people I care about."

Jenny walked over and kissed him on the cheek. "Thank you, Enos."

"There's something else."

"What's that?"

"Making that decision was easy, but sticking to it I think will not be so easy. Help me, Jenny. I need someone better than me who won't judge me to help me keep my promise."

"And you think that's me?"

Enos nodded. "I know it's you."

Chapter 31

August 22, 1922

By late August, the coal companies were fighting back hard against the attacks on the strikebreakers the companies had brought in to replace striking miners. Up to this point, the companies had been reactive to the strike, but with some momentum gained from the end of the nationwide strike, they went on the offensive, sometimes to the extreme.

Coal mine guards shot one striking miner who wasn't even on mining property. The guard said the man was armed and eyeing shots he could make from where he stood. Another guard threw a grenade into a marching crowd of striking miners. The miners scattered and only two wound up with minor injuries. What was becoming obvious was that although David Lakehurst had fled town, his brand of protection had filtered out to other Pinkerton agents in the county, at least the ones who were assigned as guards for the mines.

Things got so bad that the federal government started talking about taking over the mines and operating them until peace returned to the western end of Allegany County. Governor Albert Ritchie also traveled to Frostburg to tour the coal region. He spoke with local officials and mine owners. Paul Tomlinson tried to get a meeting with the man to present the union's side of things in the strike, but he was refused.

Governor Ritchie also examined the water system in Frostburg while he was there. Mayor Olin Rice spoke to him about getting state aid to create a reservoir or at least drill more wells. Under normal circumstances, Frostburg had plenty of water for its citizens. These weren't normal times, however, but the water shortage had nothing to do with the coal mines and striking miners.

Water was being consumed at three times the normal rate. Frostburg typically used about 110,000 gallons of water daily, but it was using 330,000 gallons in 1922. The reason? The estimated 100 stills operating within town boundaries. The newspaper did the math, estimating that each still used an average of ninety gallons of water an hour or nearly 2,000 gallons to make a batch of moonshine. The average still was using the same amount of water as twenty families.

Paul Tomlinson knew things were set to change. The national coal strike had ended, so inevitably, things would change. The question was, would they change in his favor? Yes, the Allegany County miners had voted to continue their strike, but how long could they last? Coal was flowing once again. While some of the small coal companies in the county still suffered because they couldn't get their product to market, Consolidation Coal was strengthening its position. Its other mines in Kentucky, West Virginia, and Pennsylvania were making up the losses from Maryland. It was even operating some of its Allegany County mines with strikebreakers and scabs, and the mines were shipping a decent amount of coal. It also didn't help that the nearby coal mines in Garrett County were operating with enough men. The pressure for the company to unionize here was lessening.

Paul needed to find a way to bring the company, as well as the others, back to the negotiating table and to allow the United Mine Workers in. Paul needed to secure a contract. The coal companies had even offered to pay 1920 wages, which was appealing to the miners because it had only been dropping since then. Of course, it wasn't the union so much that had won that concession. Even with other mines operating across the country, it looked like there might be a coal shortage this winter. The companies wanted to increase production as quickly as they could, even if it meant paying higher wages. It was an attractive proposal for the miners, but the companies were insisting that their mines stay open free from the union. That wasn't acceptable.

Paul thought he had an ace in the hole, but that ace wanted out of the hole. Matt Ansaro's future was in Paul's hands. Paul wanted nothing more than to reveal Ansaro's undercover work for the Pinkertons and leave it to the miners to deal their justice against the traitor. However, Paul also recognized the value of a secret. Ansaro knew things about what the coal companies were planning. If Paul could learn that information, he knew that he could parlay it into something useful for his cause.

He was tired of waiting. He just needed to make sure Ansaro knew he was trapped and his only choice was to cooperate with Paul.

Laura sat in the parlor with her feet up on the couch, staring over the back out the large front window of the house. There wasn't much to see, especially for as long as she had been looking out. A few people walked past along the road. The trolley passed every hour, and cars occasionally drove past.

Although she was dressed, she kept a blanket pulled around her. She shivered, but she wasn't cold. She just didn't want to feel she was exposing her body.

Her throat felt dry, and she wanted a drink. She had been through the house this morning while Mrs. Middleton had been shopping for groceries. Laura had gone through all the cabinets in the kitchen, thinking she might find a bottle of cooking sherry tucked away. She hadn't. She knew it wouldn't do any good to go through the rest of the house. Joey had made sure to lock all the alcohol away.

She needed a drink.

She didn't even have any money left over from her visit to the speakeasy yesterday.

She stood up from the couch and looked around. She knew how to get a drink. It was worked once before. It would work again.

She walked into the bedroom and looked at herself in the mirror. First, she would need to put on some make-up and dress nicer. Then she would be ready for another trip to Frostburg.

Part of her sobbed at the thought, but she pushed that part of her away. She needed a drink, and she knew how to get it.

Chapter 32

August 23, 1922

Samantha Havencroft stood at the door to the model school and greeted the students as they entered for the first day of the new school. The model school was a public school operated by the Frostburg Normal School. It educated students in the area for a minimal cost to the county school system. In exchange, prospective students from the normal school spent a semester teaching at the model school as a final class before graduation. The school was also used to try the new forms of instruction the prospective teachers learned.

Because of the summer courses Samantha had been studying, she would be able to graduate from the Frostburg Normal School at the end of this semester. Once she graduated, she even had a job waiting for her in Annapolis. Since it was the middle of the school year, she would work for a semester at the different schools in Anne Arundel County, acting as a substitute teacher or assistant as needed. Then she would be assigned her own classroom for the next school year.

Things were going according to her plan, so why wasn't she happier?

She rang her school bell once again and then glanced at her

watch. It was nearly eight o'clock. She walked into the building, which had four classrooms. Each one contained students from two grades.

Samantha walked into her classroom and over to her desk. She looked around the room at the children talking at their desks, the posters she had hung on the wall, and the books on the low bookcases that ran along one side of the room. She had already written her name on the blackboard. She looked over at her class. She had twenty students who were eight and nine years old. A few of them were watching her, but most were still talking amongst themselves.

Samantha clapped her hands together. "Good morning, students. Welcome to your first day of school."

The children quieted down and turned to face her. Samantha picked up a sheet of paper from her desk and glanced at it. She was going to use assigned seating in her class to keep friends from clustering together, where they might be more inclined to talk amongst themselves when they should be listening to their teacher. Since this was a mixed grade class, she wanted to add something that would make instruction easier.

"Students, please stand up and take your books with you to stand at the side of the class."

Some students grumbled, knowing what was coming, but they all obeyed. Samantha walked to the first desk.

"Melissa Bailey, you will sit here," Samantha said.

A third-grade girl walked over and sat down at the desk. Samantha stepped to the next desk.

"John Harmon, this is your desk."

That surprised some students. They were expecting to be seated in alphabetical order. Samantha's plan was to alternate between boys and girls because they were less likely to talk to each other. It might not solve all the problems with students talking and not paying attention in class, but she thought it would help. She had also assigned seats so that the third graders were on the left, while the fourth graders were on the right side of the room.

When all the students were seated, Samantha said, "These will be your seats for this semester."

The students' teacher for the next semester might change them, but this was Samantha's class for this semester. She had the opportunity to experiment with some ideas she had before she put them into practice on the job, and she planned to do just that.

She then called on two students—a third grader and a fourth grader—to pass out the primers to the other students in their grade.

Samantha looked over at her class. She wondered if she would ever be a mother. She knew she wanted to be a teacher, and she believed she wanted to be a mother. However, if she ever did have a child, she would have to give up her teaching position. And if she did have a child with whom would it be? Matt? Did she want to be a miner's wife?

She didn't think so. She wanted to be a teacher and eventually a principal of a large school, or even a school district superintendent. That had been her dream for years. She wanted to shape children's minds and open them up to new possibilities. She wanted them to believe that women could be anything they wanted to be.

And if she ever did have children, Samantha wanted them to be proud of their mother. She wanted her children to see that not only had their mother taught equality, but she also had achieved it.

The children finished passing out the primers and sat back in their seats.

"Now, children, I want you to take out a piece of paper and a pencil. We're going to start today with English, but first I need to find out how much you remember from last school year. I'm going to say a word, and I want you to write it down."

"Not a test," one boy grumbled.

"That's right," Samantha said. "It's not a test. I won't grade you on this. I will use it to see where you are with your spelling. Then we'll do something similar at the end of the semester, so I can evaluate your progress. Ready?" She paused to make sure she everyone's attention. "The first word is schoolhouse."

Samantha walked out of the model school with her books in her arms. She thought her first day of classes had gone well, although she was exhausted. Keeping twenty students focused on their work wore her down. She hadn't realized it would be so diffi-cult, but she guessed that was the point of student teaching. It was one thing to talk about how to keep a student engaged, but it might not always work in practice.

She headed down the walk to the street that would lead her to her house. She saw two miners approaching her. She didn't give it a second thought that they were miners in this area of town, which was not a place they would normally be. They weren't dust cov-ered, as miners typically were, but then the strike was still going on.

They walked up to her, and one miner asked, "Are you Saman-tha Havencroft?"

That took her back that they would know her name. Her next thought was for Matt. He must be in trouble for them to come looking for her.

"Yes, yes, that's me. Is there a problem? Is Matt all right?"

"No, problem. We just need you to come with us."

"Where?"

The miners looked around, and she began to get nervous. A car pulled up beside them. One man suddenly grabbed her by the arm, spun her around, and put his hand over her mouth so she couldn't yell. He dragged her toward the car.

She remembered her training from Matt and slammed her heel onto the man's toe. He yelled and released his grip on her. She kicked the other man in the crotch as he ran at her. He doubled over and fell, but then the first man grabbed her again and shoved her head first into the car.

Meanwhile, people seeing the commotion ran toward her to try and help. The car sped off, leaving the man she had kicked in the groin behind. She screamed for help, and the miner slapped her hard across the face.

She tried to jump from the car, but miner laid on top of her. She screamed and struggled.

"Gag her! Gag her!" the driver yelled.

The miner grabbed his handkerchief and shoved it in her mouth. She tried to spit it out, but he held her mouth closed until he got a length of rope and tied it around her head to keep her from spitting out the handkerchief.

The miner fought with her. He slapped her more than once until she was sobbing. Then he tied her hands behind her back and left her lying face down on the back seat of the car.

Samantha lay in the seat as the car drove. She tried to raise up to look out the window and signal for help, but every time she tried, the miner in the backseat with her pushed her down. The car bounced around, so she figured they had moved off the main roads. The bouncing knocked her off the seat and into the footwell. She managed not to bloody her nose by turning her head to the side. Because her hands were tied, she wasn't able to push herself up. The miner with her just laughed.

The car finally stopped and Samantha heard the doors open in the front. Then the back door opened and she could see grass and a man's legs.

"Get her up from there," someone said.

A man leaned over and pulled her by the shoulders. Samantha kicked out and connected with the man's crotch. He yelped and fell backward. Samantha smiled behind the gag.

Another man pulled her up and slapped her across the face. "You think that's funny?" Then he slapped her again and dragged her out of the car and onto the grass.

Samantha watched a well-dressed man walk out of a nearby house. He buttoned his jacket and straightened the cuffs on his sleeves.

"I told you not to hurt her," the man said.

"She fought us, Mr. Tomlinson," one miner said.

"One woman against three miners caused you trouble?"

"She caused trouble, but we got her here."

"Where's Dodson?"

"We had to leave him behind. The girl made too much of a scene."

"Idiot," Tomlinson said. "He can identify us."

"He wouldn't."

"He's a miner. Even if he doesn't say anything, the police will assume the union is involved."

Tomlinson walked over to stand next to Samantha. She looked up at him, and he smiled.

"Don't worry, Miss Havencroft. You will be all right as long as Matt Ansaro does what we tell him to do."

Matt answered the knock at the front door and saw John Havencroft standing on the porch. He looked panicked and angry.

"Is she here?" he asked.

"Samantha?" Matt shook his head. "No, I haven't seen her all day. I had to go into Cumberland."

"Matt, people said three men took her on her way home. One of them is in jail, but I was hoping it was all a misunderstanding and Samantha was here."

"What does the man in jail say?"

"He's not saying anything. Why would they take her? She's just a student."

Matt could think of many reasons, and he wasn't sure he wanted to share them all with Samantha's father.

"Have you had a ransom demand?"

Havencroft shook his head. "No. Do you think they took her because they want money from me?"

Matt shrugged. "That's the best answer, but I doubt it."

Somehow, he knew Samantha had been taken because of him and the threat Paul Tomlinson had made. He had John drive them both back to the police station. When the two men entered the station, Police Chief Collins was talking to another officer, and they didn't seem in agreement about things.

When the chief saw John, he said, "We still don't know anything, Mr. Havencroft."

John pointed to Matt. "This is Matt Ansaro. I brought him to help. He is dating my daughter."

The chief looked Matt over. "I don't see how he can help."

"Can I see the prisoner you have?" Matt asked.

"Of course not! You're not his family or lawyer. You're also not a police officer," the chief said. "What's more, you have a personal relationship with the missing woman."

Matt needed to question the prisoner, but first he needed to get into the back room where the man was being held. He looked over at John. The man was desperate. Matt had to help.

"Chief, may I speak with you over in the corner... alone, please?" Matt asked.

"This is not the time, Mr. Ansaro. If you want to help us, go home, and let us work."

"Please, chief. It's important."

Chief Collins rolled his eyes. "Make it quick."

He walked with Matt over to the corner of the office.

"Chief, I'm a Pinkerton Detective," Matt admitted in a low whisper.

The chief's eyes widened. "What!"

"Quiet down. I'm undercover. I'm here because of the strike. I think I can help, but I need to talk to the prisoner first."

Chief Collins rubbed his face and stared at Matt. "You're being honest with me."

Matt nodded. "I can show you my badge if you want, but not out here where others can see it. I am trying to maintain my cover."

The chief held up a finger. "Fine, I'll let you back there on one condition. I want to know anything he tells you."

Matt nodded. "Of course."

The chief turned around. "Bill, let Mr. Ansaro question the prisoner."

The officer looked surprised. "Really?"

Chief Collins nodded. "He might be able to help us."

The police officer unlocked the door to the cells in the back. Matt started for the door, and John followed him. No one objected.

Matt stood in the hallway and looked at the two jail cells. Only one held a prisoner.

Matt walked up to the bars and looked at the man inside. He was short and thick, although Matt wouldn't call him fat. He had the slump-shouldered look of a coal miner, and he squinted against the sunlight that came into the room. Matt also guessed that he was a union miner, which wasn't much of a leap of logic.

"I'm Matt Ansaro."

The miner just smiled.

"What did you do with her?"

"We'll take care of her until you finish doing what you need to do."

"What's he talking about?" John Havencroft asked. "What do you have to do? What's going on?"

Matt pushed John toward the door. "Mr. Havencroft, you need to leave."

He pushed his way back toward the cell. "I'm not leaving until I find Samantha."

Matt had work to do here, and not that of a miner or gentleman, or even a lawman.

"That's what I intend to do, but you can't be here. You can't see what might happen."

"What might happen?" He stared at Matt, who just stared back at him. Havencroft's eyes widened. "This is not about coal mining, is it?"

"It is, but not how you think. You don't know the whole story."

"But Samantha's in trouble because of all this."

Matt nodded.

John grabbed him by the shirt. "Why? Why has my daughter been kidnapped?"

Matt sighed and decided he had nothing to lose. His cover had been blown. He pulled his badge from his pocket and showed it to Havencroft.

"You're a…"

"Don't tell anyone. But I want you to know, so you will also know I have a lot of resources I can call on to get your daughter. Now, please, wait for me outside."

Havencroft stared at the badge. Then he nodded and left. Matt turned back to face the miner. The man was standing near the bars of the cell.

Matt jumped forward, grabbed the man by the shirt and jerked him forward so his face slammed into the bars. Before the man could yell, Matt grabbed him by the throat and squeezed.

"You're going to tell me what I want to know."

"Or what? You're going to kill me? I'm in jail. They'll know it's you."

"Perhaps. Perhaps they won't care. Don't you wonder why they've left me back here alone? The police and I have an understanding, but maybe you're right. Maybe I'll just pay your bail, wait for you outside, and take you away in a car like you did Samantha, but if I do that, you'll never be seen again."

"Neither would your girlfriend."

"Yes, so you're going to tell me where she is."

"No, I'm not. You're going to do what Tomlinson tells you to do."

"When I was in Europe during the war, a shell hit a foxhole I was in. I was lucky. I was partially buried. My friend, Cal Hanson, wasn't so lucky. Shrapnel ripped through his middle. He was left on the ground with his intestines hanging out. He was too hurt to get help and there was none nearby. I couldn't get to him because I was trapped, but the rats could reach him. There was nothing he could do but scream and plead while they ate his insides. Then, after a while, all he could do was cry. And finally, not even that. He died quietly."

The miner said nothing as Matt stared him down.

"If you don't tell me what I want, we will go down one of the closed mines and I'll gut you. Somewhere between the screaming and the silence as those hungry mine rats feast on you, you'll tell me what I want to know. If you aren't too far gone at that point, I may even take you to a doctor."

He poked the man's stomach with his free hand and felt him flinch.

"So, do we talk now or later?" Matt asked.

When Matt walked out of the back room, John Havencroft stopped pacing. The chief and police officer looked over at him.

"Do you know where she is?" John asked.

"Maybe. He told me where they were taking her. Can we take your car? It's a place in Mount Savage."

"I'll call the county deputies to meet you there," Chief Collins said.

"It will probably be over and done with before they arrive. We can't wait around for them to get here."

Chief Collins pointed at John. "You can't take the president of the college on a raid."

John straightened up. "Yes, he can. It's my daughter who is in trouble. I'm going to help." He turned to Matt. "Let's go."

Matt drove as fast as he could to the address in Mount Savage. He wanted to floor the accelerator, but the roads were windy, and once he got off the main road, it was also rough. He forced himself to ease up, though. It wouldn't do Samantha any good if he rolled the car while he and John Havencroft were driving to help her. He could have used Enos's driving skills to speed along the windy road.

As he neared the location, Matt pulled over and stopped the car.

"Are we here?" John asked.

"Almost. I don't want to get any closer because they will hear the car coming."

Matt climbed out of the car and checked his pistol. Then he shoved it into his waistband behind his back.

"You can't go in there shooting," John said. "You might hurt Samantha."

Matt nodded. "I know. That's why my weapon isn't drawn right now. I want to see what we're up against. Then I can decide how to proceed."

"*We* can decide."

Matt stared at the older man and nodded. John might not be young, but he had been a soldier.

They crept up close to the house, staying in what Matt figured were blind spots if lookouts were stationed at the windows. He pulled out his field glasses and scanned the house. He didn't see anyone or any movement.

Had the miner lied to him? Matt didn't think so. The miner hadn't seemed that good a liar. He'd been a blow hard, confident that Tomlinson would keep him out of trouble.

Matt and John scurried, keeping low until they were standing on the side of the small miner's house. Matt crouched and worked his way around the wall to peer into the house through a window. He was looking at the main room, and it was empty. They might be in the bedroom, but it was doubtful. If Samantha was being held here, at least one person should be in this room, acting as the lookout.

"It's empty," Matt said to John.

"What? But this is the address that miner gave you."

Matt nodded.

He straightened up and walked around to the front door. He turned the knob, and the door opened. He walked inside.

"This is small," John said.

"It's a miner's house."

"Your house isn't this small."

"It's a boarding house."

Matt looked over the room. The furniture here was well used. The sofa had a rip in it and stuffing poking through. He saw no dishes waiting to be washed. It smelled of cigarette smoke. Someone had been here recently.

He walked over to the bedroom door and opened it. It was also empty. The bed was made. So was the miner who lived here at work?

And where was Samantha?

"Matt."

Matt turned. John was bending over next to the sofa. When he straightened up, he was holding a stack of school books.

"These are Samantha's," John said. "She was here."

"But where is she now?" Matt asked.

He continued searching the house to find some clue of where the miners had taken Samantha. A note telling the miners where to take her or a map showing them how to get to another hiding place. They must have realized the miners who took Samantha would be identified—especially after one of them had been recognized in town—and Samantha would be traced here. Now, they had switched the group watching Samantha and taken her some place where she could be hidden away. It would most likely be in a coal town that solidly supported the United Mine Workers. Hiding Samantha there meant that everyone in town would watch out for police or Pinkerton agents.

Not finding anything inside, Matt went back outside and circled the house to see if he could make anything out. He examined the ground. He could see that there had been a lot of activity around the house. He saw at least four different sets of footprints, including the sharp point of a female's heel. He also saw at least two sets of tire tracks in front of the house.

He could garner nothing more from them. The tire tracks disappeared once they merged onto the main road, where other tracks crisscrossed them or obliterated them.

When he walked back to the house, Matt saw John standing in the doorway.

"Anything?" John asked.

"Nothing we can use."

"She was here, though." John said it more to himself than Matt, but Matt nodded.

They climbed into the car and drove in silence back to the Frostburg police station. Matt stared at everyone they passed, wondering if that person was conspiring in Samantha's kidnapping. None of them seemed suspicious, but it didn't mean they didn't know something about what had happened.

At the police station, John filled out a missing person report about Samantha.

Chief Collins said, "I didn't think you'd find anything out there, but I guess you needed to check it out."

"Paul Tomlinson is involved in this," Matt said.

"Maybe. Maybe not. I sent an officer to bring him in," the chief said. "That much we could do."

"Are you arresting him?" Matt asked.

The officer shook his head. "We have nothing to hold him on. We are going to question him."

Matt knew that wouldn't work, either. Tomlinson knew there was no proof he was involved in the kidnapping. He also knew the police would be careful with him since he was a union representative who could create problems for the police.

The door to the police station opened and Paul Tomlinson walked inside with another police officer. He removed his bowler and looked around.

"Hello, Matt. I heard your girlfriend is missing," Tomlinson said.

"You should know," John said. "You had her kidnapped."

Tomlinson arched his bushy eyebrows. "I am not in the business of kidnapping, Mr...."

"Havencroft. I'm Samantha's father," John said.

"Well then, you have my condolences, sir. I hope she is found safe, but I am sure what happens to her is out of my control."

"I'd like to ask you a few questions," the police officer said.

"I don't think so."

"Don't you want to help us locate Miss Havencroft?"

"She is not my responsibility."

"Then why did you come here today?"

"I was under the impression that if I did not accompany your officer voluntarily, I would be arrested."

Movement outside caught Matt's attention. He looked out the window and saw miners gathering in front of the police station. To attack or protest? How far was Tomlinson willing to drive the miners?

"He's trying to build his reputation," Matt said.

"What?" the police officer asked.

"I'm sure as soon as Tomlinson left the hotel, one of his assistants ran off to spread a rumor that the coal companies had the police in their pocket and they were going after the UMW."

Tomlinson chuckled. "Not bad."

"But that's not why we asked you here at all. A woman has been kidnapped and you are interfering with the investigation now."

Tomlinson held out his hands. "Then by all means arrest me."

The officer grumbled. He stomped over to the window and looked out. Most of the men looked upset. Matt guessed more than a few of them were armed.

"If they start shooting, you might be hit," Matt said. "In fact, I would guarantee you would be hit."

"This play is not without its risks, but I have been shot before. Painful, but I survived. I have also gambled before and lost, as have you."

"So you came not to help us but to make yourself look good?" Chief Collins asked.

Tomlinson looked around the room. "No, I came because I wanted to help locate this innocent young woman."

"Then help us and stop playing games."

Tomlinson looked around the room. "I need to speak with Matt."

The chief pointed to Matt. "He's right there. Say what you have to say."

Tomlinson stared at Matt. "I need to speak with him alone."

"What are you playing at, Tomlinson?"

"Let me speak with Matt alone, and we may find a solution to this problem," Tomlinson said.

The chief looked at Matt. "Do you know what he's talking about?"

Matt nodded. "Probably. Let me talk to him, Chief. I doubt he's as concerned about Samantha as he says, but I am."

The chief looked back and forth between the two men. "Fine. Go in the back room. Talk, but you had better bring me some answers."

Tomlinson stood up and walked to the door that led back to the cells. Matt followed him.

As he neared John Havencroft, John whispered, "Did he do it, Matt?"

"He's involved. Otherwise he wouldn't want to talk to me."

"Is she in danger?"

Matt hesitated. It would be easy to lie, but he chose not to. "She may be. You know the violence that has been happening around this area. However, I think Tomlinson knows that if she is hurt even accidentally, not only will you call a lot of unwanted attention to the UMW, but I will end him and anyone who hurts her. He doesn't want that."

John nodded. "Then find her, Matt."

Matt followed Tomlinson into the back room and closed the door.

Tomlinson walked over to the miner in the cell. "How are you doing, Dobson?"

"He threatened me," Dobson said, pointing at Matt.

"No doubt. Did he do anything to you?"

"Not really."

Tomlinson turned to face Matt. "You know you are going to have to release me."

"I don't have to do anything," Matt said. "It's the chief's call."

"I didn't take her."

Matt poked a finger at Tomlinson's chest. "You know who did. You probably ordered it."

Tomlinson grinned and Matt wanted to smash his teeth in. "Oh, I did."

"Where is she?"

Tomlinson held up a finger. "It won't be that easy. If you want to see her again, then you are going to have to help me."

"What do you want?"

"Information."

"I don't know what the coal companies are doing. I am just one agent in Eckhart. I am not even the only undercover agent."

"But you know who they are."

He barked a laugh. "I don't. We are compartmentalized. Only the main office knows who they have working out here. It helps avoid this situation. Why do you think David Lakehurst went after me?"

"He's the one who told me you were an agent."

"He didn't know it at first. He found out after he started investigating me."

Tomlinson rubbed his chin. "I can believe that. He certainly hates you."

"The feeling is mutual."

"Then what I want you to do is send information I give you to the Pinkertons and the coal companies."

"What information?"

Tomlinson shrugged. "I don't know yet. I have to decide on what will best help the UMW."

"Fine. Let Samantha go."

"Oh, no. It's not that simple. If I let her go, I lose my leverage. I will give you the information I want you to plant. Once you do it, and it has an effect, then I will have her released. Until then, I need my leverage to ensure your cooperation. I will come by your home tonight and tell you what I want you do." Tomlinson straightened up and put his hat on his head. "Until then, I am going to eat dinner."

Matt could tell Tomlinson was desperate. Everywhere else in the nation had settled the strike, except for Allegany County. He had committed a kidnapping to try to keep his job.

"How long do you think you can hold her?" Matt asked.

"As long as I need."

"Her father won't let that happen. He'll have every local law officer and the state police going house to house searching for Samantha."

"Then you had better hurry and help me before the men holding your girlfriend get nervous."

He walked out the room and headed to the front door.

"Wait a minute," the chief said. "Where do you think you are going?"

"Let him go, chief. There's nothing we can do right now," Matt said.

"Is he involved or not?"

Matt looked at the chief and then Tomlinson. Matt couldn't let this continue. He had to end it. Samantha's safety was at stake.

Tomlinson grinned at him.

Matt said, "Yes, he's involved." Tomlinson's smile fell. "I changed my mind. Arrest him."

"You're making a mistake, Ansaro," Tomlinson said. He turned to get out the door, but the police officers grabbed him.

Matt walked to the front door and opened it. He stepped outside and saw about two dozen miners. They were yelling and frowning. Matt held up his hands.

When the crowd quieted down somewhat, Matt said, "Paul Tomlinson has been arrested for the kidnapping of Samantha Havencroft. I know someone in this crowd knows where she is. This won't help the UMW. In fact, it is going to do quite the opposite. I have no doubt that when John Lewis hears about this, he will separate the union from Tomlinson. Samantha is not a miner or from a coal company family. In fact, her father is a state employee. Samantha's kidnapping will bring the law enforcement from the state governments here. You don't want that. If Samantha is harmed in any way, it will only make things worse. Don't try to help Tomlinson, he'll be fired within the week and on trial for kidnapping after that. You don't want to be associated with him. It won't build support for your cause. If you don't know who has Samantha, find out who does. Help free her. That will help your cause more than what Tomlinson is doing."

"How do you know he's involved?" someone called out.

"Because he told me so," Matt said.

"Why would he do that?"

Matt needed to do this. It was for Samantha. It was the best thing he could think of to help her. He only wished he could have warned his family first. He might simply be transferring the miner's attention from Samantha to his family.

"I'm a Pinkerton agent."

"You're a miner. You're from Eckhart."

"I am, but I was undercover."

"Traitor!"

Matt let them vent.

"From your viewpoint, yes, but I was not lying when I told you what Tomlinson did will stop the union from organizing here. The government won't allow it. The only chance you have is to make yourselves look like the honest people most of you are and help Samantha. Don't make this another Matewan because of a few foolish people."

Matt turned and walked back into the office. He felt like a weight had been lifted from his chest, but another was hanging over his head. Whether or not it fell depended on what happened with Samantha.

The inside of the police station was just as quiet as the outside was noisy. He looked around the men in the room.

Finally, the chief asked, "What did you do?"

"It was what needed to be done." Matt pointed to Tomlinson. "He wanted leverage over me. I took the benefit of that leverage away from him and created my own leverage."

"What if they don't let her go?" John Havencroft asked.

"That was a risk from the moment they took her, but it was a risk with little consequence. I just created a consequence. I made it clear that if Samantha is harmed, not only will hell rain down on the UMW, but it will guarantee Maryland will not unionize, and the UMW will probably lose some of the ground it has been gaining. It won't mean that they will release her, but it will keep her safe."

"You're risking her life. They will be after you, too."

Matt shook his head. "Better me than Samantha. Tomlinson risked her life to try to compromise me. Go home, Mr. Havencroft. Wait there. Someone may contact you with information about where she is, although it's more likely they will contact me, which is why I will also go home."

"You won't break us, Ansaro," Tomlinson said.

"I'm not trying to break an 'us.' I just need one person who has information I can act on. I think I can find that person."

"You need to include the police in this," the chief said.

"She is probably not being held in Frostburg. She may not even be in the county or the state. I know I would have taken her into West Virginia where the union is strong, and it would have muddied the jurisdictional issues."

"You let me know when and where you believe she is, and I will make sure there are no jurisdictional issues," Chief Collins said.

Matt nodded. He would probably need help to free Samantha, but the more people who were involved in the operation, the more likely it was that someone would be hurt.

"Thank you, Matt. I know you're risking yourself," John told him.

"I got her in trouble. I didn't mean to, but the result was the same."

Matt left the station. He turned down a ride from John. Matt wanted to walk the distance to his house. It would help clear his head so that he could think about possible outcomes to this situation and how to overcome them.

He was passing Maple Street when three miners walked out from the between the buildings. Two of them carried bats.

"There's the traitor," one the miners said.

Matt shook his head. "I'm not in the mood for this right now, boys."

"Afraid of being beat up? You deserve it."

"I have better things to do." He drew his pistol from behind his back and pointed it at the miners. "Leave me alone."

The miners froze and stared at the pistol. Then they broke and ran. Matt had guessed they would. Courage was easy to find in a group when the consequence was getting punched. It was an entirely different matter when one faced a pistol and possible death.

Matt didn't chase after them. He wasn't looking for a fight, but the UMW was bringing one to him.

As he approached the boarding house in Eckhart, he could see that news had already reached here about what he told the miners. A large group of them were gathered around the house, shouting at each other and at the house.

Matt swung around to Porter Road and then cut across people's yards until he was in front of the house behind the boarding house. He hurried through the backyard of the adjacent house, jumped the fence and then entered the boarding house yard. From here, it was easy enough to enter the house through the backyard without being seen.

Toni and Samuel stood at the front window. They jumped when Matt came in through the kitchen and Samuel grabbed for his rifle. Matt thought his uncle was a bit slow in lowering it even after he saw Matt.

"What did you do, Matt?" Samuel asked.

"I'm trying to get Samantha back from the miners who kidnapped her."

"Kidnapped?"

Matt nodded. "Tomlinson had her kidnapped to get me to help him."

"And so you had to tell them you're a Pinkerton detective?"

"It took away the leverage he had over me."

"And endangered this family."

"So now you admit it is dangerous for people to know who I am."

"When you're a Pinkerton among miners, it is."

"I was very selective about what I reported back to my bosses because I do understand coal miners. When men like Lakehurst went too far, I fought back against them. I kept the President from being shot at."

Samuel shook his head. "They wouldn't have done it."

"How can you say that? You were at the meeting with me. You heard Tomlinson."

"They wanted to scare, not harm the President."

"The President wouldn't have known that. The police certainly wouldn't have known that. It would have been disastrous for the miners in this county. The only reason it didn't happen was because I got to the shooter before he had a chance. Now, the UMW has had Samantha kidnapped in an effort to force me to set up an ambush of other undercover Pinkertons like me."

"Spies like you."

Matt nodded. "Yes, but I haven't gotten anyone killed. Can the UMW say the same thing?"

"I didn't kill anyone."

"And I haven't betrayed anyone. I have been trying to do what I can to keep the peace."

"Stop arguing, you two," Toni said. "It's not helping Samantha."

Matt nodded. "That's why I'm here. I need the family's help to find Samantha."

"What can we do?" Toni asked.

"I haven't heard anything about where she might be," Samuel

added.

"But you all can ask around, especially you, Aunt Toni."

"Why me?"

"Because Samantha is probably being held with a bunch of women. I don't think Tomlinson wants anything bad to happen to her because he knows it would bring down more trouble on the union. He can't risk keeping Samantha with miners because things might get out of hand."

"You haven't run into angry miner wives then."

There were plenty of stories not only from this strike but earlier ones in Maryland where miners' wives had attacked strikebreakers and scabs because they had known the men would be reluctant to fight back. The women had shown no such reluctance.

"That's not the sort of out of hand I was talking about."

Toni paused and then nodded. She understood Matt was worried about angry miners raping Samantha if no one was around to keep them under control.

"If you, Jenny, and Myrna could ask around…"

"Jenny's not from a mining family."

"Actually she is, but she has other contacts who may be able to help." Matt looked over at Jenny who was standing on the stairs. She nodded.

"What will you do if we find her?" she asked.

"I'll get her back," Matt said.

"How? You don't know how many people will be watching her."

"I'm a former Marine and a Pinkerton detective. This is what I've been doing for the past five years. If I find her, I will get her."

Chapter 33

August 23, 1922

Samantha sat at a kitchen table in a house somewhere. It was too big to be a miner's house. It was about the size of the Starner Boarding House.

Two women were in the kitchen with her. One was preparing a meatloaf while the other kneaded bread. They had said nothing to her. In fact, they had said very little even to each other. They were older women, about the age of Matt's aunts, although they didn't look nearly as cheerful as Toni and Myrna did.

Samantha stood up. The women stopped their work and stared at her. One of them reached for a carving knife.

"I just wanted to get a glass of water," Samantha said.

"I'll get it," one of the women said.

She pulled a tin cup from the cabinet and filled it with water from the sink. It sloshed a bit when she set it on the table in front of Samantha.

"Sit down," the woman said.

Samantha did so.

She had been in the house for two hours now after having been driven around the countryside for at least an hour.

These people were coal miners. She had seen a miner's helmet hanging on the wall, so it must have something to do with Matt and his family. She had also heard some of her kidnappers talking about the union, so it probably had something to do with the coal strike. She had no idea what they hoped to get Matt to do, though. He was only one man, and he hadn't taken a stand strongly in one direction or the other as far as the strike went.

A man poked his head into the kitchen. "Make sure you make enough for everyone. We have four more men coming for dinner."

"You can tell those men to feed themselves unless they are also bringing money to pay for all of my food you're planning on eating," one of the women said.

"You should be happy to help the miners."

"You're here, aren't you? I'm not running a boarding house for lazy miners, though."

"Lazy?"

"All you've been doing is sitting around my house this afternoon."

"We're guarding the girl."

The woman snorted. "Four men to guard one girl. My, aren't you doing dangerous duty?"

The man frowned. "Just cook the food and watch the girl."

"I thought that was your job."

"Just do it." He walked back into the living room.

"What's going on?" Samantha asked. "Can someone please explain it to me?"

The women ignored her and went back to seasoning a roast.

Samantha took a deep breath to calm her nerves. She needed to get away from here, but she would never get past these two women and any miners who were around the house.

The women continued working on the meal and one of them went into the dining room to set the table. When the second woman walked out of the kitchen to help set the table, Samantha saw an opportunity.

She stood up and walked quietly to the back door. As she reached for the door knob, she felt sharp pain along her scalp as her head yanked back.

"Get back here, missy," one of the women shouted as she

yanked on Samantha's hair.

Samantha staggered backward. The woman slapped her across the face.

"Sit down and don't try that again. Besides, the men are patrolling around the house. You won't get far."

"Behave yourself and you'll get back home safe and sound," the second woman said.

"It won't work. You won't get what you want," Samantha told them.

The woman nodded. "I know. I want my son back. He died in a mine cave-in because the company didn't care as much about safety as they did about getting coal out of the ground. And after he died, I had to pretend like it didn't matter. I couldn't raise a fuss or my husband would have lost his job in the same mine that killed his son, and we would have lost our home."

She wiped away tears.

"Then why are you doing this?"

"So someone else's son won't have to die. So another man like Elsa's husband won't be crippled for life. So all miners can earn a decent living. The company owes us that much."

"And you think kidnapping me will get you that?"

"I didn't kidnap you, missy. You should be thanking me and Elsa. Otherwise, you would have had those *men* out there watching over you. No telling what they would have done. I wouldn't trust any of them. They are as dark as the mine."

Samantha glanced at the entryway to the kitchen almost as if she expected one of the men who kidnapped her to appear.

What would happen to her if Matt didn't do what they wanted him to do? Would they let her go? Certainly they wouldn't kill her, but they might send these women away and then what would happen to her?

Chapter 34

August 24, 1922

Patrick Kennedy leaned against the bar in the speakeasy in the basement of one of the houses on Beer Alley in Eckhart. The speakeasies in town had tried to bar strikebreakers, but the strikebreakers had threatened to bring in the revenue agents. Faced with closure, the bar owners had relented. The miners weren't happy, but they were visiting less and less anyway as they ran low on money. The strikebreakers had money and so they were fast becoming the primary customers of the bars.

Patrick nursed his beer, which tasted like water flavored with piss, but it was hard to get a good beer during prohibition. Most of the moonshiners made hard liquor, which carried a greater profit margin and was easier to hide.

The two men next to him were neither nursing their drinks nor drinking beer. They had whatever the owner was trying to pass off as his latest batch of moonshine.

"I don't like it," the one man said. "We're asking for trouble. She's the daughter of the college president, not another miner's daughter. And he's got her hidden here in town."

"It's the last place they'll look. Paul said we needed to do this. We need that Pinkerton's help to get rid of the rest of them," the second man said. He finished his drink and asked for another. "I don't like it either. If she gets hurt, it's on us, not the Pinkerton."

"Exactly."

The men quieted down after that. Patrick leaned in to try to hear more, but he wound up leaning in so much he was up against the man next to him.

He pushed Patrick away. "Hey, what are you doing?"

Paul straightened up. "Sorry. I may have had a wee bit much."

"You may have. If you can't stand up, get out of here."

Patrick nodded. He wasn't drunk, but better if these men thought so. Patrick didn't want them to know he had been listening in on their conversation. They knew about the kidnapped woman. Toni had told him to ask and look around to see if he heard anything about the woman.

The men finished their drinks and headed for the stairs to leave. Patrick let them get ahead of him, and then he followed them.

He came out the rear door of the house that hid the speakeasy and looked around. Where had those men gone? He wanted to follow them to see if they might lead him to Samantha Havencroft.

Hands shoved him from behind and Patrick went staggering across the alley and fell to his knees.

"Why are you following us?" one man from the bar asked.

"I wasn't following you," Patrick said. "I was going home."

"You were next to us in the bar and followed us out when we left."

"No."

Patrick started to stand, but the miner punched him in the jaw, jarring his teeth. Patrick fell sideways onto the ground. One miner kicked him in the backside.

"You had better stay away from us. You're a strikebreaker. You don't belong here," the miner said.

The miner kicked Patrick again. Patrick saw this kick coming and moved his head mostly out of the way. The kick from the heavy boot grazed him across the temple and he saw stars.

He heard the men running away, but he couldn't focus his

blurry vision enough to even see what direction they ran off in.

He pushed himself to his hands and knees and retched onto the ground. It was probably a good thing the beer came out of him. It had been no good. He leaned against the side of the building to pull himself to his feet. He checked his balance and then staggered off toward the Starner Boarding House.

He walked out of the alley and headed down Neff Street to the boarding house. A few people on the street saw him and shook their heads. They probably thought he was drunk.

He went up the stairs to the boarding house and knocked on the door. When no one answered quickly, he pounded harder.

Samuel Ansaro opened the door. Patrick slumped against the door frame.

"I need to see Antonietta," he said.

Samuel drew back a bit. "Who are you?"

"Patrick Kennedy. She knows me. I need to talk to her. I need to talk to you all. It's about the kidnapped woman."

Samuel's eyes widened. He took hold of Patrick's arm and helped him into the living room. He helped Patrick sit down in a rocking chair.

"Matt! Toni! Come to the living room," Samuel called.

Patrick slumped into the chair. He rubbed his sore head. He hoped he wasn't bleeding on Toni's new furniture. It was bad enough that he was dirty.

Toni walked in from the kitchen. She saw Patrick and ran over to him.

"Patrick! What happened to you?" she said.

She started looking at the side of his head. He wondered how bad he looked.

"I was in a speakeasy. I heard two miners talking about Samantha Havencroft," Patrick said.

"Did they mention her by name?" Matt asked as he walked in from the hallway.

Patrick shook his head. The motion made him dizzy.

"No, they called her the daughter of the college president."

"Who were they?"

"I don't know. I didn't know them. I tried to follow them, but they did this to me," Patrick said, pointing to his head.

"It doesn't look like you broke anything," Toni said.

"How do you know this man, Toni?" Samuel asked.

Toni straightened up and look at Samuel. "I've been seeing him."

Samuel's mouth dropped open. "Really? Why haven't you ever mentioned him?"

Toni put her hands on her hips and glared at her brother. "Is that really the important right now?"

Samuel shook his head. "No, but it is something I would like to hear more about later."

"Did the miners say anything else?" Matt asked.

"From what they were talking about, the woman is being held someplace here in Eckhart."

"Eckhart? We would have known about that."

Even as he said it, he doubted it. The family had been isolated from the rest of the town since word had spread about Matt's announcement at the police station.

"They believe you wouldn't look somewhere you thought was too obvious," Patrick said.

"That makes some sense, Matt. You said you followed the kidnappers to Mt. Savage, but they weren't there. What if they are trying to throw you off?" Samuel asked.

Matt said nothing. Then he finally nodded. "We need to look around."

"How are you going to do that?" Toni asked. "You can't go door to door. People don't really like us right now, especially you."

"I still think they will have her with women," Matt said. "But they will also need lookouts. Even if they are staying in an obvious place, they won't want anyone getting too close. They can't risk someone stopping by to visit and telling what they saw in the house."

"We'll have to look for a place—a house, maybe—where miners are gathering in town but usually don't," Samuel said.

"That's still a lot of places to look," Toni said.

"It is easier to search Eckhart than the entire county," Matt said. "We've got to find her."

Chapter 35

August 24, 1922

Matt, John Havencroft, Enos, and Samuel sat in the tree line on the hill above Eckhart, watching the house on Angel Street. Matt lowered his field glasses and passed them to Samuel.

"I count four guards and two women in and around the house," he said.

After getting the tip from Patrick Kennedy, Matt and Samuel had scouted the town. They had identified seven possible homes on their fast pass that might have been some place where Samantha could be held. Two additional walks through town had narrowed the choices to this home.

Samuel had wanted to bring in the police, but Matt was more cautious. He had sent Toni and Myrna to get the deputies, but it would still be a while before they arrived.

Matt worried that the miners might start shooting and injure Samantha. He could see the men were armed, and he knew some miners had shown little restraint during the strike. Matt had alerted John, and then the four of them had taken their rifles, circled around, and come to the house from above.

"I can see her," Samuel said. "She's sitting on a chair in the center of the room."

"They're keeping her away from the windows and doors in case she tries to run," Matt said.

"Why not tie her up?"

Matt had wondered that himself. "I don't know. Maybe they are doing their best not to hurt her since it would only make them look worse."

"Maybe the women have something to do with that," John suggested.

Matt nodded. "Could be."

"So what are we going to do?" John asked.

Matt had been watching for patterns and openings in how the miners were protecting Samantha. He thought he saw both. First, they weren't watching the rear of the house because it backed up against woods and they weren't expecting anyone from that direction. They were only watching for people approaching from town. Second, because the guards didn't want to draw attention to themselves, only two of them sat on the front porch. The other two watched from upstairs windows. The two guards on the front porch were also keeping their weapons hidden. They wore pistols tucked in the back of their waistbands.

He looked at his watch. With any luck, Myra and Toni should have reached the police. The Frostburg Police wouldn't have any authority in Eckhart, but they could notify the Sheriff's office.

"Enos, John, can you handle the two on the porch?" Matt asked.

"What do you mean handle?" Enos asked.

"Get the drop on them before they can pull their pistols and tie them up with the rope we brought. Try to stop them before they yell. If we can, I don't want to alert the lookouts upstairs."

Enos nodded, but he looked doubtful.

"Samuel, we'll go in through the back door. I'm not sure whether those women will be helpful or a hindrance. Can you handle them?"

"I suppose so, but I don't want to shoot a woman."

"I don't want to shoot anyone, but we have to be ready. I'll take care of the men upstairs."

Matt took a deep breath. "Let's go."

The four men scurried out of the trees, down the hill and to the side of the house the miners weren't watching.

Enos and John went around opposite sides of the house. They stayed close to the walls so that no one looking out the windows from the second floor would see them. Hopefully, no one passing by or in a nearby house would suspect something was going on and call out a warning to the two porch sentries.

Enos came around the corner on his side of the house first. He had his gun out and pointed at the two men.

"What are you doing?" one man said.

"Making sure you don't reach for those pistols you're hiding behind your backs."

Hearing Enos, John hurried around his side of the house, pointing his gun at the men.

"Raise your hands out in front of you," John said. "You wouldn't want us to think you're reaching for your gun."

"Who are you?" the second man asked.

"The father of the girl you kidnapped."

The man shook his head. "I didn't take her. I was just asked to watch her."

"Shut up," the first man said.

"Enos, get their pistols," John said.

Enos walked up on the porch and behind the men. He pushed each man forward so he could reach down and grab their hidden weapons. Then he tucked them in his waistband.

Only then did he put his own pistol away. He grabbed the first man's hands and tied them together behind his back. Then he did the same with the second man's hands.

"Do you still have plenty of rope?" John asked.

"Yea."

"Tie their feet together, too. We don't want them running off before the deputies get here."

"Deputies?" one miner said.

"Kidnappers go to jail," Enos told them.

"We didn't kidnap her."

"She's sitting in the house, and you're out here with guns. I don't think many people will believe you."

As Enos and John disappeared around the side of the house, Matt and Samuel went up the back stairs. Matt turned the doorknob. The door was locked. It wasn't surprising. They wouldn't want to take a chance that Samantha would get away and sprint out an unlocked door.

"It's locked," Matt whispered.

"So what do we do?"

"I can kick it in, but they will know we're coming. I'll rush the stairs and try to head off anyone coming downstairs. You need to find Samantha and get her out of the house. Take her out the way we go in. We know this door will be open."

"You'll need help."

"I'll call for Enos. He should have the two miners out front tied up soon."

Samuel took a deep breath and nodded. Matt stepped back and slammed his good foot against the door. The lock held. He quickly kicked the door a second time, knowing they were now fighting against a ticking clock. The door slammed open and the two men rushed inside.

Matt saw two startled women in the kitchen. He wasn't worried too much about them at the moment. He ran into the dining area and then peered around the corner. He saw one of the miners from upstairs starting down. Matt fired a quick shot up the stairs, not aiming at the man. He just wanted to send him scurrying away from the stairs.

"Matt, we've got a problem," Samuel said.

Samuel had run into the house behind Matt and then past him into the living room. Matt glanced up the stairs to make sure the miner hadn't come back. Then he ran into the living room.

A miner was holding Samantha in front of him and had a pistol pointed to her head. Matt froze.

"He must have come down right before we came in," Samuel said.

Tears ran down Samantha's cheeks.

"Put your guns down," the miner said.

"No," Matt said.

"I'll shoot her."

"If you do, you'll be the next one to die. The UMW will be blamed for her death, and all the miners will suddenly find themselves with the whole country against them. That doesn't even include how any of your family will be treated for murdering an innocent girl."

Matt was making this up as he went along, but it made sense. Tomlinson had made a series of bad calls and had put the UMW in a bad position.

"Deputies should be on their way here now," Matt said. "There's no way you walk away from this. The best thing you can do is surrender now. If you tell the police who put you up to this, things will go a lot easier for you in court."

"Court?"

Matt nodded. He looked at Samantha. "Are you all right? Did they hurt you?"

"I'm fine. They hit me, but I'll be fine."

"You need to let her go," Matt told the miner.

"No. You need to leave now, or I'll shoot her." He moved the pistol down to her side. "She doesn't have to die right away. If she suffers, it will be your fault."

"Samantha, do you remember our classes?" Matt asked.

Her eyes focused on him. "Yes, but I don't—"

"Just stay calm. You'll know when to use it."

"What are you talking about?" the miner asked.

"She's a student. I didn't want her to worry about her classes," Matt lied. "Just put your gun down."

"I can't do that."

The front door swung open as Enos and John came inside. The miner swung to the right to see who was coming in. As he did, the pistol left Samantha's side. She saw her opportunity and grabbed his wrist with both of her hands. Then she slammed her heel down onto his foot. He yelled, and she drove her elbow into his stomach.

Enos saw what was happening and darted forward, grabbing for the pistol. Meanwhile, Matt ran up and put his pistol in the man's ear.

"Stop! It's over," Matt said.

The miner froze. He loosened his grip and Enos took the pistol away from him.

"Samuel, make sure those two women we saw in the kitchen haven't pulled out their own weapons. Bring them in here. Enos, watch the stairs. There's still another miner up there."

Enos walked over the stairs and shouted, "You might as well come down. Even if you get away, I'm betting one of these other men will tell us who you are."

There was silence.

"Suit yourself, but the police will be here soon. They might not be as nice as me."

"Fine. I'll come down," said a voice from the second floor.

"Just make sure you leave your guns up there and that I can see your hands."

The miner walked slowly down the stairs with his hands raised, and Enos waved him over to the living room.

John Havencroft hugged his daughter and kissed her on the forehead. Matt let the two of them have their time together.

When the sheriff's deputies arrived about ten minutes later, Samuel was waiting on the porch to show them inside.

A crowd had gathered around the house at the sound of the fighting in the house. They watched events and talked amongst themselves.

"This is not the way to do things," Samuel shouted at them. "We're miners. We're not killers. We're not kidnappers. There are better ways to get what we want. People—innocent people—could have been killed here today. Is a bigger payday worth that?"

The police led the handcuffed miners out of the house and loaded them into the backs of their cars. They decided not to do anything with the two women for now unless it was determined they were more involved with the kidnapping than they appeared to be.

When the police drove off, Matt walked back inside to Samantha. She hugged him.

"You did well. You kept your cool and did what you needed to do when the opportunity opened up," he told her.

"I was scared."

"I was, too."

"Matt…"

She had a sad tone in her voice that he didn't think was there because of the kidnapping—at least not directly.

Matt held up his hand. "We can talk tomorrow. Why don't you go home with your father and rest? There are still some things that need to be wrapped up with your kidnapping."

She hesitated and then nodded.

John walked over and shook Matt's hand. "Thank you for getting her back."

"I had no other choice."

"This strike is getting dangerous."

"It always has been. You just haven't had to experience what the miners go through."

"I suppose not. What happens now?"

Matt thought for a moment. "Samantha will need to give the police a statement about what happened to her. Did she recognize anyone?"

John nodded. "She said one of the men was a union man you introduced her to in town one time."

Tomlinson.

Tomlinson had made another mistake and let Samantha see him. He had been too sure that Matt would give in and become his mole in the Pinkertons.

"Make sure she tells the police that. There's something else I need to do before word gets out about this failed kidnapping."

Chapter 36

August 24, 1922

Paul Tomlinson hurriedly shoved his suits into his suitcase then closed and locked it. He looked around his room in the Hotel Gunter to see if he had left anything behind.

He needed to get out of town quickly. He was already suspected of Samantha Havencroft's kidnapping. He couldn't wait until they found her, although he doubted that wouldn't be for some time.

If only Matt had given in and agreed to help him. It would have only helped the Ansaros.

Now Paul needed to get out of town before the police arrested him.

He heard a knock at the door. Paul walked up to the door but didn't open it.

"Who is it?" Paul asked.

A high, youthful voice said, "It's the bellhop, sir. I have a telegram for you."

"Slide it under the door."

The bellhop hesitated. "Okay, sir. I also brought your mail and newspaper up. Should I try sliding that under the door, too?"

Now Paul paused. He didn't want to open the door. He could have the bellboy leave everything outside the door, but the bellboy would also want a tip.

He unlocked the door.

It slammed open, knocking Paul back. Matt ran into the room. He grabbed Paul by the shirtfront and punched him in the face. Paul raised his arms to protect his face, but Matt slammed him up against the wall.

Matt swung low and punched Paul in the stomach. Then Matt threw him across the room.

Paul hit the floor and rolled up against the wall.

He felt Matt's knee on his back. Then his right arm was yanked behind him and a cuff closed around it, followed by the same thing happening to his left arm.

Only then did Paul feel the weight against his back lift.

"It's over, Tomlinson. I told you it wouldn't work. We found Samantha, and she saw you. She can testify you were part of this. The miners will probably break, too," Matt said.

Matt yanked Paul to his feet.

"You ruined everything," Paul said.

"No, you did. You went too far."

Matt pushed Tomlinson toward the door.

Chapter 37

August 25, 1922

Toni knocked on the door to the miner's house. She looked around nervously, feeling like every eye in town was watching her. They probably were. She just wasn't sure whether they were curious whom Toni was visiting or no longer trusted her.

The door opened, and she saw a strikebreaker wearing pants and a t-shirt. His suspenders hung at his waist and he was barefoot.

"Yes?" the miner asked.

"I was told Patrick Kennedy lives here," Toni said.

"Yea, but he's not feeling too well. He was on the wrong end of a fight yesterday."

Toni nodded. "I know." She held up the small pot of soup she held. "I came to bring him some soup and bread."

The miner inhaled deeply. "Lucky him." He stepped back and opened the door wider.

Toni entered the house and was surprised to find it was a bedroom of sorts. What was generally the living area in a miner's house now had four beds in it and a large dining table near the kitchen area.

She saw Patrick pushing himself up to a sitting position. He looked pale from the effort.

"You don't need to get up," Toni said.

"Of course I do," Patrick said. "Leroy Thomas, this is Antonietta Starner. Toni, this is Leroy."

"How do you do?" Toni said to Leroy.

"Apparently not as good as Patrick," Leroy said, grinning.

Patrick swung his legs over the side of the bed. He motioned to a nearby chair for Toni to sit.

"You didn't have to come to see me," he said. "I know you don't want people in town knowing that a strikebreaker is courting you."

Toni nodded. "I did feel that way, but after what you did for my family, I have changed my mind. You are a good man, Patrick, and if people, including me, can't see past the fact that you work for the coal company, then we don't deserve you."

Patrick grinned. "And all it took was for me to get beat up."

Toni chuckled. She held out the pot of soup. "It's homemade beef and vegetable soup."

Patrick took it and raised it to his nose and sniffed. "Smells delicious. I always suspected you were a great cook."

"You haven't even tasted it yet."

"I don't have to. It certainly can't be worse than the stuff we cook for ourselves around here."

Toni wasn't sure how much she liked the comparison. She knew how badly most miners cooked for themselves.

"How much longer will you be in bed?"

"I can get out now. Nothing's broken. I'm just bruised. It can hurt to move, but I can."

"That's good to hear."

"Why?"

"I thought you might want to go for a walk this evening."

Patrick smiled. "That I would. I tell you what. I'll eat your soup for lunch and return the pot to you about seven o'clock. Then we can walk and talk about your cooking skills."

Toni stood up. She hesitated and bent over and kissed Patrick on the cheek. "I look forward to it."

Matt walked Samantha to the model school. She was determined to get back to a normal life as soon as possible. Matt kept scanning the people they passed, the vehicles that drove past, and the windows.

"Your father said you could take time off just like any sick student would," Matt said.

"I'm not sick, though," she told him. "I need this. I need to feel in control again."

"I guess I can understand that."

Samantha put a hand on his shoulder. "You didn't have to walk with me, Matt. I'm fine. Really. I'm not worried about being kidnapped again. You said the police arrested Paul Tomlinson."

"He's just one person. There are other things that could happen."

"There are always other things that could happen."

Matt nodded. He had come to the same conclusion when he was fighting in the war. No matter what he might do to protect himself, a stray bullet could have ended his life. Although the shrapnel that had nearly killed him hadn't been meant specifically to end his life it nearly had.

And she was right. Matt didn't expect the miners to strike out at Samantha. They wouldn't have done so in the first place if it hadn't been for Tomlinson. He hadn't lied when he said most of them were good people.

"There is something I need to talk to you about," Samantha said.

"What's that?"

"I decided to take the job in Annapolis."

Matt nodded. He had expected that. It was a good opportunity for her.

"Well, I don't have a job in the mines anymore. The Pinkertons will fire me as soon as they realize what I was doing here. I'm surprised I haven't heard from them yet. The kidnapping made the newspaper."

"I'm sorry about that."

"It means I'm free to move to Annapolis. I can get a job there."

Samantha shook her head. "Don't. Please. We could certainly see each other if you moved there, but we couldn't marry. If we did, I would have to stop teaching. I told you when we met, I'm not interested in raising a family. I don't know what I want to do with my life yet, but it's not be a housewife."

Matt couldn't say he was surprised. She had been honest about her goals and dreams all along. If he was surprised at anything, it was his own reaction. He expected to be more upset than he was, especially given how he had reacted at her kidnapping.

"What are you thinking?" Samantha asked him.

He sighed. "I'm not sure."

"I don't mean to upset you, especially after you rescued me from the kidnappers."

He had thought he loved Samantha more than he had Priscilla. He had even rejected Priscilla to stay in Eckhart with Samantha. Now that she was breaking up with him, though, it felt very different than it had when Priscilla broke up with him. He had felt like a part of him had died then, but now, it simply seemed like Samantha's decision was simply the inevitable end.

"I will be fine. I'm disappointed, but somehow, I feel like you're right. It wouldn't have worked for either of us if I had moved to Annapolis."

"What will you do now that you don't have a job either in the mines of with the Pinkertons?"

Matt shrugged. "I don't know. I've got time to think about it. I like the Pinkerton work mostly. Maybe I can find a job with another agency."

"Will you stay here or go back to Baltimore?"

"Here. I used a lot of my savings to keep my family in the hotel while the new house was being built, so my funds are limited."

Samantha squeezed his arm. "I'm sure you'll be great at whatever you do."

They reached the school and Samantha said goodbye.

"Good luck," he said, and he meant it.

Chapter 38

August 31, 1922

Matt and Toni walked up the hill from Eckhart toward Frostburg. Matt took deep breaths, trying to prepare him for any scenario that might play out.

"Are you sure you want to do this?" Toni asked.

Matt stopped and turned to his aunt. "You thought it was a good idea when I told you about it."

Toni nodded. "It is. It makes sense, but she is going to have certain expectations. For that matter, I'm curious about your expectations."

"I just want to help."

"Uh-huh."

Matt started walking again. They walked up to Joey's house. Matt straightened his back, walked up onto the porch and knocked on the door. A middle-aged woman answered.

"May I help you?" she asked.

"We're here to see Laura Spiker," Matt said.

The woman frowned. "Oh."

She started to close the door, but Matt held out his hand to stop her. "Are you going to get her or take us to her?"

"I don't work for that tramp."

Matt gritted his teeth. It wouldn't do to vent his anger on this woman, and she probably knew that. Instead, he pushed into the living room of the house. Mrs. Middleton protested, but Matt ignored her.

"Laura!" he called.

"Matt?"

He followed the voice upstairs and saw Laura coming out of Jacob's bedroom.

"What are you doing here?"

This was the moment he had worried about. "I came for you and Jacob."

"What are you talking about?"

He hesitated, but Toni laid a hand on his arm. He glanced at her, and she nodded. Then she started walking towards Jacob's bedroom.

"Toni and I came to take you Jacob to the boarding house," Matt said. "You don't belong here. You don't want to be here. We want you at the boarding house."

Laura shook her head. "I can't. What about Joey?"

"What about him? Do you love him? Do you think he will complain if you leave?"

Laura looked at her feet and didn't say anything. What had Joey done to her?

Matt stepped forward. He put a hand on her chin and lifted it so that she was looking at him.

"I am here for you. I want you to come with me. I'm not asking for anything else. Do you understand?"

She nodded slightly. "You don't understand, though. You don't know what I've done. What I've become."

"I think I have a good idea. I might not know all the details, but I can figure out enough." *With a little help from Jenny.*

"Then you know I can't come with you."

"I don't know anything of the sort. If you truly want to come with me, and I hope you do, then come with me. You deserve to be happy."

"I don't."

"Yes, you do. I don't know if you will be happy with my family, but I can guarantee that you'll be happier than you have been here."

Laura nodded and then shook her head. "I don't know. I keep making bad decisions. I need Pete. I miss him."

"He was a good man. You made a good decision when you married him, but can't you see you need to get out of here, Laura? I know you aren't happy and that you've made some wrong decisions. Let us help you. We'll get you someplace safe where you can think and make decisions with a clear head. Enos and Jenny will be there to help you."

She blinked and stared at him. "Enos and Jenny?"

"They are having to deal with similar problems that you are. You may think I don't understand what you're going through. That may be true, but they do understand."

Tears started running down her cheeks. "Why are you doing this, Matt?"

It wasn't that he hadn't considered the question himself. Laura had made bad choices and was now suffering the consequences. That was life. He could say that, but even he didn't believe it. If he saw someone in need, he tried to help.

"I have a few reasons. You need help. I can help. You're a good friend. You have a young child who doesn't deserve to be hurt. You don't deserve it. I can go on."

She leaned against his chest and sobbed.

"What's going on here?"

Laura jumped back as Joey walked into the living room. His suspenders hung loose at his side as if they were reins. Matt was tempted to jump on Joey's back and pull on those reins.

Mrs. Middleton stood behind him with her hands on her broad hips. She wore a smug smile, and Matt understood why she liked her work here. She and Joey were two sides of the same coin.

"He and that other woman just pushed their way in here," the older woman said.

"Get out of my house, Matteo," Joey said, pointing at the door.

Matt took a deep breath and forced a smile on his face. "Happy to oblige, but Laura and Jacob are coming with me."

"I don't think so, Matteo. You had your chance with her. She's mine now," Joey said.

"Yours? She's not a piece of furniture or a car, Joey. She's a woman you've been mistreating." Matt realized that it was not unlike the way Joey treated his miners. They were things to move around to accomplish his goals. They weren't people to him.

Joey snorted. "Mistreating? Is that what she's told you? How am I mistreating her? I have given her and her brat a home, and a good home at that. I've fed them and clothed them. It's far more than she deserves. She's nothing but a whore. I guess I should have expected as much from a miner's woman."

Matt felt Laura shaking beside him. It wasn't the first time she had seen this side of Joey. Matt wasn't sure if she was sobbing or shaking in fear. He laid an arm around her shoulders to try to calm her.

"You used her, Joey," Matt said.

"Believe me, I had to pay for it. She's a drunk who went through of some of my best liquor."

Matt had no doubt Laura was trying to forget what Joey had lured her into doing.

Toni came down the stairs with Jacob. He saw his mother crying and ran over to hug her legs. She patted him on the head.

"Laura, why don't you Jacob and Toni head down to the boarding house?" Matt said. Although he directed his comment to Laura, he knew Toni would have to take the lead. Laura was too scared, too uncertain.

Joey reached out for Laura's arm, but Matt's arm darted out, snagging Joey's wrist. Then he twisted it down and under, forcing Joey to his knees.

"Go ahead, you three," Matt said, as if he wasn't on the verge of dislocating Joey's shoulder. "I'll catch up in a bit. There's something I want to tell Joey."

Toni glanced at Joey on the floor and at Matt. "Don't do something you'll regret," she whispered to him. She paused and added, "But you can make him hurt a little bit."

Then she took Laura and Jacob by the hands and led them out of the house. When they had left, Matt twisted Joey's wrist a bit further. Joey gasped and twisted his body, trying to ease the pain.

"You're hurting him," Mrs. Middleton said.

Matt shook his head. "Not yet, but I'm thinking about it."

"You'll never work in Eckhart again!" Joey blustered. "I'll have you blackballed."

"I don't care. I was never really working for you in the first place. Now that you've fired my family, you can't even hold them over me." Matt pressed up on Joey's arm. "But, David Lakehurst was working for you, wasn't he? You sicced him on me. He tried to kill me and hurt my family. You saw what I did to him. Maybe I should do the same to you."

"No!" Joey shouted before he could stop himself.

Matt put a foot on the back of Joey's neck and pressed his face to the floor. "Here's what is going to happen, Joey. If I hear any-one talking bad about Laura that I think sounds like it could have come from you, or if I hear any rumors about her, I'm going to come back here and break your arm. Just let her go and live her life. No one has to know what is happening here. You won't lose any respect in town, if anyone respected you in the first place. Do you understand me?"

"Yes."

Matt hesitated. Then he stepped back and released Joey's arm. Joey rolled over and gently moved his arm around, as if to check Matt hadn't really broken it. Mrs. Middleton hurried over to him.

"Are you all right, Mr. McCord?"

Joey waved her away with his good arm. "Yes, yes, I'm fine." He looked at Matt. "You know, I won't have to do anything. The miners know you betrayed them. They'll run you out of town themselves."

Matt shrugged. "I don't have to live here to come back and visit you. I could live in Cumberland and ride the trolley right up to your front door." He stepped closer, so he and Joey were nearly standing nose to nose. "Don't try me, Joey. I had to put up with you before because of my work. That's all over now, and so is your hold on Laura."

"I can always find someone else."

"You can try, but it won't be anyone who knows you."

Then Matt turned and left.

Enos walked down to the second floor of the boarding house and knocked on the door to Jenny's room. She opened it and smiled when she saw him.

"Good morning," she said.

"Good morning. I wanted to know if you will do me a favor," Enos told her.

"What's that?"

He held out a small canvas bag and opened it. He reached in and pulled out a large roll of bills. Jenny gasped and put her hand to her mouth.

"This is all the money I was able to save while I was driving for Vincent Gambrill. I want you to go with me to buy a car. I am going to start my taxi service."

"Enos, that's a lot of money. Do you know what you're doing?"

"I'm going to do something I enjoy doing and turn it into a business, and I want you to help me."

"I know nothing about cars."

"But you know about money, probably better than me. You can help me get a deal. I'm not against you flashing your legs and smiling if it helps." Jenny swatted his arm. "Then you can help me run my taxi service. I have to figure out what to charge, how to let people know what I'm doing, and how to get a hold of me."

Jenny put her hand on her chest. "I don't know. That's a lot of responsibility."

"You're the one who encouraged me to quit driving for Vincent and follow my dream. Don't you think you should see things through?"

"Me?"

Enos nodded. "I trust you, and I believe in you like you believed in me."

She looked into his eyes and nodded. "Let me get dressed."

Chapter 39

December 15, 1922

The conductor called out for the train to board. Samantha looked over at Matt.

"Time to go," she said.

"I'm sorry to see you go," Matt said.

"You won't even miss me."

"Of course, I will."

"You'll be too busy. You're not even staying here."

Matt shook his head. "You're wrong."

"I thought you wouldn't be able to stay now that the miners know you're a Pinkerton."

"I'm not a Pinkerton anymore."

"What? Did they fire you because of what happened?"

"No, Frostburg hired me because of what happened. I think your father put in a good word for me, but after I rescued you, the mayor asked if I wanted to be a police officer for the town."

"And you said yes?"

Matt nodded. Samantha hugged him. "Matt, that's wonderful."

He had liked being a Pinkerton, mostly, but he had no desire to move back to Baltimore. He wanted to stay near his family. He had been away from them for too long. He also suspected Laura was going to need a friend to help her get back on her feet.

"So Professor Williamson isn't going with you?" Matt asked.

"That was never the plan. He has his work here, and I need to find my way without having someone look out for me. I am a modern woman after all."

"Having people look out for you doesn't mean you're not a modern woman. It just means you have people who care for you."

The train whistle blew. Samantha kissed Matt. Then she picked up her suitcase and walked to the train. Matt watched until she got on board.

He took out the badge he had been given this morning and pinned it on his shirt. He would need to get his uniform, but for now, the badge was enough. The badge and his family.

The train started pulling out as he headed up the hill to Frostburg. This was his town now, and he would protect it.

Matt walked back to his room at the boarding house in Eckhart. He was looking for a home of his own, but he hadn't found the right place yet. He knew he needed to leave, though. The strike was still going on, and the people in Eckhart didn't trust him. His family might be able to remain, but not if Matt kept living in the boarding house.

He walked into the room and Jacob ran over to him.

"Matt!" the boy said.

Matt tousled Jacob's hair. "Hi, little man."

"Did Samantha get off okay?" Laura asked. She stood up from the chair where she had been sewing a patch over one knee of Jacob's pants.

Matt nodded. "She's on her way to Baltimore and then Annapolis."

"Are you disappointed?"

Matt looked at Laura. She was looking at the floor, afraid of what he might answer.

"Laura, everyone made their decisions. Sure, I will miss her, but even if she had stayed in Frostburg, we would have only been friends. I made my decision, and I don't regret it. Do you?"

Laura looked up. "To be free of Joey's control?" She shook her head. "Definitely not."

Matt walked over and hugged her. He felt her stiffen for a moment, and then she relaxed and hugged him back. What had Joey put her through or was it the other men?

Matt helped her where he could, but he suspected Jenny and Enos were more help than he was much of the time. They had been through some of the same things Laura was going through. Matt could say he knew what Laura was feeling, but he didn't, not really. Jenny and Enos did. If the three of them could be enough support to each other, then Matt was fine with that as long as it helped the three of them.

"I have to get ready for work," Matt said.

She followed him to his room. Laura walked over to the closet and pulled out the blue serge police uniform. She handed it to Matt, and he walked into the bathroom to change.

"I will be looking for a job this morning," Laura said through the closed bathroom door.

"Anything promising?" Matt asked.

"Not yet."

"Don't get discouraged. I'll keep my eyes open while I'm on patrol."

He would also be looking for a new home for himself while he worked. Frostburg Police were required to live in town in case they needed to be called for an emergency.

Matt walked out of the bathroom wearing his police uniform. He looked at himself in the wall mirror and tugged at his jacket. It had been some time since he had worn a uniform.

Laura walked around him, straightening the sleeves and smoothing out the fabric. "You look fine. Now you had better get going, or you'll be late for your first day."

Matt gave her a quick hug and headed out for the streets of Frostburg.

Author's Note

Thanks for reading the Black Fire Trilogy. I hope you enjoyed it. It has taken about fifteen years to get to this point. I had the original nugget of an idea for this trilogy back on 2007. At that time, the story was about an undercover Pinkerton agent who was spying on union miners in Western Maryland during the 1922 coal strike. I even had a title for the book, In Coal Blood.

I'm sure you can see how the original idea is still a major part of the trilogy. I started writing the story, but it ground to a halt about 50 pages in. I put it aside to work on other projects. I came back to it time and again. I would write a few more pages, edit what I had written, and work on the outline.

I knew something was wrong with the story, but I couldn't put my finger on what it was. I hoped I could write what I had planned and that would make the problem I was missing apparent.

It didn't, but I kept trying.

Then I had a breakthrough when I was riding my bike four years ago. I often come up with ideas while exercising. I guess the endorphins ramp up my creativity. Anyway, I turned on the recording app on my phone, which acts as my GPS when I bike, and I started recording my thoughts about what the story needed.

The key was I needed to make the story more personal for the protagonist. I had to raise the stakes he had in the game. That is when I made him a former resident of Eckhart Mines, and he was spying on friends and family.

That broke the log jam and after that, I quickly put together a new outline with new characters. The story expanded even more as I wrote the first draft. Some characters increased in importance. New situations came into play. As the draft grew in pages, I soon realized the story was too long for a single book, and hence, the Black Fire Trilogy was born.

Every book has its own behind the scenes story. This trilogy was my greatest challenge to date. It took me years to solve the problems with the story and make it a reality, but I'm glad I did. Our biggest challenges can lead to our greatest satisfactions.

James Rada, Jr.
January 5, 2022

About the Author

James Rada, Jr. is an Amazon.com bestselling author of historical fiction and non-fiction history. They include the popular books *Strike the Fuse, Canawlers,* and *Battlefield Angels: The Daughters of Charity Work as Civil War Nurses.*

He lives in Gettysburg, Pa., where he works as a freelance writer. James has received numerous awards from the Maryland-Delaware-DC Press Association, Associated Press, Maryland State Teachers Association, Society of Professional Journalists, and Community Newspapers Holdings, Inc. for his newspaper writing.

If you would like to be kept up to date on new books being published by James or ask him questions, he can be reached by e-mail at *jimrada@yahoo.com.*

To see James' other books or to order copies on-line, go to *www.jamesrada.com.*

PLEASE LEAVE A REVIEW

If you enjoyed this book, please help other readers find it. Reviews help the author get more exposure for his books. Please take a few minutes to review this book at *Amazon.com* or *Goodreads.com*. Thank you, and if you sign up for my mailing list at *jamesrada.com*, you can get FREE ebooks.

If you enjoyed
Frostburg Burning,
try these <u>FREE</u> novels by James Rada, Jr.

Visit *jamesrada.com/newsletter-email*
and enter your email
to receive your FREE novels.